# NONCOPOREAL

## A. BALSAMO

Inkd
Publishing

# NONCOPOREAL

# CONTENTS

# INTRODUCTION

*W*elcome to *Noncorporeal*, an eclectic collection of ghost stories and other oddities. If you like spooky tales and plot twists this is for you. We have put together a curated selection of anecdotes and yarns that will make you laugh, cry and give you chills. The authors in this anthology come from a wide range of backgrounds, genres and writing experience. Some are published authors that you may recognize, others are previously unpublished. If you find a story that you love, please consider looking up the author and giving them a like on their social media!

A. Balsamo, Editor

# SHADOW IMAGE

## KAT FARROW

California, 1998:
Charlie Tanaka rocked the developer over the forming image and sighed.

There it was again.

Every time he tried to replicate the mirror portrait he'd found of his grandpa, a smoky figure showed up behind him on his left.

The old Kodak he used, inherited from the same grandfather, checked out fine at the camera shop and every other photo he'd taken with it came out great, even the mirror portrait of his cat, Pudge.

He transferred the photograph to the stop bath, then the fix. He stared at the picture. Everything except the edges were in sharp detail: the pattern of the armchair, even the hairs on his head, but that...thing was still there...though now closer and with a more defined shape.

A person shape.

He shivered, slipped the photo into the water bath and hung it on the line to dry. He had one last picture he wanted to print tonight.

The day before he had complained about the problem to his best friend, Freddy, who had suggested, "Pudge's came out fine. Try one with him in it."

So, he had. It took several treats to get Pudge to settle, but Charlie finally got the picture. He was looking forward to this one. Until he slipped it into the developer.

There he was, sitting in the armchair, Pudge sitting calmly on his lap, but there was a double-exposure image of the cat's head turned in a silent hiss over Charlie's left shoulder. The ghost image was there, much closer and more distinct.

A woman with bobbed hair.

Charlie slipped the paper into the stop bath. He went to the corner of his bathroom, grabbed his phone and flipped it open to dial Freddy.

"Hey, I took a picture with Pudge and it's still there. And it's clearer this time. It's a woman, I think. It's—" he said in a rush.

"Whoa," Freddy said. "Calm down, dude. Take a few deep breaths and explain in a less freaked out way."

Charlie took a deep breath and described the image.

"Yeah, that's trippy. I don't think you should stay in your apartment tonight."

"Are you offering?"

"No, man, I'm meeting Charlene. Why don't you ask Mrs. Garcia."

"What?"

"She loves you, man. You've taken like a dozen pictures of her Pekinese. Ask if you can sleep on her couch."

"What am I supposed to tell her? What about Pudge? I don't know if she'll let me bring him."

"Just ask." Freddy's doorbell rang in the background. "Look, I'll come by Mrs. Garcia's in the morning and we'll figure things out."

\* \* \*

Mrs. Garcia opened her door.

"Freddy! Como estas?"

"Bueno, Mrs. Garcia. Is Charlie here?"

"Yes, he's coming. You are a good friend to help him. You're not allergic to hornet?

"Uh…no?"

Charlie slid past his neighbor into the hallway. "Thanks again, Mrs. Garcia."

"You let me know if you need to stay again, Charlie." Mrs. Garcia waved and closed her door.

"Hornet?"

Charlie fished his keys out of his pocket. "I told her there was a hornet in the apartment and I was very allergic."

"Are you?"

"I don't know. I've never been stung."

Freddy looked him over. "You look like crap, dude."

"I'm worried about Pudge," Charlie said, unlocking his apartment door.

"He's fine. Probably just pissed you weren't here to feed him."

The door swung open and they stepped inside.

"Pudge?" Charlie called and clicked his tongue twice.

When no cat appeared, Charlie started checking his typical hiding spots. Freddy opened a kitchen cupboard and grabbed the kitty snack bag.

"Pudgie? Treat time." He shook the bag.

Charlie started toward the bedroom, but Freddy grabbed his arm.

"Did you put him outside?" Freddy asked, pointing his chin toward the balcony.

Charlie shook his head. He saw Pudge curled into a

striped gray ball in the corner furthest from the balcony door.

Freddy tried the door. "It's locked." Opening it, he stepped out and reached for Pudge, who let out a soft growl. "Aw, hey buddy, it's me. You're okay."

Freddy took a step back and knelt down, shaking the treat bag. He tossed one to Pudge. It landed a few inches from the cat. Pudge stared at it for a full thirty seconds before pulling it toward him.

Several treats later, Freddy was rubbing the cat's chin. He picked up the cat and headed inside, but the moment they reached the doorway, Pudge began squirming.

"Grrrr…hiiissssss!"

"Whoa, easy boy." Freddy set the cat down and he returned to the balcony corner.

Freddy put his hands on his hips and stared at the skittish feline.

"I'll, uh, get him some food and water," he said. "Show me that photo, okay?"

Charlie retrieved the photo from the line in the bathroom and handed it to Freddy.

"Okay, yeah. That's freaky." Freddy glanced around the apartment. "Seems all bright and sunny in here now. Why don't you take a couple more pictures?"

Charlie's mouth hung open and Freddy clapped him on the shoulder.

"We're just gonna try to figure out what's going on, man. Take a couple of those mirror pictures. One with just the chair, one with you, one with you and me, and maybe some with a different camera."

"I've tried—"

"I know, I know. Just try it again while I'm here, like a test." He flashed a smile, dimples appearing in his freckled cheeks.

5

Charlie rolled his eyes. "This is gonna take a while."

"I've got all day, man. We'll order takeout while the film's drying."

\* \* \*

BEADS OF SWEAT ran down Charlie's neck as he slipped the exposed sheet into the tub of developer. So far, every print without him, the mirror, or using the Kodak, had turned out fine. But there was definitely something on the other negatives.

"How's it looking?" Freddy asked, holding his Walkman earphones away from his head. He sat on the toilet leaning against the tank, legs crossed in front of him. The red light of the room gave him an eerie glow.

Before Charlie could answer, an odd thump came from outside the bathroom.

They shared a look. Freddy stood and started for the door.

"Don't open it! It'll ruin the print."

Freddy dropped his outstretched hand and stared at the door. The towel laying across the bottom edge of the door kept light from getting in, but also prevented them from seeing anything moving on the other side. No other sound came from the apartment.

Freddy peered over Charlie's shoulder.

"Do you think Pudge came back in?"

Charlie sighed. "I don't know. I was surprised he didn't come in during lunch."

He checked his timer, then rocked the developer over the paper. He didn't like what it showed. He picked it up with his tongs and slid it into the stop tray.

"It's there again," Freddy said.

"Yeah."

This was the picture of just him in the armchair. The shadowy figure was more distinct and even closer to his shoulder.

Charlie shivered. "I'll do the one of us next."

A few minutes later the hairs on the back of his neck prickled.

The photo showed him sitting on the cushioned seat of the chair and Freddy perched on one arm with a cheesy grin. On Charlie's other side was definitely a woman, although there were no clear details other than bobbed hair and some type of dress.

He slipped the paper into the stop.

"Hey, how come I look all ghosty. Did you process that right?"

It was true. Charlie looked perfectly solid in the image, but Freddy was a touch translucent. About the reverse amount of the ghostly woman.

Charlie rubbed his stomach. "I don't want to do any more prints."

He slipped the sheet into the fix, then the water bath.

Freddy flipped the light switch. Fluorescent light flooded the room then all went dark. Even the red safety light went out. He tried the switch a few times, but nothing happened.

"Just get the door," Charlie said and hung the photo on the line using the light from the doorway before joining Freddy in the living room.

Something was off.

"Where's the chair?" Freddy asked.

They found the armchair blocking the apartment door.

"Okay. We're leaving now," Freddy said. "Go grab some clothes, I'll grab Pudge."

Charlie dashed to his bedroom and pulled a duffle bag from his closet. He shoved a handful of T-shirts, sweats, socks, and a couple dress shirts and slacks for work into the bag. He slung the strap over his shoulder and frantically looked around for anything else he might need.

Pounding came from the living room.

Heart racing, he peeked around the bedroom doorway and saw Freddy hammering on the balcony door from the outside, Pudge's carrier in one hand.

Charlie ran to the door, but couldn't open it, even though it wasn't locked. He pulled and Freddy pushed, but it wouldn't budge.

Charlie felt a cold breath on his bare arm, and he jumped away, but there was nothing around him.

The balcony door burst open, and Freddy stumbled inside. Pudge yowled from his carrier.

"Did you see anything just then?" Charlie asked.

Freddy just shook his head and hurried toward the apartment door, Charlie close behind. They slowed and stared at the armchair a moment before each grabbed an arm and drug it into the living room.

Charlie grabbed his day-planner off the entry table. "What about the camera?"

"Leave it," Freddy said. "I don't want that thing in my car or my apartment."

\* \* \*

LATER THEY WERE SITTING at Freddy's kitchen table and he asked, "Does your grandmother know anything about the camera?"

Charlie shrugged as he pushed potatoes and corn around his plate. "She's not doing that good, Freddy. I didn't want to bother her."

"I think you need to," Freddy said, dropping another dollop of coleslaw on his plate.

Charlie offered some chicken to Pudge.

"You know that's why Pudge got his name, right?"

"Who knows what he went through last night." Charlie rubbed his cat's ears.

"You're sure you didn't leave the balcony door open?" Freddy asked, tapping his fork on his lip

Charlie nodded. "What about the chair?"

"Let's not talk about the chair." Freddy took a bite of potatoes. "You need to talk to your grandmother, dude. I don't know what else it could be. Maybe the camera is cursed or something."

Charlie sighed heavily. "Fine, but in the morning. I don't want to upset her this late in the day if there's a problem."

* * *

FREDDY PARKED his red Miata in front of the Eternal Spring Care Center.

"You bring any of the pictures?" Freddy asked.

Charlie patted his day-planer. "Yeah, some of the earlier ones. I don't feel right about this."

"I don't feel right about some ghost-curse thing lurking around you and your camera."

They checked in at the desk. "Mrs. Tanaka is in the rec room," the nurse said, frowning, "playing mahjong."

Charlie grimaced. "Has she been betting, again?"

"We can't seem to stop her, so we've negotiated: no money."

"What's she betting with then?" Freddy asked.

"You'll see," the nurse said with a slight roll of her eyes.

They headed down the hallway until it opened up on a long, low-ceilinged room. Mrs. Tanaka was sitting at a table, a pile of mahjong tiles at its center. Three grumpy seniors were scooting their chairs away from it.

"Better luck next time," Grace Tanaka said, gathering up her booty.

"Snacks," Freddy said. "Grandma Tanaka is betting with snacks."

There was a pile of fruit cups, Doritos, juice boxes and pudding cups piled on her side of the table.

"Grandma Tanaka," Charlie called, walking toward her.

She reached up to give him a hug. "Charlie! No one ever comes to see me. You come for mahjong?"

"No, Grandma. I wanted to ask you a couple of questions."

"Good to ask your elders. Why do you still hang out with this red-haired devil?"

"You're looking good, Mrs. Tanaka," Freddy said. "Nice haul."

Grace tsked and patted the chair next to her.

Charlie sat and glanced at Freddy who nodded encouragingly.

"Grandma, you know that camera Grandpa gave me?"

"What camera?"

"The old Kodak. The one that collapses down?"

"Oh, that old thing. Your grandpa knew you like those old cameras."

Charlie looked again at Freddy, who mouthed, "Go on."

"Did he ever mention having any problems with it?"

Grace popped open a chocolate pudding cup. "Problems? Is it broken? He hadn't used it since we first came here, before WWII."

"No, it works fine most of the time, it's just... You know that picture of him, the self-portrait he took using a mirror?"

Grace frowned.

Charlie brought out his day planner and flipped through the photos he'd brought along.

"Here. This one."

She took the photo and the corners of her chocolate-covered lips curled up. "Oh, yes. He was such a handsome devil back then. Much more than my sister deserved." She patted Charlie's cheek. "You look a lot like him."

"Sister? I didn't know you had a sister, Grandma."

Grace's eyes clouded, then she looked at Charlie with the most vacant expression he'd ever seen on her face. "I don't have a sister."

"But you just said…"

She handed back the photo. "Do you want a pudding?"

A chime sounded.

"Lunchtime!" She dabbed her mouth with a napkin. "You staying, Charlie?"

"Um, no, I don't think I can."

Grace stood shakily and the movement triggered a coughing fit. The deep racking made her lose her balance. Charlie and Freddy caught her and helped her steady herself until a nurse came over.

"Are you all right, Mrs. Tanaka?" the nurse asked.

She waved the nurse away and patted Charlie's arm. "Tell your father to come visit. Don't let Freddy take any of my snacks."

She tottered off to lunch, the nurse following a step behind.

* * *

CHARLIE'S MOM was filling a large pot in the kitchen sink when he and Freddy walked in.

"Hi, Mom," Charlie said.

"Charlie! You didn't say you were coming." She shook her head at Freddy. "There are no more cookies. Jill had her college friends over to study yesterday."

"Aw," he said, replacing the lid of the cookie jar.

"Mom, do you know anything about Grandma's sister?"

"You mean Grace?" She carried the pot to the stove. "She didn't have a sister."

"That's what I thought, but she just said she did, but then said she didn't."

"You weren't bothering her, were you? She hasn't been doing well."

Freddy said, "She was raking in the snacks when we saw her."

"Snacks?"

Charlie sighed. "She's been playing mahjong for snacks."

Mrs. Tanaka mumbled a curse in Japanese.

"I didn't catch that one," Freddy said.

"You're not learning that one from me, Freddy. Go talk to your father, Charlie. He's out in his shed."

* * *

CHARLIE SLID the shed door aside enough for him and Freddy to enter.

"Hi, Dad."

"Hey, boys," Mr. Tanaka said. He sat in a lawn chair, his feet propped up on the mower, watching a baseball game on a small, grimy TV. "Want a cola?"

"Thanks, Mr. Tanaka," Freddy said, grabbing one from the small fridge.

"We went to visit Grandma today," Charlie said.

Mr. Tanaka's eyebrows disappeared under his baseball cap. "Did you?"

"She said you should come visit," Freddy said.

He sighed. "Yes, I should. Is she still playing mahjong?"

"Yeah," Freddy said. "She's playing for snacks."

Mr. Tanaka chuckled. "She never loses. Dad said that's how they got the down payment for their house."

Freddy choked on his soda. "Seriously?"

Mr. Tanaka nodded.

"Dad, did Grandma have a sister?"

"Sister? Why are you asking about that?"

"So, she did have a sister?"

Mr. Tanaka nodded. "She did. From what my dad told me, she was quite the beauty. She was a couple years older than your grandmother, but she died and Dad ended up marrying your grandmother instead."

Charlie and Freddy looked at each other.

"You know that camera Grandpa gave me?"

"Yeah, though I don't think I ever saw him use it. I know he took a lot of pictures when he first got it. Still have a few of them. Are you having problems with it?"

"Sort of. Could we see those photos?"

"Um, sure. Sure." His gaze went to the shelves covering one wall of the shed. "I think they're in here, actually."

He rose and shuffled over to several dusty banker boxes, his flip-flops slapping his heels. He slid a couple out and peered inside.

"This one has several. I should go through them I suppose; put them in an album. Your grandma went into the care home so soon after Dad died I didn't really sort through things very well."

Charlie took the box from his dad and looked inside. There was a pile of folders and loose papers and a shoebox resting on top. Popping the lid off the shoebox, he saw stacks of old black-and-white photos. He could tell some had been taken with the old Kodak.

"Can I take this?" Charlie said.

"Sure. You need anything else?"

\* \* \*

CHARLIE AND FREDDY sat in a booth, empty pie plates and half-full coffee mugs pushed to one side. A pile of photos lay between them.

"You really do look a lot like your grandpa," Freddy said, tapping the photo in his hand. "Different style of glasses and his face is a bit leaner, but otherwise..."

"Look," Charlie said. "This must be her."

He held out a photo of two young women. They wore floral print kimonos, but had styled and bobbed hair. Charlie pointed to the one on the right. "This is Grace. She's in a couple of the other photos with Grandpa when she's a little older."

Freddy took the photo. "Wow, her sister was a looker. Check out that smile."

"And look..." Charlie handed him a photo of his grandpa and the sister in a mirror self-portrait. Her hand was resting on his shoulder, his arm crossing his chest to touch his fingertips to hers.

Freddy set down the photos and took a swig of his cold coffee. He grimaced, waved at the counter waitress, and pointed to his cup. Then said jokingly, "So, your grandmother offed her sister so she could marry your grandfather and now the murdered girl's spirit is haunting your camera."

"Dude!"

They fell silent as the waitress set down two new cups of coffee and cleared away a few of the used dishes.

Charlie rubbed his neck. "I don't believe in this kind of stuff."

"Yeah, I don't either, but it's happening."

They sipped at their fresh coffees.

"Maybe it's 'cause you look so much like him," Freddy said.

Charlie raised an eyebrow.

"Your grandfather. Maybe she wants to say something to

him. She's been dead a long time, maybe she's confused. I don't know… I'm just throwing out suggestions. What else is in the box?"

"Papers and stuff."

Freddy spread his hands as if to say "And?"

Charlie shuffled through the loose stack of papers on top of the folders.

After a few minutes, Freddy asked, "Well?"

"Some of it's really old…maybe letters."

"Maybe?"

"They're in Japanese. I don't read Japanese."

"Who does?"

Charlie shrugged. "Well, I don't want to ask my parents, not if what you're suggesting is true."

"What about Jill? Isn't she studying linguistics or something?"

\* \* \*

CHARLIE OPENED Freddy's apartment door.

"So," Jill said, "my big bro needs help from me. How come we're meeting at Freddy's?" She followed Charlie down the hall to the living room. Pudge meowed from the couch. "How come Pudge is here? You get kicked out of your apartment or something? Gas leak?"

Charlie shook his head. "I need you to read through some of Grandpa's stuff."

Jill set her bag on the couch. "What am I looking for?"

"Tell her, Charlie," Freddy said from the kitchen doorway.

Charlie took a deep breath. "You know that old Kodak Grandpa gave me?"

Twenty minutes later, Jill was sitting on the couch looking through the photos, old and new.

"Jesus, Charlie. You don't even believe in ghosts and

curses and stuff." Jill bit her lip and shook her head. "I never heard anyone talk about Grace having a sister." Pudge nuzzled Jill's elbow until she rubbed his ears. "Poor, Pudgie. Did Auntie scare you?"

"You think it's true?" Charlie asked.

Jill shrugged. "Something weird is going on. Did you notice how close a match the ghost image is to Auntie? That bob is almost identical in length. Probably the right height, too."

She picked up the picture of the sisters and one with the clearest ghost image next to Charlie.

"Here, look. This looks like a kimono sleeve. And Freddy's right, you do look like Grandpa when he was your age."

She sipped her soda. "In folklore, mirrors show the true nature of things. Maybe that's why she only shows up in the pictures taken with the mirror. You look like Grandpa and she's trying to show some truth."

Charlie shivered. "Will you help us?"

"I'm here, aren't I? Where are the letters?"

* * *

"GRACE'S SISTER'S name was Rose. This is a picture of them," Jill said, picking up one of the photos. "Those are some pretty nice kimonos. Probably for a festival or something. Do you think Grandpa took this one?"

Charlie shrugged. "Possibly."

"I wish they had dates on the back. If we spread these out like a timeline…" Jill arranged some of the photos across the coffee table, then set a couple stacks of letters next to them. "Rose looks almost identical in the one with Grace and the one with Grandpa. So, they were probably taken pretty close together time wise.

"In this picture of Grace with Grandpa, she's older, maybe

a year or two later. I also noticed there aren't any more of the mirror portraits after those first ones."

She tapped the two larger piles of letters. "Most of these are from Grandpa to an Uncle Ito. I've never heard of him and don't know why they ended up back with Grandpa. The early ones talk about marriage arrangements with Rose. Then, Grandpa talks about marriage arrangements with Grace. Between the two events, there is one odd letter." She tapped the middle pile, only a few pages thick.

"Odd how?" Freddy asked.

"It's Grandpa grieving over Rose's death, but he also says 'Why would she think I would have gone along with such a bet?'" She picked up the top letter from the right-hand pile. "One of the last letters to Uncle Ito says 'I've never seen Grace lose a bet before. I hope I never do again.' It goes on to say 'I'm very sorry to have lost the beautiful bowls you gifted us.'"

Freddy asked, "Have either of you ever seen Grace lose a bet?"

The siblings shared a look, then shook their heads.

Charlie's phone rang and he flipped it open.

"Hi, Dad." He paused. "Oh, you did. Um, yeah, it might be. I'll stop by."

Charlie closed his phone and looked at the other two. "Dad said he found some more of Grandpa's old photos. Some of the images are kind of blurred, and he wondered if that's the trouble I was having."

"I'll go get them," Jill said, grabbing her bag. "I need to pick up some study notes I left there yesterday."

* * *

THEY SAT ON THE COUCH, eating the pizza Jill had brought back with her, and looked through the new photos.

"Wow. So, what do we do now?" Freddy asked.

Out of the eight pictures, five were mirror portraits. All five had blurred images; two with just Grace, two with just his grandpa, and one with...

"All three of them," Charlie said, leaning close to the image. A ghostly Rose had her hand almost resting on his grandpa's shoulder.

"Dad said they were in an envelope," Jill said. "He had to break a wax seal to see what was inside."

Charlie sat back and crossed his arms. "I don't know. Do you think Grandma made a bet with Rose over who got Grandpa?"

"But who lost?" Freddy asked. "Did Rose kill herself from grief or did Grace lose and attack Rose?"

"I also asked Dad if he had ever seen Grandma lose a bet. He did, once. He was ten and she went berserk; broke a bunch of stuff and swore in English and Japanese. The next day, it was like it never happened. She just calmly cleaned everything up."

Charlie hung his head. "What do we do about the camera? I don't want to take any more pictures with it."

"What do we do about Rose?" Freddy said.

"I think we should talk to Grandma," Jill said.

Charlie looked at his sister. "I don't want to upset her. Her lungs are getting pretty bad."

"I have a feeling, Charlie. She brought up her sister on her own. She's nearing the end of her life. Maybe it's something she needs to talk about." Jill checked her watch. "We can just make it before visiting hours end at eight."

"Tonight?" Charlie said.

"Yes." Jill stood. "I'll meet you there. Bring the camera, you might need to take a picture."

\* \* \*

GRACE WAS SITTING up in her bed, an oxygen tube below her nose.

"So many visitors today!"

Jill leaned in and kissed her cheek. "Hi, Grandma. We found some pictures Grandpa took with that old camera."

She grabbed the top one from the stack in Charlie's hand and gave it to Grace. "This is you and your sister, Rose, isn't it?"

Grace was quiet for a while, then nodded.

"Grandma, Rose has been showing up in Charlie's mirror portraits."

Charlie held out the last one he developed, the one with Freddy.

Grace took it and traced the transparent image of her sister with a shaky finger.

"We think this one was the last one Grandpa took," Charlie said, holding out the photo of his grandparents and a ghostly Rose. The young woman looked almost identical in both images.

Grace looked at them both and a tear ran down her face.

"What happened, Grandma?" Jill asked.

Grace looked into her granddaughter's eyes, then down at the photos. She turned them over.

"I don't lose bets," she said in a quiet voice. "I didn't lose that one, but Rose laughed at me and said it was a silly bet and she wasn't going to give him up—your grandpa. We argued and I pushed her, harder than I meant to. We were standing on the end of the bridge near our home. She went over the railing and hit her head on the rocky bank."

Another tear traced its way down Grace's cheek.

"I wrote a suicide letter, but Grandpa burned it after he read it to spare the family from disgrace. It was left an unsolved death."

After a few minutes, Jill broke the silence.

"Grandma, would you let Charlie take a mirror portrait of you and him?"

After a moment, Grace nodded.

"You sure?" Charlie asked his sister.

Jill nodded. "It's a feeling."

\* \* \*

CHARLIE SAT NEXT to Grace on her bed, his left hand clasping hers. He felt her tremble as he adjusted the camera in front of them.

"A bit more to the right," he said to Freddy.

They had taken the mirror off the wall and propped it on the frame at the foot of Grace's bed. Freddy shuffled to his left, trying to stay still.

"This thing's heavy, man. Aren't you ready, yet?"

"I'll take two, Grandma. Just to make sure."

Grace nodded and Charlie snapped the shot. The room's window blew open and Jill ran to close it.

"You moved the mirror," Charlie said.

Freddy rolled his eyes.

Grace said quietly, "She was here."

"What, Grandma?" Jill asked.

Grace shook her head and waited for Charlie to take the second picture.

Afterward, Jill helped Freddy hang the mirror back on the wall and Charlie straightened Grace's blankets.

"It'll probably be Tuesday before I can bring the photographs by, Grandma."

Grace smiled and patted his hand. "It's all right, Charlie. You come this weekend and play mahjong with me. Bring your father."

"Okay, I'll try."

Grace hummed a soft tune as the three left her room.

"That was weird," Freddy said. "Do you think it did something?"

Jill nodded, then saw Charlie heft the camera in his hand.

"What's up?" she asked.

"It's...uh, it feels lighter."

"It's not coming back to my apartment, dude."

"That's okay. I think I'll stay in mine tonight."

\* \* \*

CHARLIE DEVELOPED the film the next day after work and stayed up late printing the two photos.

In the first one, Rose appeared at Grace's side, opposite Charlie. Transparent, but in nearly full detail. Her hand rested on her sister's shoulder and a double-exposure image of Grace's hand was reaching up to hold it.

The second photo showed only Grace and Charlie.

Charlie went into his living room and placed his grandpa's Kodak on the bookshelf.

He turned to his cat, who watched him. "Everything okay, Pudge?"

The cat gazed at the camera. Then he stood and walked away, flicking his tail.

*KAT FARROW IS a multi-genre author whose works range from fantasy, sci-fi, mystery and historical, to children's stories.*

*Her short stories have appeared in several anthologies, including Parliament of Wizards (2022), Witches of a Certain Age (2022), Particular Passages 3 (2022), and The Librarian Reshelved (2023). Her first children's book, Bobbin and the Magic Thief, is scheduled to release in 2023.*

*A former Interlibrary Loan Librarian, Kat spends her days writing, reading, gardening, watching anime, and being herded by her cats. (...they are far better at doing the herding than being herded.)*

*Find out more about Kat and her latest releases at* www. LoreWeaver.com

# CHARLIE BOTTOMS AND THE GHOST COACH

## COLBY WOODLAND

*I*f Charlie Bottoms was honest with himself, falling down a flight of stairs and snapping his neck in three places was not the worst day of his life. Sure, his spine stabbed right through his neck, but being a ghost had its perks. A lot less stress than a day job, plenty of free time, and the IRS still hadn't quite figured out how to tax ghastly apparitions. When his soul woke up from his little stumble, he was pleasantly surprised to find out he got to enjoy a seemingly permanent staycation in the countryside manor he had been hired to renovate.

Charlie still wasn't sure what the rules for being a ghost were. There were no "New Ghost Orientation" meetings, no paperwork from an ethereal (un)human resources department, not even an ice cream social for newly departed individuals. On days he got bored, he would float over to the nearest town—he was getting pretty fast—and he was able to find a couple of other lost souls inhabiting hotels and hospitals. Unfortunately for Charlie though, most these deadites had no more information on being dead than he did.

There were rumors of an old lady ghost, a gal that had

worked at a day care, who had figured out how to move on to *somewhere*. Ironically the debate of the afterlife still raged among the ghosts. No one was sure if there was somewhere to move on to, or how you even became a ghost. It was clear that not all folks were destined for this ghoulish fate, and this was confirmed when all the local ghosts excitedly huddled around a dying grandfather and waited to see what would happen upon his death, only to be given the apparent cold shoulder.

Despite the directionless nature of being a ghost, Charlie really didn't mind it at all. He got to be a fly on the wall wherever he wanted to be. He quite enjoyed watching local drama unfold as his own private soap opera. He did get bored sometimes, but that was the worst of it. At least it *was*, until the day a dusty red car snaked along the gravel driveway towards his own private place of haunt.

The older sedan had "Williamson Property Development" written across its doors, and Charlie had recognized it as the company who had hired him to renovate the property. The manor itself had been foreclosed upon after the previous owners had neglected it, and it was bought up for cheap at auction. He couldn't be sure, but he figured his untimely demise had put a halt on the further renovation and sale of the house, and he knew that one day the project would inevitably resume.

Charlie hadn't tried to interact with living beings very much. He didn't want to admit it, but upon his death he fell into the cliché trap of trying to talk to the ambulance workers who stretchered off his body. He even moaned the classic line: "Why can't anybody see me?" After that, he didn't feel the need to contact anyone living. He didn't have much of a family or a social group, so he couldn't even participate in a good-natured spiriting like many other ghosts do.

When the renovation resumed on the manor, Charlie had

to face his options. He could either find a new place for his otherworldly residence or stand his ground. The local ghost community had mixed feelings on a proper haunt. Some think it's antiquated practice that harms their reputation as specters, but many agree that it's their natural dead right to usurp their place of passing from the living.

"Don't let the bastards take it from you," advised Tim Jefferson, a local fire chief who died during the school building fire of '87. "We died here, it's only right for us do our duty as a ghost."

Tim was considered to be the most hardline member of the local ghost community. When an elementary school caught on fire after an electrical malfunction, Tim had personally saved half a dozen fourth graders from the consuming blaze. He was lauded as an unequivocable hero among the community, but to him, his duty didn't die there.

The building was quickly condemned, and another elementary school was promptly built on the near side of town. Like many abandoned buildings, the spot became quite popular with teenagers and other types of people who like to look for trouble. Tim reckoned that he was doing a service to the community by keeping people from the building. After all, it was still condemned and was a helluva safety hazard.

"You got to put the fear of God in them," continued Tim. Charlie and the fire chief were floating around a cemetery, a favorite location among the dead. "Play to your strengths. Make a name for yourself. Everyone knows who haunts that damned school building. You know who?"

"Uh," Charlie mumbled, unsure if it was a rhetorical question or not.

"You know who?!" Tim said raising his voice further. Apparently, it was not rhetorical.

"You do," Charlie sighed.

"You're goddamn right I do!" A flock of birds flew off a

branch in the distance as Tim responded. "So, when I hit them kids with an 'ahhh help me, I'm burning,' or a 'get ouuuuut,' or 'hot-hot-hot-hot,' they know it's serious! They know I don't mess around."

Charlie realized this was turning into more of a bragging session for Tim than it was him receiving haunting advice. He began to tune out the fire chief, but refocused as Tim turned his attention back on Charlie.

"Do you know how to materialize your form?" asked Tim.

"What?"

"You know," Tim waved his arms around his translucent body, "become visible for a second or two."

"No," Charlie paused, "wait, do you?"

Tim scoffed, "What kind of ghost do you think I am? Of course, I do."

Charlie rolled his eyes.

"Watch this," said Tim, separating himself a few feet away from Charlie for a proper showing.

Concentrating, Tim closed his eyes and bore a strained look on his face. He began to flex certain muscles, seemingly at random. After a few deep breathes, his translucent figure began to flicker into a solid form. The ground beneath him had a sudden weight upon it, as the once undisturbed leaves crunched and crumbled under flame retardant boots.

"Holy shit," whispered Charlie.

"I'm not done," Tim said with his hand raised. "I'm just a fat old man, nothing scary about that. Just sad." He tilted his head towards Charlie. "You think I died like this?"

Charlie assumed this wasn't rhetorical. He had to think about it though.

"You died in a fire, so you probably would have been burnt up pretty bad."

"You got that right, kid," replied Tim. "I was just a bit crispier." Tim closed his eyes again, and more muscle spasms followed. Suddenly, his physical form was engulfed in flames. His pale, rashy skin blistered and popped. His eyeballs burst out his skull followed by rush of liquified brain matter pouring out of the sockets. By the end of show, his form was a dark husk with skin dripping off the skeleton.

Charlie jumped back and gasped. "Holy shit!"

"Pretty good, right?" asked Tim, who had flickered back to his ghostly form now.

"You weren't kidding."

"Imagine a couple of teenagers running into that in an abandoned building. I'm telling you fella, they shit bricks."

Charlie was astonished. He was still getting a handle on learning how to fly and move physical objects ever so slightly. What Tim could do was beyond his imagining.

"And you learned to do that all by yourself?" he asked.

"Well," Tim became evasive, "something like that."

"I can't do half of that," said Charlie with dejection. He put one hand on his hip and rubbed his mouth with the other before giving a quick shrug. "I'm screwed."

"Hey, you got time," assured Tim. "The development project will take some time."

Charlie nodded, if he could scare the contractors off, the realty group may just give up on the property and let it decay. He didn't know how, but he was going to haunt the shit out of that house.

The weeks following were a frustrating time for Charlie Bottoms. His usually secluded manor was now a bustling worksite for various contractors across the entire state. Electricians, plumbers, and general contractors cycled in and out of the house constantly. The sound of hammers and power drills shook the antiquated building from its basement to its shoddy roof.

The ghost looked for opportunities to instill fear in the workers at every turn, but something about a group of construction workers in the middle of the day made it a formidable task. They weren't teenagers in an abandoned building, that's for sure. Charlie tried some beginner's steps: flickering the lights, stomping on the floor, and slamming doors. All things he realized were actually very common on construction sites. He even tried to unplug a few cords, tip over a few shelves, and even grab a few shoulders with his cold, ghostly grip, but that still required a little more finesse than he could muster. He was running out of time before the home would be ready to sell, and he was aware of that.

After a month or two of failures, he was getting desperate. Charlie made his way back to town to find Tim on a dark autumn evening with a cold whip in the air; an evening that was made for haunting. Charlie was sure Tim would be stalking the school building waiting for an unlucky group of kids to wander onto the property.

As Charlie entered the condemned building, he saw how perfect it was for a haunt—something he wouldn't have noticed before trying his own hand at the game. The intertwining hallways that venture deeper and deeper into the building are the perfect trap for getting lost in. The fire had scorched the walls of recognizable markings, creating the illusion of going in circles. Individual classrooms seemed to be a great place to trap and separate prey as well. As Charlie was reveling in envy, he heard voices echo throughout the empty halls.

"Shut up!" whispered a voice harshly. It was high pitched. A girl.

Hushed laughing followed the girl's scold, and then a second feminine voice spoke up.

"I *cannot* get in trouble. If we get caught my dad is going to flip-the-fuck-out."

"Relaaaax," said a much deeper voice.

Charlie floated around the corner of the hallway and spied a group of four motley youth creeping slowly through building. He watched as the two girls clung to their respective dates, whose hands seemed less worried about a secure grip, and more worried about navigating to areas of soft exposed flesh.

"We should have just gone into the city and found a haunted house," spoke the blonde.

"Fuck that," cursed the boy she was attached to. His black hair draped out of a worn grey beanie.

The other boy parallel to the couple spoke up.

"Those blow. They're all just a bunch of cringy theater kids playing dress up," he laughed.

"Don't be a dick." The girl with a blue streak in her hair gave him a punch in the arm.

Charlie flew past the foursome looking for Tim. He waited for a light to flicker, or the sound of footsteps, but whatever Tim was planning it seemed that he was taking his time.

After a few minutes passed, the door to a classroom the four had just walked by slowly creaked open.

*There you are*, thought Charlie.

As the teenagers debated whether or not it was just the wind, Charlie curved his path into the room and found the surly fire chief posted up against the wall. The larger man furrowed his brow at Charlie and spoke with an annoyed venom.

"Get out of here."

"Wait," Charlie began. "I'll get out of your hair in a minute. I just need advice."

The teenagers had begun walking along the corridor again, causing Tim to curse beneath his breath at the missed opportunity.

"Leave. Now," Tim growled.

"I need help. I can't haunt for jack-shit on my own," Charlie pleaded.

"Not my problem. Leave," Tim replied bluntly as he began to trail the four.

"Please," he begged. "Or, can you just do it for me? I'll... pay you?"

Tim craned his neck around and gave an incredulous look to Charlie, who now realized what an incredibly stupid thing that was to offer. What was he going to pay him with? Ghost money? Other than the nasty look, Tim ignored the asinine proposal and continued to fly after his victims.

Charlie was panicking, Tim was his last shot. "Tim, please!" he begged. Just help me learn how to materialize. Help me do ghost shit." His voice was growing louder.

Tim felt his heart race and his muscles tense.

Charlie lost control. "Help me!" he screamed.

There was enough energy behind the voice to cross the threshold into the physical realm. The noise echoed off the lockers lining the scorched hallways. The four teenagers halted at once, their curses and gasps followed Charlie's plea. They began to talk over each other.

"What the fuck was that?"

"Did you hear that?"

"Guys..."

"We should leave."

Tim spun around and glared at Charlie with a deadly fire in his eyes. He pointed a single index finger at Charlie.

"Get out!" Tim's voice dwarfed Charlie's previous vocal expulsion.

Without hesitation, the four teenagers sprinted down the charred hallways, scrambling to find the nearest fire exit that wasn't blockaded by collapsed building material—a touch that Tim had added post-mortem.

Charlie couldn't help but be overcome with a wave of guilt.

"I'm sorry, man," he said with his head down. He felt guilty for ruining what seemed like a solidly spooky haunt.

Tim let out a deep sigh. "It's fine." He pinched the bridge of his nose, like a father who regretted scolding a child. "You ruined the haunt, and they probably won't be back, but it's fine."

Charlie was silent. The realization that he may have burned his only bridge was sinking in.

"Look," Tim began. "I wasn't always what I am today." He actually sounded apologetic. "I didn't just..." He paused, trying to find a way to explain. "...die and automatically know how to do what I do." Sincerity was a vulnerable thing for Tim. "I had to train, you know?"

"I have been," replied Charlie. "It's useless."

Tim let out a deep sigh. "Look man," he said uneasily. "There's this guy... when I was a new ghost, he may or may not have helped me out a little bit."

Charlie looked up at Tim, trying to decipher where he was going with this.

"See, he was my football coach in middle school back in the 60's. Actually died of an aneurism during the championship game." Tim reached up and stroked his mustache. "When I passed, I didn't know what to do with myself. So, I reached out to him, and this guy gave me my new purpose." He took a solemn pause. "To harass the shit out of minors, and women who are showing up alone in an empty house."

"You think he can help me?" asked Charlie

"If anybody can, it's him. I have to warn you though Charlie," began Tim.

"What?" he asked with caution.

"He's a little rough around the edges."

Coming from Tim, Charlie had a tinge of concern what being "rough around the edges" meant. Most people would describe Tim himself as "rough around the edges," if not outright jagged and abrasive. Despite the air of caution though, Charlie took Tim's offer to reach out to Coach Casper (no relation). Tim didn't mention how long it would take, only that Coach pretty much worked on his own time-line, and when he shows up, he shows up.

The concern in Charlie grew as the contactors finished up their renovations on the manor. The decaying walls and water-stained ceilings had been gradually replaced by pris-tine alabaster sheetrock and glistening plaster. The cold wind that drafted through the house had been extinguished by the installation of a brand-new central heating unit. Every little detail that had once made the house a great beginners haunt, had been systematically extinguished. Charlie had wasted home field advantage while he had it.

When the morning was still orange and brisk, Charlie's eyes caught a glimpse of a round translucent figure cresting the horizon. As he got closer, Charlie was able to make out the details of Coach Casper. He was bigger and surlier than his previous student, and his mustache remained unkempt. His pasty face was adorned with bright red cheeks that were flanked by two powerful sideburns, that had no doubt been in style at the time of his passing. A bright red collared shirt —that was just short enough to show a sliver of stomach hair —was stretched out thin around the towering man's gut.

In life, Charlie was sure he was a man among men. Having played for Notre Dame following a stint in the Pacific Theater of WWII, Coach Casper came from a genera-tion of leather headed football players who had never even heard of the words "concussion" or "CTE" before. If Tim Jefferson was of one school of ghost, here was its headmaster.

Charlie greeted Coach with his hand extended, but the ghoul only looked him up and down while tonguing his cheek, seemingly playing a pinch of tobacco that had long been decaying with his body.

"You Chuck?" he asked, spitting ectoplasm between his teeth.

"Uh, Charlie, yeah."

"Yeah, I 'spose yer havin' trouble with ghostin', huh?"

"That's, uh," Charlie struggled to process the strange apparition in front of him. "Yeah, that's right. I see what Tim can do and I—"

"Ha!" Coach interrupted. "Little Timmy wouldn't know ghostin' if it kicked 'em in the pecker."

Charlie was beginning to connect some dots.

"Well, I see what he does, the materializing, and how he plans everything down to specific times and locations and—"

"Look son," Coach interrupted again. "It's Simple. Let me spell that for you. Ess. Eye. En. Pee. El."

Charlie was speechless.

"It's 'bout spooks! Scares! Hoodwinks 'n' how-do-ya-do's. None of that 'elevated horror' rigmarole horseshit." Coach pointed to a contractor unloading power tools. "Watch this." He floated over to the prey, who was exiting out the back of a work van, then let out a *SHRIEEEEK* an inch from his face.

Startled, the worker cursed and stumbled backward into the back of the work van, tripping over his own heels. In a swift flick of the wrist, Coach had turned on a power drill that was left in the back of the van. Charlie realized the worker's head was a on a direct path for the spinning tool.

"No! Wait!" he yelled.

In a quarter of a second, the workers skull had been penetrated by the tool, which had begun to make a strawberry milkshake out of his brain matter.

"Jesus Christ, you didn't have to kill him!"

"Oh boo-*fucking*-hoo," replied Coach. "Oh my gosh, can you believe it?" He was feigning shock. "Oh, a ghost killed somebody! Oh, my word!" Coach was now prancing around with his arms flailing. "I ain't never heard of no such thing," he said in a falsetto.

It had been all but five minutes of meeting this man, and Charlie was already regretting it. Maybe leaving the manor wouldn't be so bad. Surely not worth putting up with this idiot.

Coach straightened up and pointed a finger at Charlie with a sharp whistle from his mouth.

"That's what it takes be a goddamn ghost, son. I just saved your ass about a week before they continue finishing this house."

"Thanks," said Charlie reluctantly.

"The way I reckon, this place will sell real quick, meaning we got maybe a month or so 'fore the new owners move in." Coach turned to face the manor, assessing it. "A month to get ya ready."

"What?" Charlie asked. "So, we're just going to let them finish renovating?"

"Yes, we are. Think about the targets?" Coach tapped his temple. "Construction workers? Tough scare. But if we get lucky, and a family or a young couple moves in," he rubbed his hands together and licked his lips. "Them piggies are ready for market."

Charlie was confused. "Then why kill that worker?"

Coach jerked his head back and acted accosted. "Come on, son. A story!" He balled his hands into fists and shook them in the air. "You got a beautiful, haunted manor out here like this, and you got to put some damn lore behind the place."

Charlie turned and looked at the manor. He was beginning to understand.

"See, you got to lay down a foundation," said Coach while making a low sweeping motion with his hand. "Let the rumors spread jus' a bit. A couple construction workers have mysterious deaths, the house gets sold for cheap, a family moves in, *but* 'spite strange things happening, they don't want to move because they won't be able to afford another place as nice."

"A couple deaths? So, you plan on killing another?" asked Charlie.

"Shit son, you already took care of the first."

"But that wasn't mysterious."

Coach shook his head. "They don't know that."

Regrettably, Charlie was beginning to see how Coach might be considered a savant.

Upon his request, Coach was given a tour of the house. He inspected doors, flooring, windows, cupboards, anything and everything that could be slammed, smashed, or thrown open. He studied the layout of the house, drew maps, took notes, all to the surprise of Charlie who still couldn't get over the absolute ludicrousness of the way this man walked and talked.

The training regiments were, admittedly, rigorous. Coach had Charlie pushing his spectral abilities to the absolute limit. Flickering lights, materializing as a decayed corpse, even infiltrating some unlucky training dummy's dreams.

Slowly over the course of the training, the contractors ceased visiting the manor, and a bright blue "For Sale" sign was planted square in the yard. As potential buyers filtered in and out, Coach had Charlie use this as a "pre-game."

"Fundamentals," Coach told Charlie. This upset the younger ghost, as he truly did feel much more confident in his abilities now than before. He had mastered the door creaking open, the lights flickering, even the cupboard openings. He was ready for more. He knew it.

The family who ended up snagging the place up was young. The father, no older than his early 30's, had professionally styled black hair brushed to the left, while the sides remained closer to their roots. His dress and demeanor also spoke to the fact that it was important to him to be viewed by the world as both professional, and fashionable. By the looks of him, Charlie assumed he worked in some marketing or finance position, ideally something that would take him away from home quite often. If you get the wife to notice paranormal activity, and the husband to deny it, that's a recipe for success. Maybe Coach really did know what he was doing.

The mother seemed naïve. She had been carrying canvases and boxes of paint in. If she was a stay-at-home mother like Charlie had predicted *and* had some artistic sensibilities, it wouldn't take much before she would assume a poltergeist. The baby was the key to that.

The child was around a year old or so. Coach was strict about not overdoing it with her. Charlie's interaction with her had to be just little enough to warrant strange behavior, but not enough to send her into frequent wailing fits that would warrant a doctor's visit.

The pair of ghosts hovered above the child's crib, who was close to outgrowing it.

"Okay," Coach said. "Momma's been down for 'bout half an hour or so. She's gonna be real sleepy."

"Don't we want her awake?" asked Charlie. "To be aware?"

Coach waved his finger in there. "Nope. Not right away. Make her question if she's really seeing what she's seeing."

At Coach's signal, Charlie waved his translucent hand through the child's abdomen. A trivial thing, but enough to disturb her spiritual equilibrium to start the waterworks.

\* \* \*

As THE CRY bounced across the newly finished walls, the mother begrudgingly lifted herself from her bed. She was tired. Tired of being alone in a new home, tired of being the one to constantly be cleaning, feeding, changing, caring, and especially waking, for the baby.

She was almost asleep too. Tessa had been sleeping well enough since she turned one, so it wasn't a big deal for Mary to have to go in and calm her down on the occasional off night. To be frank, Mary had sort of missed the feeling of being needed since Tessa had become slightly more independent. Her husband thought the baby growing up would help her depression, but he also thought moving her out here to the middle of nowhere would help as well. He had heard it from a "doctor friend," though Mary was pretty sure she knew what friend he was referring to and it didn't give her any comfort.

She put her hair in a quick ponytail while striding down the hallway towards the nursery. Her eyes weren't completely open yet, but the layout of the house was fairly easy to learn. As she turned the corner into the child's room, she felt warm. Despite the frustrations that come with motherhood, she couldn't resist the happiness she felt when comforting her squirming child. She liked feeling needed. She liked feeling loved.

Crossing the threshold into the nursery, the warmth receded from her body. She shivered. She didn't remember the room being this drafty before, and she approached the two windows facing the north yard to check for any air flow. Waving her hand across the creases and edges of the windowsill, Mary couldn't identify exactly where the chill was coming from. Regardless, she put the investigation on pause and returned to her child.

Mary hovered over her daughter, admiring Tessa's scrunched up face. The little hairs on her head were barely more than white. Mary's hair had looked similar as kid, but eventually her blonde locks had darkened into a standard golden as she grew. She lifted the child out of her crib and brought her close to her chest. Mary wanted to give the babe her own warmth, but quite frankly was having a hard time fighting off the chill herself.

"Shhhhh," she soothed, bouncing the child in her arms.

As the mother cradled her daughter, a noise softly crept behind her. The door that led into the hallway slowly, and steadily, began to close shut. The aged wooden frame gave out a groan.

*Creeeeeeeeeek*

Mary sucked in her breath. It was an old house. *It was the draft* again—nothing more. She held on to Tessa tighter. Her steps towards the door were slow and deliberate. Her hands trembled as she reached for the doorknob. As she touched the frigid brass, another noise arose mere steps behind her. A soft wind chime rung out across the room. She turned her head just enough to see it out of the corner of her eye. The decorated mobile hanging above the crib began to turn, and it was accompanied by electronic noise that mimicked a wind chime.

The mother froze. *It was the draft.* Even though not one hair on her body could detect the movement of any air what-soever. *It was just the wind.* Inside the house. This satisfied her for a moment, until the mobile began to spin faster.

As the mobile spun, the musical chimes lowered in pitch. The animals and flowers hanging by threads began to spin rapidly, knotting with each other and bouncing wildly. Tessa had seemed to go from a simple child's cry, into a violent wail. Mary clung tightly to her child, not moving an inch. Was she hallucinating? This can't be right. None of this seemed right.

In a decisive motion, Mary pivoted around and bounded

out of the bedroom, slamming the door behind her—shutting out the madness. With her back against the frame, she listened carefully as the distorted chimes seemed to fade out of sound. With one hand still pinning her child to her chest, she moved the other over her mouth and let out a soft sob.

\* \* \*

CHARLIE AND COACH stood quietly in the nursey, neither one of them making a sound. Charlie's chest heaved with exhaustion. He hadn't felt this tired since he died. As he let off control of the mobile, he heard the woman slowly march back towards her room with the baby.

Still panting, Charlie looked over to coach, whose eyes were wide with excitement.

"Was that…" Charlie started.

"That's what I'm *fucking* talking about, son!" yelled Coach.

Charlie grinned. "I don't think I did too bad."

"Absolutely not." Coach floated over and put his hand on Charlie's shoulder. "If I had a corporal body, I'd be hard as a goddamn rock right now."

Charlie laughed as Coach gave him a little shake. He was beginning to understand him a little better.

"This ain't the end though. Hell, first quarter isn't even over with," began Coach.

Charlie nodded.

Coach's eyes narrowed as he shifted moods. "You were a little early on the mobile spinning, and a little fast. It got a little sloppy." Coach's wheels were turning. "And you forgot to give the lights a little flicker at the end there, son, but that's alright. We got her on the ropes." A smile was fighting through his stern expression, but it wasn't a smile for Charlie, it was pure love of the game.

"Yes sir," responded Charlie. He was surprised at his own reaction.

"We *do not* let up." Coach turned to stare directly in Charlie's eyes. "Whose house is this?"

Charlie studied Coach. Was this question rhetorical or was he genuinely curious about the ownership.

"My house," responded the younger ghost hesitantly.

Coach raised his voice. "Whose house is this?"

He understood now.

"My house!" Charlie responded, slamming his fist into his chest.

"Whose house is this?!" There was a hellfire in Coach's eyes.

"My house!"

The pair went on like this for minutes. Charlie realized that this first set up was a test. Coach wasn't going to truly invest in him if he didn't buy in to what he was selling. Charlie had passed the test.

Coach emphasized the importance of pacing. Charlie had to take a few nights off to get the woman to settle down before acting up again. It was important to sow seeds of doubt. The immediate weeks would be simple stuff. Fundamentals. Heavy footsteps, knocking stuff of cabinets, etc. Nothing to give the wife proof to show the husband. "Divide and conquer," Coach would say. And oh, was it easy.

Being a ghost allowed Charlie to get a pretty good idea of the relationship between the spouses. The woman may not have been perfect even before the haunting, but good lord was the husband a dick. Part of Charlie felt guilty for driving a rift between the two, but maybe this could present the two an opportunity for divorce. Wouldn't be the worst thing to come out of this, Charlie thought.

After a month or so, Coach instructed Charlie to ramp it up. Bloody handprints, whispering in the mother's ears at night, real exorcist shit. He felt like Coach was beginning to trust him to call plays, which was a bigger honor than Charlie imagined. They were getting close to the finish line. Both knew that.

On a particularly stormy night, Charlie and Coach had watched the family have an uncomfortable dinner. The wife sat across from her husband, while the child sat in a high-chair at the end of the table. There had been screaming matches recently about leaving the house and moving back to the city, but the husband wasn't having any of it.

The atmosphere inside the house was hot—almost flammable. The scene outside the house was dreary. Rain pattered against the windows as periodic lighting gave glimpses to a landscape littered with dead trees and puddles of mud. The two ghosts had not said a word to each other, but both knew tonight was the night to finish it.

Charlie watched as they argued. The woman was pleading with her husband to leave—begging him to. Charlie was going to see to it that he would regret not listening to her.

He needed the lights to go out. Charlie had flickered them before, but never all at once. He focused his spectral energy into the surrounding lightbulbs. Only a few of them went dark. He cursed himself.

The couple went silent.

Charlie looked at Coach, who was glaring at him.

"The breaker, son. Don't split your focus on all the lightbulbs. Focus on the breaker in the basement and flip that," instructed the older man.

Charlie nodded. He closed his eyes and found the breaker in the basement below. With a flick of his wrist, the house went dark.

The couple's necks craned upwards, investigating the power outage. "This fucking piece of shit house," said the husband, already tense from the dinner conversation. He pushed himself away from the table and began towards the basement door.

"John, please don't." There was fear in the woman's voice.

"I'll be fine," he sighed as he turned on his phone's flashlight.

As he opened the door to the stairs, Charlie waved his ghostly hand through the child in the highchair. Tessa let out a soft whimper at first, but it quickly developed into a cry that pierced through the blackness of the manor. Charlie saw the husband stop before taking his first steps.

*Good,* the ghost thought, *he's beginning to feel it.*

As the husband crept down the stairs slowly, Charlie turned his attention the mother and child, who had found a flashlight in the drawer and was now panning it around the room slowly. Perfect.

Just in the sightline of the woman was a hallway leading down to the bedrooms on the first floor. About halfway down the hall, there were two open doors across from each other leading into opposing rooms. The space between the rooms was just small enough that if Charlie could materialize for a brief second and walk across the hallway in sight of the woman, it'd be a hell of a play. He needed this.

As Mary swept across the kitchen with her flashlight, Charlie waited in one of the bedrooms. He had to time this perfectly. He still wasn't great at materializing, but it wouldn't have to be long. He closed his eyes and focused.

"You got this son," whispered Coach in his ear.

Charlie jumped. Even though he was a ghost himself, he still got occasionally spooked by the master.

"Focus," Coach continued. "Put all that unnecessary bull-crap away. You ain't sitting under a shade tree drinking lemonade and eating fish sandwiches with your fat girlfriend no more. You are a ghost. A spook. A specter. Show me you're worth it."

Some stuff Coach said still caught Charlie by surprise sometimes.

Charlie caught a glimpse of the sweeping light and moved. He felt his physical feet hit the hardwood. He turned his head away from the woman. He only wanted her to get a glimpse of him. Let her fill in the rest with her imagination. As the flashlight filled the hallway, he took two quick strides across the hall and into the other room. Not even half a second. He was hoping he wasn't too quick.

Suddenly, the mother expelled a loud gasp, and the flashlight came crashing to the floor, rolling away from her. Charlie didn't plan this, but he was calling an audible. He looked at Coach and they gave each other quick nods, both understanding the opportunity in front of them.

As the mother scrambled for the flashlight, she reached out and gripped the handle. Hovering behind her, Charlie quickly materialized his right hand, and gripped the mother's trembling hand holding on to the flashlight. He made sure to make his hand a sickly pale green, and his touch to feel icy cold.

As Charlie, gripped her hand, the mother let out a scream and jerked the flashlight away from him.

"Mary!" yelled the husband from down the stairs. "Mary!?"

"John please!" she screamed, trembling in the corner with her child clung to her chest. "John please! Please! Please! Please!"

As she wailed, Charlie heard the husband stumble in the dark, rushing up the stairs.

"Charlie, the door!" yelled Coach.

Stretching out his hand, Charlie swung the basement door shut right before the husband reached the top. To

Charlie's surprise, he struggled a bit keeping the door shut as the husband fought in the pitch black to open it.

"I know you're tired," yelled Coach on the sidelines. "Fight through it, son. We're at the two-minute warning."

The couple were yelling through the door. They were scared. The husband was confessing his love for her, for their daughter, for his own life. They seemed beaten and broken. When Charlie was sure of this, he let off control of the door and the husband burst through. Simultaneously, Charlie flipped the breaker back on and the house was once again illuminated.

The husband sprinted over to his wife and knelt by her side, his hand brushing back her golden hair that her tears had matted to her face.

"It's okay baby," he said fighting back tears. His voice was hoarse and shaky. "I'm here. I'm here."

The wife was trying to get something out between her sobs and the baby's cry, but Charlie could not quite make out what. It didn't matter. All that mattered was timing and atmosphere.

As the couple cradled each other, Charlie caught his breath. This final push was going to take everything he had in him and more. He waited till the air seemed calmer and looked at Coach for the signal. *Is it time?* Knowing his thoughts, Coach gave him a commanding shake of his head.

Charlie glared at Coach. Pleading with his eyes for the go-ahead. Again, Coach shook his head and raised his hand up in the air in a "wait" gesture.

In a quiet breath, Charlie heard the husband speak.

"It's over," he said. His wife's face was buried into his neck. "It's okay Mary. It's over."

With a sudden ferocity, Coach slammed his hand down through the air, letting Charlie loose on the trembling spouses. Charlie took a deep breath and raised his right hand in the air. He extended his spectral presence to each lightbulb on the bottom floor of the house, like a puppet master's strings emanating from the translucent figure.

To the couple's horror, the once fully lit room was now assaulted by antiquated strobing lightbulbs. The hopeful silence of the room was now buried under the screams of the occupants, who had begun to resign themselves to the poltergeistic torture.

With his right hand still raised in the air, Charlie took his left and swept across the room— thrusting the doors of the cabinets open, and launching their glass contents across the room, shattering themselves upon the stained wood walls.

The woman screamed, "What do you want?!"

Charlie Bottoms was going to tell them exactly what he wanted. Using his left hand once more, Charlie raised it parallel to his other. The chairs that had flanked the dinner table levitated to shoulder height and began to rapidly spin.

"Finish it, Charlie!" yelled Coach. "Bring this 'sum bitch home!"

He strained. He had to materialize while maintaining the flashy show. He was running out of energy. Charlie wasn't even aware ghosts could sweat, but damn was he sweating.

He strained between words. "I'm. Trying."

"There's no goddamn trying," replied Coach. "What do you want?"

"For them to get out!" Charlie yelled back.

"What?" asked Coach.

Charlie's arms were shaking. "Get... Out!"

Coach put his palm behind his ear, "I can't hear you, you fucking *pussy*."

Charlie's wrath flared. He felt an unknown hellfire of energy surge through him. Suddenly he felt his feet hit the kitchen tile. His face was grey—decayed. His eyeballs were rotten out of his head. He had hit the ground hard when he died, and his spinal cord protruded out of his neck, dangling dead flesh like flag on a pole without wind.

Charlie raised one dead finger at the terrified couple and whispered.

"Get out."

Within three seconds, the pair had bounded out of the kitchen door and onto the brown yard. Just for fun, Charlie made sure it took their SUV a couple tries for the engine to turn over. As the Chevy Tahoe tore through the rain and wind into the black of night, Coach floated over next to Charlie, admiring his work, and gave him a firm "good game" pat on the ass.

*Colby Woodland is a part-time author and full-time teacher out of Topeka, KS. His short stories have appeared in Dark Horses Magazine, and Schlock! Webzine. He enjoys writing speculative and supernatural fiction, often with a humorous tint, and looks forward to more of his work being published in the near future.*

# BOSQUE BELLO

## KEVIN A DAVIS

"*J*ames, dude, it's after midnight."

Focused on the frogs and insects chorusing the cemetery, I hadn't heard my roommates pull up in their Prius. The pungent scent of smoke overtook the musk of the woods. I'd spent the last five hours on my stool without a single glimpse of a ghost, spirit, apparition, specter, shade, or phantasm. Not even a wisp of fog. The incorporeal favored me, but not every night.

"Thanks Rick. Let me pack." I sighed and slid my gangly legs off the stool to a wobbly stance. The night wasn't cold for April, but my constitution has never been an asset. Balancing the case on my stool, I disassembled my equipment and tucked each piece into their foam slots.

"We're going to drop by Palace Saloon for a quick drink." Erin had exited the passenger side and leaned on the top of the Prius.

I sagged slightly, continuing to fold up the tripod. "Any chance of dropping me off first?"

Rick snorted. "You haven't come out in two weeks. See the living."

So, no, they'd hijack me to the bar. "I work at 8:00 a.m., with the living." I snapped the case shut. Both of my room-mates believed I needed a social life. At thirty-four, I had more social interaction than I wanted between them and work.

Erin had moved to the back to open the trunk for me. "Any pictures?" They thought ghosts were cool, along with ancient aliens, vampires, and myriad government conspiracies.

"Not tonight." I slid the case inside and covered it with a sandy beach towel.

I had some poor pictures where the spirits had offered me an electronic glimpse. My attempt to submit them to a New England journal had indeed ended in a story. They featured the quirky, but harmless, ghost hunter who believed he met with ghosts in western Massachusetts. My employer of eight years had shunned the negative press and terminated me. Yearning for warmer nights to pursue my interests, I found a position as a statistical analyst in Fernandina Beach, moved to a cheap room with two stoners, and kept my photography to myself.

"See anything?" Erin's lidded eyes widened slightly and they flicked their brown ponytail back over their shoulder.

I frowned and shook my head, closing the hatch. "Not tonight."

The back seat of the Prius always had an abundance of detritus, some more identifiable as trash than others. Squeezing in behind Rick, I folded my long legs up against his chair and took off my flat, ivy cap, brushing a dead leaf off the herringbone plaid. With one last languishing study of Bosque Bello Cemetery, I watched the road as Rick drove off the grass swale.

The Palace Saloon had historical value in the area, and I appreciated that one aspect more than the others did. The pirate at the door begged posing tourists and their cameras while the glass above promised that it was the oldest bar in Florida. I enjoyed history, but had never confirmed the boast.

My interest in Fernandina Beach was who had died, and possibly not left. The most interesting possibilities were those who had been separated from their mortal bodies during the Spanish-American war, but there were other notable figures. The spirits abounding at Bosque Bello Cemetery enjoyed my company, if not my equipment. One local had warned me from the place, firmly believing that a grave robber, their cousin, had disappeared within the gates.

I jolted when Rick chirped to a stop in one of the downtown parking spots.

He swore, then giggled. Fresh salt air assailed my lungs as I slammed open my door. I had legs unfolded and squeezing out by the time he found park. In another two months I'd have saved up enough to get my own car, if I could avoid buying any more equipment. I leaned toward a safer transit at the moment.

The bricked downtown was quiet except for a few rumbling cars. When Erin opened the front door to the bar the exploding clamor stopped me in my tracks and raced my pulse. "C'mon," they said after Rick slid inside.

I swallowed and stepped into a room full of talking people and the scent of stale beer mixed with salt air. The décor ranged from bare-chested maidens holding up various things to historical items from every period. I did enjoy that.

Peering at the patrons, some of whom I knew as regulars, I paused at one of the most arrogant. Duncan proclaimed a noble heritage with a chiseled jaw, a regal bearing, and a perfect build. A head shorter than myself, his proportions were complimentary to a muscled physique. An intolerably affluent Adonis who did his best to belittle me at every excuse.

I strode tangent to him in a vain attempt to avoid a confrontation, but my head loomed over any possible cover.

"Ichabod!" He yelled with a rich laugh that drew in other locals.

"Ichabod." At least a third of the room joined in and the rest turned to find me, the gangly, awkward creature who searched for a low, empty chair.

One lone table had the leftovers of a single patron and I dove to seat myself. If I'd mistakenly taken someone's place, I could relocate once the attention dwindled. Rick and Erin had settled in with one of their friends, probably the reason they'd planned the outing. A couple of the other patrons still gawked, but most had gone on to more interesting chatter. Duncan, I couldn't see, but at least he did not hunt me down.

When a brown-haired woman settled into her spot at the table I startled hard enough to knock my knees. "I'm sorry," I said in a fluster. Racing heart and stiff limbs betrayed me as I somewhat flailed attempting to arise.

She laughed lightly. "I can share." Her wide eyes were a deep brown, her smile subtle, and her voice a melody. "It looks like you haven't ordered yet. I'll take another rum and Coke. As rent."

I blinked a few too many times and her smile just grew. My cheeks flushed warm and the tips of my ears burned. "Rum and Coke."

Her face had a pleasant symmetry, though her eyes dominated my focus. She wore a simple blue blouse, two rows of tiny jeweled studs on pink earlobes, a single silver bracelet, and tiny silver ring – on her right hand. "My name's Cynthia. You're not Ichabod."

I stiffened even as I managed to rise halfway out of my seat to head for the bartender. Rum and Coke was a simple straightforward drink. "It's not Ichabod." I gestured down my body. "They just call me that."

"A school teacher, are you?"

Had I stopped blinking? If I had, I started again then smiled. "I'm not, but good guess." I liked her light humor and quick wit. "My name is James."

"Light on the ice." She handed me her unfinished glass. "James."

My heart pounded as I turned and approached the bar. I had not been taken with a woman's attention since high school and that had been enough of a failure to cure me, so I had thought. Cynthia's simple demeanor had entranced me in a mere minute. Emotions I had considered long dead boiled in my chest and it tightened, near bursting.

Before I turned from the bar with our two drinks, I felt two quick dreads, first that she'd be gone; and second that she would have seen the scrawny height of me and wish she had left. Instead, she watched me with just a corner of a smile playing at the outside of her lip.

"How tall? Six-four?" Cynthia asked.

"Six-six." My throat was dry but I had to be careful, alcohol did not do well with my metabolism. "I got the same drink." I placed two rum and Cokes on the table before I folded down into my seat.

"Smart. I've always been partial to rum. It's best in the islands." Cynthia studied her glass.

"Do you have a favorite? Island?" My left arm became an awkward extension that I could not place in an appropriate position. The pulse of my heart beat loud enough that I hoped I might hear her response.

"Jamaica. Though it can be dangerous. The culture there is deep enough to be intriguing. I remember an excellent play. *Pocomania*."

I preferred Barbados and the Chase Vault, but I'd rather stay off the topic of my obsession with spirits. "Marson, correct?"

Cynthia's laugh tinkled with delight. "You know the poet?" She leaned forward and I thought I might swoon. "So few people know of her."

Her rapt focus on me made it difficult to speak. "Toward the Stars was my first read of her work. A distinct shift from her earlier work. You like poetry?" Her smile spread and I added, "Who are your favorite poets?"

Cynthia expounded on the virtues of many, to my own excitement as we overlapped. We barely touched our glasses as the light, sweet scents filled the air between us. I had never been so enamored by a person who could speak intelligently on the arts. Perhaps Beth had been right and I did need more social time. My anxiety had converted to sheer delight.

"Ichabod." Duncan scraped a chair to our table, sat with fluid grace, and draped himself onto the wood and into our conversation. "Have you been boring this beautiful woman with your ghost stories? Invite her out to the graveyard with your equipment?" Casually, he raised his hand and offered it to Cynthia. "Duncan MacGregor."

I peered at Cynthia. She'd straightened and turned herself toward Duncan with a growing smile. Her eyes flicked to the muscled arm he offered and she quickly took his hand. "Cynthia. Pleasure to meet you."

"It's a cemetery," I said. My ears burned hot. How the words had come out, I did not know. I had been careful not to mention my spectral interests, for fear of driving her away. Duncan had quickly torpedoed that attempt. Cynthia did not seem to care. I couldn't be sure she even remembered I was here. She certainly didn't argue his assumptions on what we were speaking about. A hollow formed in my chest.

My eyes flicked to my drink and I grabbed it. Warm, flat Coke with a spike of sweet rum flushed into my dry throat, stemming any other nonsense that could escape.

Duncan chuckled in a deriding tone. "Whatever. It's the

childish behavior that comes from a lonely nerd. We live in a seaside paradise of shopping, culture, and natural resources. Do you like to sail, Cynthia? My family has a catamaran that is a dream on the water. I rarely bother with any of our larger ships as I like to be in control instead of leaving that to a captain."

I sagged as she leaned forward with an impish smile. "I love sailing, Duncan."

Rick's hand on my shoulder made me knock my knees on the underside of the table. The warm rum had started to filter down to fill the hollow in my chest.

"They're closing up, dude. I figured you'd be bouncing off the walls by now." Rick's voice proved how oblivious he was to my plight.

Erin stepped to my other side, closer to Duncan. They studied Cynthia and Duncan, then their face saddened as they glanced at me. "Let's go, James." Their tone coaxed and sympathized.

I stood, swaying and rattling the chair with the back of my leg. Duncan described his mastery of sailing and the various amenities available on his boat. Cynthia didn't look up as I prepared to depart. My ears hurt and my heart felt as if it were breaking.

"Say goodbye," Erin whispered.

I had already stepped toward the door. Rick let in a breath of salt air as he exited. "Goodbye," I said with a thin croak. "Cynthia."

It took her a moment, and she used a slight pause in Duncan's bragging to turn up to me. "Have a good night, James. Thank you for the drink." She picked up her glass and sipped as Duncan continued.

I'd been a fool to think a woman would find me interesting, especially compared to the worldly Duncan. She'd been happy to have someone buy her a drink. That was all. I stumbled into the night, missing the pirate statue at the last moment. The streets had too many lights when I wanted darkness.

"It looked like you were really hitting it off," Erin said.

"Who?" asked Rick. His Prius beeped as he opened his car door.

"We *were* having an enjoyable conversation."

Erin patted my shoulder. "Maybe she'll be there tomorrow night."

I said nothing as I squeezed in behind Rick. There was no reason for me to go to the bar with Duncan taking her out for sailing cruises. The evening had been a glimpse at my own loneliness and I couldn't afford to trick myself into hope. As we drove away, Rick began a sluggish banter that made me question my present safety over all else. I closed my eyes and barely opened them fully until I was safely in my 10x10 bedroom that I rented from Rick.

My clothes were ready for the next morning, so I slid my equipment into the closet and stripped. My heart beat slow and empty with a melody not unlike a funeral march. It fit the sparse accommodations. I placed a glass of water on the nightstand and climbed into the only other furniture, a lumpy single bed with a worn blanket. Any thought of Cynthia I slammed back down, refusing to give it any light. I could not change who or what I was, and that would never compete with Duncan. Curling on my side so that my feet fit, I turned out the light.

The next morning I found it easier to ignore the previous night. Work provided all the usual frustrations and routine to keep me preoccupied. During an egg salad sandwich lunch, I considered my evening's activities. I would forego the equipment tonight and merely stroll the cemetery grounds. The police and other authorities had grown accustomed to my excursions and ignored me. I might as well be one of the spirits.

Erin dropped me off before dusk and I set down the narrow roads. The air had the comforting, earthy smell of graves, though most soil here was clay. Within fifteen minutes a small wisp, no more than a child, paralleled me among the trees and headstones. They disappeared into deeper shade and I kept strolling. I appreciated the early gratification; something that would keep my mind off other more troubling questions concerning the mortal world.

The next spirit proved far more cohesive. Shadows marked eyes and a turn of his face gave me a sense of masculine features. A soldier from his ephemeral gear. I did not approach, but paused to let him march across the graves ahead of me. His glance in my direction sent a light shiver up my back. Some ghosts wanted nothing to do with mortals, and they could be quite persuasive in their reproach. I'd learned my lesson with a broken arm in tenth grade. Worse for them were people such as myself, who could see and interact with them. I considered my fear healthy.

Two more spirits appeared to me. I should have been elated at the abundance this evening, but my emotions were stunted. Morose, I had done what I could to subdue all feelings.

I managed to speak with one, a young woman in ragged form. She trailed up to me to investigate. "Good night," I said to her. They never spoke back, at least not in words, but I always tried to be polite.

She flared to twice her size and height, then hissed. Fluttering she threw herself back from me and I remained motionless. Something had bothered her, but she dispersed into the shadows without another approach.

It was 10:00 p.m. when the ghost I'd dubbed the Colonel turned directly toward me. He had solid definition and I named him by his hat and clothes. Even his goatee had form. His eyes were black pits as he strode toward me, blocking my path deeper into the cemetery. An animosity poured out from him and I began to take steps backward. I could smell my own sweat.

As he continued with such purpose, I rose my hands. "I'll leave. I'll leave." Perhaps I gave off something they didn't like tonight. Sadness. Loneliness.

I braced as the spirit smacked into me. The force knocked me a long step back. They did not want me here.

The form dissolved upon impact, either overtaxed or secure that its message had been sent. Despondent over a wasted night I turned for the entrance gates. I had hours before Erin would drive the half hour to pick me up, unless I called them early. My phone in hand at the boundaries of the cemetery, I peered back at the activity I missed. More than one shape moved in the shadows and trees. My mood had been too dark, it brought out the worst in spirits. How long before I forgot Cynthia?

Instead of dialing, my fingers tapped up a map and located the Palace Saloon. The walk would take half an hour. Standing a full minute, I did not start the directions. I knew them, generally. I couldn't imagine subjecting myself to more embarrassment, but I appeared to crave the punishment.

The door let out a warm scent of beer and the loud laughter of the Palace Saloon. I took a hesitant step inside. Duncan did not appear to be here. Heart in my throat, I turned to our spot.

Cynthia waved me over, tapping the top of the table in an invitation. My breath caught and I forced a smile on my face and shuffled.

"Duncan said you didn't come here much. I'm happy to see he was wrong." She tapped her glass. "Buy me a drink?"

The mention of the arrogant Adonis stiffened me, but I

tried to crack a smile. "Of course." Drinks weren't so expensive that she'd suffer through a conversation with me just for the cost. It could be possible that we had both enjoyed our talk. Could she actually be happy to see me? I wanted to stab the bubble of hope that lifted in my chest. My face tightened as I walked to the bar.

The bartender took in my expression and grimaced back. "Same as last night?"

I searched the entry for Duncan. "I hope not." The bartender had meant the drinks. "Yes, rum and Cokes." Pasting on a smile, I resisted the urge to see if Cynthia still sat at her table.

She watched me as I returned, and a truer smile lifted my lips and step. "I'm not here that often. Usually with my roommates. What brings you back tonight?" I set our drinks down. "Are you on vacation?"

"I'm teaching middle grade, and writing, of course."

Folding limbs into place, I sat. "So you live here." I stated the obvious and quickly turned to a question. "What are you writing?"

"Contemporary fiction. Chick lit." She smiled. "Do you write, James? Maybe about your ghost hunting?"

I flinched. My cheeks were hot, and I took a sip of my drink. "No" Bringing up my proclivity could be dangerous as I tended to ramble. "Some poems in high school, but they never amounted to anything. Have you published?" I asked.

She hadn't, but we talked about her many attempts and few successes with writing. We'd both taken college courses in literature, though she had far more opportunities with her degree. Once again, we became engaged in our discussion to the exclusion of all others. I had cringed at each opening of the door early on, but it seemed Duncan was occupied elsewhere and I carefully did not mention him. Basking in the first engaging interaction I'd ever had, my heart danced at every smile and twinkle in her eyes.

We had moved on to talk about her new teaching career and I began to calculate a near decade difference in our ages. I never heard the front door of the saloon open.

"Ichabod!"

A good quarter of the room chorused with Duncan's call. Heat flushed up my cheeks and ears. Cynthia looked around my shoulder, smiled broadly, and waved. My heart stopped its lively dance and raced in attempt to flee. When we were alone, I could believe she only had eyes for me, but when Duncan arrived that illusion faded like a surprised spirit. Gloom descended like a thick fog. Why had I done this to myself? Not wanting to see the expression on her face, I studied the table.

Duncan wore stylish polished brown leather shoes that clacked on the floor as he strode to our table. He smelled of sharp perfume as he stopped beside my chair and placed two well-formed hands on the table. I withdrew my bony left hand and dropped it to my lap.

"Should you be digging up graves or something?" Duncan's rich voice boiled with satisfaction at his own humor. In the next instant, he dismissed me as he spoke directly to Cynthia. "The crew will have the catamaran ready Saturday morning. We need to discuss provisions. I'm planning for a day of it."

"Lovely!" Cynthia bubbled, suddenly sounding her age.

I shuffled the chair back. "My ride will be here soon." Time had lost all meaning during my conversation with Cynthia. Hopefully, I wasn't too late to redirect Erin. I stood with a hollow chest.

Duncan slid into the chair, brushing me aside with dense muscles against scrawny bones. "Wine is going to be an important selection and will depend if you want to go with a simple cheeseboard or want to add smoked fish to it."

I stumbled for the door. The clamor and scent of beer made me nauseous. Once again, I'd put myself in a painful situation with Cynthia. There couldn't be anything between us considering my age and poor appearance.

Drawing in a deep breath of salt air, I fumbled for my phone. Erin would already be driving. Trembling, I dialed their number.

They answered with a cheery tone. "On my way."

"I'm at the saloon. Sorry." My voice groaned and cracked.

"You walked?" Before I could answer, they crooned. "Cynthia. You devil."

My throat swelled and I forced a swallow. "Yes. Then Duncan. I'm ready to go."

"Oh." Erin sounded disappointed. "I was going to suggest we stop in. I'd like to meet her. Rick's crashed on edibles."

"No." I pleaded and my voice cracked again.

Erin sighed. "Okay. See you in fifteen."

I leaned on the corner near the pirate and stared up into the sky. The evening had been a roller coaster with spirits abounding who shunned my morose energy, a delightful conversation with Cynthia, and her interaction with Duncan. I couldn't keep doing this. Even if I had been lonely, I'd been comfortable and barely noticed my solitude.

By the time Erin arrived, I'd resolved not to return to the Palace Saloon and Cynthia. The next evening I brought out all my equipment. When the gloomy night ended, I refused to go to the bar with my roommates. Rick drove us there, oblivious to the argument Erin and I were having.

"I'll wait in the car," I said. "Fridays are too busy."

"C'mon, James, you can't wait outside for an hour." Erin turned in their seat, smiling, though pity tainted their expression.

"I'll walk home. I'll get my equipment when you get back."
I frowned. I hadn't done the math, but I would likely arrive
after them. "I'll sit in the car."

Erin pointed to my knees. "Folded like that?"

I didn't respond. We were driving along the street with
brick walled buildings on all sides and the tall Palace
marquee visible at the corner ahead. Erin would push to have
me go inside, but I'd resist. I needed to get past this foolish
crush.

When they got out, I did as well, leaning back in to collect
the obvious trash. "I'm going to clean up. If you don't mind."

Rick giggled. "Knock yourself out, dude. Love it."

Erin stared at me when I came back up with fistfuls. They
twisted their lips to the side and shrugged. I found a city
garbage can and strode toward it. If I cleaned enough space, I
could rest with my back on the door and legs almost
stretched out on the seat.

I had two more fistfuls when my phone vibrated.
Dumping the trash, I paused beside the fragrant bin and
pulled out my phone. Erin had sent and image and a
message. The picture was of Cynthia sitting alone.

"No Duncan. Just a lonely woman."

I scrolled up and zoomed in on the picture, then shoved
my phone back in my pocket. He'd show up any minute and
the torture needed to stop.

The items I couldn't identify as outright trash I arranged
on the floor. It still smelled like rancid chips and marijuana,
but I climbed in and closed the door. My knees still arced
and the door bit into my back, but my legs didn't fold like a
praying mantis. I stared out the window watching headlights
illuminate the brick walls, then pass. Each one I assumed
would be Duncan.

A brown-haired woman stepped around the corner at the
saloon's entrance and my heart skipped a beat. I would not

put it past Erin to tell Cynthia that I remained in the car. As the face moved under the light of the streetlamps it clearly was not Cynthia. Had she come out to the car I would have been mortified, embarrassed, and hopeful. I hated thinking about it.

I lasted about fifteen minutes, then convinced myself I was being foolish on all accounts. I found refolding and exiting a challenge. Locking Rick's car, I took in a deep breath. Even if Cynthia liked Duncan, I could enjoy conversation with her. My heart tightened at the lie, but I repeated the thought, driving it in like a stake.

I passed the pirate and stood facing the door. The low rumble of voices vibrated on the glass. Discarded cigarettes scented the entrance. Steeling myself with a false smile, I reached for the doorknob.

"Don't even bother, Ichabod." Duncan called out from the intersection behind me.

Focused on my deliberation, the passing cars had been background noise. He drove an expensive, black convertible which reflected all the lights. He paused over the crosswalk directly behind me and his expression held none of its usual humor.

"You know you'll run once I'm in there because you know there's no chance with her. What could she possibly want from a freak like you?" Duncan rolled another foot ahead. His exhaust drifted around me. "Even when I'm done with her, she's not going to see you as anything but a passing conversation."

I surprised myself when anger flushed up my neck. "Don't you hurt her." Did he really intend to lead her on, then dump her? My foot took a step toward his car on its own accord.

His smile was cruel as he noted my movement. "Please. Go for it. I will snap you like a twig." Duncan laughed when I controlled myself. "You can't protect her, or yourself. You are pathetic." He turned and gunned his car, diving into a parking spot.

My spindly arms trembled. Anger still burned inside, but I'd been bullied my entire life. No asset in a confrontation, my physique betrayed me.

His door opened and closed. Fancy shoes clacked on the sidewalk. Duncan's shadow crossed over my feet and he paused at the entryway. A rough hand pushed me toward the street and I stumbled, then dropped off balance to one knee. He laughed as he opened the door to the Palace Saloon. The sound of voices enveloped me and the scent of beer wafted past.

I stood, brushed myself off, and limped to Rick's car. My entire school years had been spent getting knocked to my knees, worse if I tried to react. Adulthood had promised an end.

Leaning on the locked car, I stared up at the night sky. Few stars showed against the haze of population. My aspirations toward Cynthia were ill conceived. We might have a multitude of similar interests, but they were of the arts, not physical. She obviously yearned for the offers Duncan tempted her with.

He would hurt her. She might believe he planned more for them, and my warning would only seem like jealousy. I could do nothing to stop this. My own pain paled in comparison to what I imagined she would feel. Somehow, the thought released my own angst.

I would be Cynthia's friend. My heart could lift with hope all it wanted, but my mind knew that if Duncan hurt her, she'd need someone she could trust. I would continue visiting the Palace Saloon and taking what conversation I could. It might hurt some days, but a small price for a friend. I saw him as evil, though he was just spoiled, rich, and selfish.

Erin touched my shoulder and I jumped. "We saw him come in. I'm sorry, James."

I smiled. "I'm just a friend. Tomorrow night I'll see if she can talk."

"Okay. That's nice." Erin cocked their head, but their smile was genuine and not sympathetic.

The next night I wandered the cemetery with a lighter heart. I met less spirits and the Colonel did not approach me at all. He watched me from under one of the trees but let me pass. I had met ghosts like him before, guardians of the graves.

Cynthia, however, was not at the saloon when we arrived. I sat quietly with Rick, Beth, and one of their louder friends, and drank a rum and Coke. Duncan had taken her on his boat. I forced myself not to imagine what activities they had engaged in, nor why they'd run so late that she did not come out. I bristled momentarily at the idea that he might have already run his course with her and she sat in her apartment crying.

"Perhaps tomorrow night," Erin said quietly.

I smiled, realizing what a frown I had been sporting. "Tomorrow night." The day had been spent reading a number of poets Cynthia had mentioned, and I still had more from the library to look forward to. The weekends were always for books.

It rained the next day and grew worse as the sun lowered to set. I grabbed one of my books and braved the smoke-filled living room. Erin grabbed their keys before I could ask.

"Saloon?" Erin smiled, lidded eyes almost twinkling.

I spent three hours reading alone before I called Erin for a ride, well short of our 1:00 a.m. plan. A bit disappointed, I smiled to bolster my attitude before dialing.

"Duncan?" Erin asked. Actors spoke from a show in the background.

"Cynthia is not here." I shrugged, though Erin couldn't see it. "She must have had other plans." She might not come back to the Palace Saloon now that Duncan had her focus. I refused to wallow in self-pity if my intention remained to be a friend. I had made the effort tonight.

"I'm sorry. Let me grab shoes."

"Text me when you get here. It's raining."

Erin grunted and the show got louder. "Will do. Give me thirty."

The rain had dwindled to an ethereal mist by the time Erin picked me up. I would have enjoyed a quick walk past the graves in this weather. Moving the passenger seat back, I compacted the junk behind it and avoided resting my bruised knee on the glovebox.

"I like that you're trying – to social and all that." Erin smiled.

I nodded solemnly. "I hope she's okay."

"Women are not that fragile. They know players like Duncan."

The next night the moon waxed bright in a clear sky as I sat with my equipment, hoping for evidence beyond my own words. I had plenty of time to consider Erin's counsel and promised to be the best friend I could be, if Cynthia showed up at the saloon. The time seemed to lag as I sat there, and when Rick and Erin showed up at midnight, I'd stowed my equipment in its case.

I followed Erin closely on the way up to the doors of the Palace Saloon. The noise seemed less raucous as Rick went inside. I breathed beer scented air, and my eyes shot to our table.

Cynthia glanced up and smiled. I swore disappointment tinged her expression, but it could be my own insecurity. Still, I strode forward, her friend. "How are you tonight?"

She leaned back, but her eyes flicked past me to the door.

"I'm fine." Tilting her head toward the bar, she started to stand. "This round is on me."

My imagination picked out differences in our previous encounters from the way she offered to pay, her less than bright smile, and glances to the front door. A friend could accept that she might be waiting for Duncan. I could fill that gap. Still, I sat awkwardly looking for places to put elbows and hands.

I drew in a deep breath as she returned with our drinks. "So, how was the sailing?"

A smile tugged at the edges of her lips and stabbed ice in my heart. "Wonderful. It's so beautiful out there. I could spend every day on the water. It's paradise here."

I'd gone to the ocean exactly twice since I'd moved. "It is amazing." Also wavy, dangerous, filled with unseen creatures, and deadly. I almost asked about the timing, trying to understand why she hadn't been at the saloon Saturday or Sunday. That wasn't a friend's business. "When do you get to go out again?"

She beamed. "Next weekend. I can't wait." Cynthia hadn't mentioned how wonderful Duncan himself was, just the sailing and ocean. I took a small solace from that.

"I read *A Woman Speaks*," I said, hoping to move into our usual conversation.

It worked as Cynthia sipped her drink and leaned forward. "What did you think?"

"Powerful." I paused, about to mention the ocean and moon imageries. "I haven't gotten through all of Lorde's pieces yet."

Cynthia snorted. "She produced a lot. How much do you read?"

"Weekends." I didn't mention my evening pursuits. "Sometimes after work. How has your writing gone?"

"That is usually my weekend, but I got nothing done." She stared into her drink and tapped her glass.

When the door opened, I didn't have to turn around to see who had come in. Her face brightened to sudden glee. I hated it. I took in a deep breath, as her friend, then finished my drink.

"Ichabod, you're in my seat." Duncan's voice was a low growl, unlike his normal boisterous tone. He dropped a heavy hand on my shoulder and I tilted into it.

"Be nice, Duncan." Cynthia chided him in a familiar, but happy way.

I put the glass down and shuffled the chair to stand, sliding out from under his weight. "I enjoyed our conversation. I'm glad you had fun."

"Thank you." She didn't take her eyes off Duncan.

He, on the other hand, only glared at me with a murderous look. His hatred burned through his skin. Duncan considered me a threat to his relationship with Cynthia. One look at her should dispel that notion. "I'm sorry," I said.

About to seat himself, he paused. "For what?"

I motioned to Cynthia. "I'm no threat."

She laughed and Duncan spun to face me. His muscles bulged and he clenched his fists.

Stepping back, I waggled a finger at her. "We're friends. Just friends. Nothing to fear."

Duncan shifted his right shoulder back, and I knew the sign of punch coming. Someone laughed at another table and he flicked a glance there, then relaxed and smiled. "Nothing to fear is right. You're a joke, Ichabod." To prove it, he shouted, "Ichabod." The room responded.

I turned for the door. Erin already stood though Rick gestured through a conversation with one of their friends.

My heart raced. Words had often been my enemy at high school when dealing with bullies.

Erin followed me outside. "James?"

I trembled. "I'm fine. A misunderstanding. Wrong words on my part."

"Hug?" Erin asked.

"No." It seemed Erin's universal answer to any disturbance and I'd taught them early on that it wasn't for me.

My eyes widened as Erin grasped me from behind. Their chin poked into my back. I took deeper breaths and finally raised my hands to touch Erin's elbows. I'd done what I came for, to be Cynthia's friend. Duncan's animosity was his own problem.

Rick spoke from behind us. "Whoa. Group hug."

I stared at the sky as he squeezed me from the side, his nose in my ribs.

The next day after a full day of work and a little reading afterward, I left my equipment behind when I headed out into Bosque Bello Cemetery. My mood was calm. I intended to head to the saloon afterward. The moon shone brighter still and I strode straight for the deepest, oldest section. To my left, toward town, I thought I glimpsed a flashlight, but it could have been a car headlight reaching through the trees from the nearby residential neighborhood.

When I spotted it a second time, I stopped at the paved road in the middle of the cemetery. Light leaked into a tree as if someone shielded the light, just not fully. They would be at the edge of the property. I'd never met another living soul here. Glancing over my shoulder, I turned onto the packed dirt road leading to the darkest part. Streetlights barely reached this far back. The moon though lit between the shadows of the treetops.

A low moan came from behind and I turned. The ghost glowed brighter than most and its form cut sharp lines. Huge dark eyes poked holes in the head. A gaping mouth actually showed teeth. I rarely saw that level of detail. The clothes were no more than a drape of luminous cloth.

"Hello," I said.

The moan lifted to a wail, though the expression never changed. One step after the next it shuffled faster toward me. I couldn't sense the animosity, but the gait appeared threatening.

I backed up deeper into the cemetery. "I'll leave." My mood had seemed calm, though it clearly wasn't now.

The ghost charged, arms raised to drape its radiant robe. The wind rustled through as it sped up.

Panic tightened my chest and I nearly stumbled trying to turn and watch at the same time. I lurched into a run for the shadows of the trees. Something felt off, but I'd been chased by stranger.

I alternated between picking a path and glancing behind. The ghost snarled between wails.

Dancing between two graves, I snagged my bad knee on a gravestone. I cringed for the blossom of pain and disturbing the dead. My breath rasped in my chest. I couldn't run for long.

The ghost seemed to have as much difficulty navigating as I did. Its robe clung to brush as it passed a gardenia. I feared it more, if it had that much substance. It did not seem winded. The ghost sprinted an open section, closing the gap I'd gained.

What rage had I inspired in it?

The Colonel stood beside a monument, partially in moonlight. If he too found fault with my mood or intrusion, I could be in serious trouble. I faltered at the sight. My right foot caught a root and I flew in the air.

My face scrubbed on stones, twigs, and dirt. I landed on my right elbow and pain shot up my arm. Bad luck found my bad knee next and then I tumbled across the ground. Neck twisted and wracked in pain, I could only watch the angry ghost bear down on me.

The face looked almost comical, not real. I'd seen distortions before, but they were more hideous than this. I had to stand.

I crab walked backwards readying myself to roll but I had no time. Face cringing against the oncoming fury, I squinted my eyes.

The white blur that hit the ghost could have been the Colonel.

The scream that came from the ghost was familiar, almost human.

As they merged, the two jettisoned to my right and up. The voice ended in a high-pitched squeal as they both dispersed into a moonbeam that cut between the branches.

I panted, becoming the only sound left in the cemetery. Even the night insects and frogs had silenced. Blurting out meaningless sounds, I scrambled to my feet. My right arm stabbed pain into my head, but I clung it to my chest and stumbled for the entrance.

That night, I did not visit the saloon. I could barely explain it all to a laughing Rick and concerned Erin without shaking and chattering my teeth. These experiences were expected, but usually a little distance kept me safe. This had been too close.

I skipped the cemetery the next night and accepted Erin's thinly disguised offer to accompany them to the saloon. My arm hurt, and I'd immobilized it with a sling, though no bones were broken.

Cynthia was there, and her smile less welcoming than ever. She was worried.

"What's wrong?" I asked.

"Duncan. He never came to pick me up last night. I

thought he'd just ghosted me, but his parents called. He's missing."

I sat without getting a drink. "Did they call the police?"

She nodded, nearly crying. "They found his car on N 14th Street Place. His phone was inside with some clothes and his wallet."

That was close to the cemetery. I sucked in a breath. Could it have been Duncan in some glowing garb who chased me? That meant the Colonel had done something with him. I remembered the local who had warned me of her missing cousin. The human scream made more sense.

"I hope he's okay," I said, knowing he wasn't. I couldn't force myself to be sympathetic, though I tried. He'd nearly scared me to death.

* * *

THREE MONTHS LATER, I took Cynthia for her first midnight walk in Bosque Bello Cemetery. Frogs and insects serenaded us in the heat of a summer night. The musk of woods and earthy clay hung in summer's humid air. A young ghost wafted along the trees to the right, keeping pace with us.

I gestured over at the spirit and Cynthia followed my direction. "Do you see it?" I asked.

She giggled and shook her head. "No." Cynthia squeezed my hand. "But I don't care. It's spooky and I'm having fun."

The Colonel appeared to our left, watching us. The protector of Bosque Bello Cemetery. I waved and as Cynthia looked, I pointed between me and her, then raised our clasped hands. His head made the slightest nod of approval.

*KEVIN A DAVIS writes the contemporary / urban fantasy series* AngelSong *and* Khimmer Chronicles *available in digital and paperback. His short stories range across a wide chasm of genres and have been published in multiple anthologies. Living with his beautiful wife and their Persian cats in north Florida, he has access to numerous conventions and comic cons which he travels to monthly.*

*Find his books and join his newsletter at* www.KevinArthurDavis.com *or follow him on Facebook at* https://www.facebook.com/KevinArthurDavis

# SOLITUDE

## MORRIGEN STOUMBOS

They always seemed surprised. Every time, even those who claimed to believe in reincarnation. Today, like any other, I collected the soul of a shocked young banker who informed me very clearly and concisely, "There has been a mistake."

Still he, like all of the rest, fell into the dark void never to be seen again.

There were times when they pondered about what life would be like on the other side. The sense of wonder and curiosity always drew strange thoughts and emotions from me. It made me curious, what would existence in the void be like?

On those days I would hover around the void's iris until it snapped shut with a spark, and I could recall my father's voice reminding me, "We do not follow the taken. We offer them solitude through the void and then continue on to the next." Still, I wanted to see what the taken saw. When they entered the void their expressions always read a gamut of emotions that I wanted to experience; fear, yearning, excitement, and, oftentimes, peace. Peace, that was the main emotion I didn't care much about, I was frequently at peace. I wanted to know what it was like to experience other feelings, happiness, interest, even fear.

I shivered, remembering the time when I asked why *we* were never given solitude. My father had gone on a long tirade, and his anger had spiked the plague of the dark ages. So many were given solitude during that time that there were not enough of us to take them. That time had propelled the living world into a time of ghosts and that sponsored centuries of stories to follow.

Still, solitude sounded nice. I liked the word and the dark void seemed quiet, comfortable, relaxing.

The banker had been gone for less than a minute's respite when faint burning in the place of the Ajna, my third eye, signaled the next soul to be released into solitude. I relaxed and felt for the pull that led me to the soul to be taken.

This one was a child of six. To my inevitable confusion, he lacked any surprise. The boy just sat there next to his body as I approached. Growing closer I understood his lack of surprise, his body was covered in bruises and broken bones. Blood covered the room of a neglected child and gauging by the gun in the young one's hands this boy had begged for solitude instead of clinging to life.

The boy looked up at me and locked eyes. "Is it time? Will it be better?"

It was rare that the taken connected so directly with me. "Yes." I said in my raspy, disused voice.

"Will I be safe?" he asked in a now shaky voice.

This gave me pause. I did not know what waited in solitude for this child. Normally, I showed up, the void opened, soul went in, and I went along my way. Summoning the void, a reflexive action at this point, the tear in space and time opened beside us. It was a large black and purple vortex that never emitted any sound or wind, for some reason I always wanted there to be wind sucking me in. Instead, it was just a huge void shaped like a cat's pupil waiting for the soul to accept its fate.

The boy looked up at me and asked "Will you come with me? I don't want to be alone."

I had always resisted the call of solitude before, but the yearning was strong and with a request from this poor lost boy it was too much to ignore. I knew solitude was not for me or beings like me, soul takers.

Almost as if another being had control of my responses, I nodded. Solitude always sounded like a good thing, even if it did sound mildly lonely, it called to me. I always thought that by stepping through, I would be more like them, more likely to feel excitement and hope, maybe… even, love. He took my hand, and we entered the void.

Once entering the iris it felt more like a vortex than a motionless void. I had seen humans empty their stomachs in wild rides, I would have appreciated this act. I remember holding tight to the boy's hand as divine forces tried to pull us apart and the boy clung to me like his life, or death in this case, depended on it. This did not last particularly long as, next, with a dull thud, we hit the ground and the spinning stopped.

Sitting in the wet sand surrounded by dense fog, I wondered, *Is this death for an Endless?* Solitude was also incredibly quiet. Attempts to speak were wasted as no sound came out, even tonal vibrations in my chest were absent. Smell on the other hand was not muted and it would have been a blessing. The scent of mildew and death was strong, and it reminded me again of the joyous experience humans must feel when they were allowed to rid their bodies of previously consumed nutrients.

The boy, like myself, was trying to say something but he, like I, was muted in the darkness of the void. I shook my head and climbed to my feet. I rid the divine sand from my now surprisingly physical form. Then the boy gripped my hand again and we walked into the fog. The destination seemed non-specific, but I knew no good story ended in wet sand.

Solitude was a fascinating place. Passing through the fog I caught glimpses of other entities, but they were all ghostly, incorporeal. The glimpses were brief, though it seemed like most were previous humans, some I even recognized. The banker was the first, most recent, then there was a hairdresser, and the longer we walked the older the souls. One thing that struck me was that they did not seem to feel. When they entered I remember their vivid emotions and in some cases their dreams, but now their faces were blank, at peace. The word bothered me, *was peace the ultimate goal?*

The sense of sound slowly returned as we walked into the mists. It was not a sudden transition but a gradual increase in volume, as if you were standing in front of a speaker and slowly turning the dial up over the course of days, weeks, maybe years.

Time has always been hard for me, as it is for all the Endless. There is no rush, or that sense that humans call urgency. *I wonder what it would feel like to desire a faster pace?*

"Where are we going?" the boy asked. His low voice broke through the feeling of cotton in my ears.

"This is the afterlife," my raspy voice responded. Almost sounded like I was talking over sandpaper. I guess this is what happens when you don't use verbal communication for over a century. What was the purpose of talking when everyone you meet is leaving for eternal solitude or an Endless with no sense of time. Communication loses its meaning to a being such as myself.

We continued forward; the sand started to turn to dirt and rocks. Eyes of the dead followed us. The hairs on the back of my neck started to rise and when I glanced over my shoulder I saw a small raven with red eyes staring back at me. It stared at me, almost as if it knew I was not supposed to be here. I had stepped out of my designated realm into something different, somewhere I had been warned against going.

"Joshua!" a voice cut through the mist. The boy at my side stopped and turned. In the direction of the voice I see a tall woman moving towards us. Her body, translucent and incorporeal, but still present. A ghost, or at least the human definition of a ghost. "Josh, what are you doing here?"

The boy, Joshua apparently, released my hand, turned and ran toward the woman. As they met, Joshua too turned incorporeal. He hugged the woman who must have been his mother, or another family member. They held tight to each other, and the woman cried while petting his hair. As the woman wrapped her arms around Joshua the two were suddenly surrounded in a bright clean light that seemed to heal them both.

"They needed each other to move on," said a melodic voice beside me. I nearly jumped out of myself, and my head whipped around to see a huge version of the Raven from before.

"Move on to where?" I ask, not entirely sure what the speaking bird was trying to tell me. This was solitude, eternal solitude from what I had been taught. There was more to afterlife than endless mist?

"For them, heaven, they look like Christian believers." The bird's shoulder feathers lifted in a shrug. "Now where do you plan on going?"

"Explore, exist, feel. I always wanted to know what divine solitude was. I want to understand more about what it means to be ..." Before I could finish the bird laughed. It laughed long with a sense of almost song. Humor had been an intriguing concept to me, to find something funny in the moment never seemed to have a long-term impact on life or the situation at large. And still to laugh or cry seemed very mortal, which this bird clearly was not.

"You cannot simply explore solitude. Once you make this journey, going forward is limited as your time here is limited. Though returning will not be the same. Whether you realize it or not you are no longer the same." The bird shook its head and something about it reminded me of an old lore.

"Morrigan?"

That had earned me a slight chuckle. "You figured that one out, did you?"

The question was metaphorical.

"Why is the chooser of the slain here talking to an adventuring soul taker?" I knew the response would not be something I wanted to hear. The only reason a goddess for all intents and purposes would be talking to me was to impart some cryptic advice.

"I am here because an Ending who has served the divine of many centuries deserves more than to simply die for a sudden curious impulse." The bird settled a bit and looked at me with a close inspection. She had called me Ending, instead of Endless. The cryptic advice was coming. "I can tell you how to leave this place, but I can also tell you that your time here is limited either way. That said, you could always choose to rule in the darkness."

At the mention of ruling darkness I shivered and recoiled, which caused Morrigan to laugh again. I had heard that Endless in the right situation could control the afterlife. It was one of the arguments against stepping into the void. The Endless lacked emotions on the best of days, given infinite power and an emotionless ruler often led to suffering. Immortals were not meant to make decisions for the mortal.

"I figured being the figurative king of hell was not in your desires." Morrigan looked back at Joshua and his mother.

This glance diverted my attention to them as well. They both had disappeared and what was left was a small glowing orb. It looked sticky in nature, almost like a fist size glob of sap, but glowed with the strength of a small star.

"If you wish to return to the world you call home, you will collect that orb and find the World tree before you completely fade. Giving the orb to the World tree will grant you passage to the land you seek. Be warned if you choose the wrong path you may find yourself in a state you did not intend. Gift or woe you will no longer be in the void."

"If I take this orb will anything bad happen to Josh and his mother?"

The raven laughed again. "Good question, not many looking to save their own skin ask those questions. Maybe you would make a good king of hell regardless of your misgiving." Sobering, Morrigan stared at me again. "No, nothing will happen to them. All you are taking is the energy left behind from their once corporeal souls."

I picked up the orb, the sappy consistency clung to my hand, which I was more translucent than anticipated. If I wanted to leave the eternal solitude ever, I had to do so soon or I would remain an incorporeal ghost. *Would I turn malevolent as the spirits from the plague did? Would being forced to observe life but not participate in it make me crazy as the ghost stories from old?*

I looked up and saw the Morrigan had left. Now the question was how do I find the World tree. As I ponder next steps I start to feel the orb pull in a direction to my left. Given that I had not many other suggestions on direction I decided to follow it.

It led me through a dark forest filled with old trees and older ghosts. Some of the ghosts reminded me of myself, soul takers, they had death and unfeeling in their eyes. Glancing down my hands were growing ever more translucent and that drove me to move faster. The trees increased in size as I continued down the twisted path.

I could not tell you how long I wandered … All I can say is that the longer I walked the more I faded. The feeling of urgency growing, it was an odd sensation, the desire to move faster but be limited by my own reality.

Without warning I burst from the grey fog into a realm of light and air. I left the land of dark mist and dying trees to a new one filled with bright, healthy trees and, strangely, lively songbirds. This was when I came across the World tree.

The World tree was an enormous willow. It was easily as wide as any skyscraper in the modern world. It was also a brighter green than anything I had seen since landing in solitude or, honestly, before my arrival. I walked to the tree and understood what the Morrigan had meant in regards to finding the root that spoke to you. As I stepped over each root, I could feel a different type of pull. One was dark and filled me with hate for everything. Another spiked my dark desire to control my destiny and that of others. The next one was almost intoxicating, making me step drunkenly as it enticed me with a loopy sort of happiness. I moved past these hoping for a future more to my calling. That is when I found it. The root spoke to me in my heart filling me with hope, joy, and the fascinating urge to laugh. As I caressed the root I could taste fine wines, but also feel the sting of regret for a future not chosen.

Regret, I knew what the word and emotion meant but it was never something that I personally felt. This felt real, like a life to be lived.

As I followed the root around the tree it led me to a hole just big enough for me to fit through and I climbed through the muddy cavern. As I did, I could feel my desire to explore and live, grow. The yearning for life was new. There was always a new day and new soul to take, but longing for experiences was different. Maybe I chose the wrong path—

I paused.

Morrigan had warned me that I would be forever changed. Perhaps this was what she meant.

The passage started to narrow. Where once I could walk upright, I now had to stoop, then eventually crawl. Finally, it felt like I had hit a dead-end, but my beating heart told me to keep going. In my very soul I knew I had to move forward. I started to scratch and pull at the dirt blocking my path. Dirt clung to my hands and got under my fingernails as I pushed the mud out of my way. Finally, my hand broke free of the earth and I could feel the warm rays of sun.

I climbed out of the hole. Mud falling on my face and braids, the damp clay feeling good because it signaled that I was almost home. Almost to the place I had spent so much time walking away from. Never again would I step into a void, divine solitude was meant for others for sure, but not me.

I pushed the remaining mud out of the way and breathed the fresh cool air of home. I pulled myself out of the hole, forever referred to as the pit of solitude, and took my first real breath of fresh clean air. Looking down at my hands, I noticed something strange. My hand was bleeding, not the clear incorporeal liquid of an Endless but red, coppery liquid much like that of human blood.

I have returned to my home, but not as a soul taker as I had been for the last millennia; as a human, to live a human life, and to die in the void. Was this the "gift" Morrigan had promised me? Was I destined to return to the solitude I had just escaped?

Pushing aside the now stifling fear of returning to that lonely existence, I turn towards the sun and see the most spectacular sunset I have ever encountered in my long life.

Gold and purple stretch across the sky as the sun sets behind a large cityscape. I had seen sunsets before, but something about this view changed my perception of them. Along with the fear, I could also feel excitement, the future now entirely what I make it.

I do wonder, when the end comes and my time on this plane is up, will I be surprised?

*MORRIGEN STOUMBOS IS a tech-industry project manager living in central Virginia with her husband and their parrot. This is her first short story publication as an author, but she is also the business manager for WonderBird Press which released their first anthology, Murderbirds, in the spring of 2023. She loves trying obscure foods and can be found on plane to a fun new destination.*

# ADIVINO

## TIM LEWIS

"*A* necklace? That's it?" Abuelita and I had been quite close for a long time, but when she and Mom became estranged a few years back, it strained our relationship too. "I don't mean to sound ungrateful, but is that all she left?" I loved my abuelita, but we hadn't talked since my mom passed last year.

"She says here in her will that the necklace is very precious, and will protect you and your family. I'm sorry this is not what you were expecting, but Mrs. Esguerra left this world with, um, more memories than assets," said Mr. Rivera, the intermediary probate attorney from Garcia, Garcia and Dunford representing my grandmother's estate from Puerto Rico.

"Yeah, the whole family knew of her escapades burning through Tito's pension to see every corner of the planet."

"Um yes, Mrs. Esguerra did travel to some rather esoteric places, I am told." His tone was flat and matter-of-fact as a person bored and just going through a process.

"Well, that is a very nice way to say she wandered chasing

freakin' bizarre and insane occult rumors, Espiritismo, and other gris-gris like an old lady that lost her freakin' mind."

Mr. Rivera just smiled, nodded, and didn't engage my rant. The firm guided him well. I am probably not the first person to sit across the desk from him and learn that a supposed inheritance was squandered, and the beneficiary had to continue their normal pedestrian life without the generational privilege afforded to so many.

His eyes darted searching for a way to bring this to a close. This was just a benign case for him. He probably had a dozen other meetings just like this one, so he wanted to round up his billable time to the nearest hour and move on to the next case.

"So, I understand your concerns..." he began, with an over-patient tone.

"Mr. Rivera, just tell me where to sign and give me the trinket so we can call this done."

Like a magician revealing a card, he produced a document already festooned with Post-it flags.

"Here," he said, pointing to an obvious place for initials with a sticky piece of pink cellophane that was labeled Sign in bold letters with an even bolder arrow.

I scratched through the few pages with a scrawl that no sane person would discern as my signature, all the while Mr. Rivera kept reciting in rote fashion "and here..."

"Is that it?" My tone didn't beguile my annoyance for a second, but Mr. Rivera had what he needed, so all pretense was gone.

"That is all. Garcia, Garcia, and Dunford thank you for your business Mr....Ayala." He had to glance back to the paperwork to remember my name. He stood from his chair and extended his hand over the desk, less to shake it and more to tell me it was time to leave.

As I stood, I could see him look me over from top to

bottom in my tan working boots, faded and threadbare jeans, and a decade old t-shirt proclaiming my appreciation for the Saints' only Super Bowl win back in 2010. Too often I dealt with people who thought they were better than me because of my station in life.

I reached my hand forward as his plastered smile broadened and then dropped my palm to the desk. Snatching up the necklace by the chain, I dangled it in front of his outstretched hand.

"Thanks," I said, while turning and exiting the room. It felt good to rebuke his handshake, but Mr. Rivera probably forgot my name again before I left the room.

I stepped out of the building and that familiar sensation of feeling your breath stolen as you moved from sixty-five-degree air conditioning into the sweltering heat of ninety-degrees and ninety-percent humidity in central Florida.

"I am Sebastian Ayala. Descendant of a proud family from the Basque of Spain who settled Puerto Rico in the seventeenth century, and you sir, are a peasant compared to my lineage," is what I should have said. I always had the best comebacks in hindsight.

I walked to the back of the parking lot to a 2009 Toyota Corolla that was a reliable gift from my uncle, after I put a grand in the black hole to fix the suspension, starter, and AC. Although I am appreciative because he kept the car in his name, so it wasn't seen by my ex-wife's creditors as an asset to acquire to cover debt.

If I hurried, I could make it back in time after my lunch break to finish my day and not burn through my limited vacation balance. I only worked at Tire Emporium because the judge viewed it as legitimate work, and I could not be considered a deadbeat to my ex subject to jail time for no alimony.

The engine sputtered a few cycles and just as the battery

reached its threshold the engine caught and the mule sputtered to life, to the same syncopation as my ringing phone.

"Seb, my love, how are you?" Gabriela's voice sung over the phone.

"Hey Gabbie," I said. "I'm good."

"So," my ex-wife drew out the word I could hear through a beautiful smile. "Are we rich?"

I laughed out loud followed by my usual truncated snort. "No Mami, but we are still more wealthy with love."

"Pendejo." She said, trying to sound stern, but she could never be mad at me. "It's okay. It would have been nice, but doesn't change anything." There was a pause as the moment passed. "Hey, could you stop at the bodega and pick up some alcapurrias on your way home, I have a craving?"

"Of course. See you soon preciosura," I said.

"See you tonight, corazón."

We both paused listening to our breaths and then I hung up the phone.

Gabbie and I got divorced a year ago. My business venture didn't quite work out the way I wanted. A lawyer advised that if we separated before I claimed bankruptcy then it would position us better in the future and enable us to keep the house. I kept my official home address, as far as the IRS was concerned, at my uncle's, but my head rested on Gabbie's pillow every night for the last decade. Despite the divorce, the collection agencies still tried to go after Gabbie as well, so we tried to keep everything out of our names.

I put the mule in gear and turned west down Highway 17 leaving Kissimmee, and back toward our home where I lived and worked in Poinciana, Florida. As I passed a variety of strip malls selling everything from sushi to recliners, my mind lingered to memories of my abuelita, or Tita as everyone in the family called her. My memories relished over days hearing stories from our time in Puerto Rico while eating homemade pasteles, thoughts eventually lingered to the night my mom dragged us from her home.

Mom wanted something more from her life than becoming the next Tita and thought her future was stateside. They argued over responsibility and the need for familia since Dad died in the Gulf War, but the arguments always ended with yelling and us leaving and not talking to abuelita for a month. But this last argument was different, and we left for the mainland the following week with just a single suitcase between us.

A horn blared as the mule drifted over the centerline while I was lost in thought. I still yanked the wheel, overcorrected, and the car fishtailed before it was back under control. I saw a pop of lights behind me as an Osceola County Sheriff pulled up on my bumper. I was back in our community, so the cops left us alone for misdemeanors if they recognized our plates as locals. They were too busy with robberies, sex offenders, Karens, and other stuff. I waved my hand, and the officer turned their lights off and signaled into the turning lane.

I picked up the little talisman from the lawyer in my palm, giving it a squeeze, "See Tita, I'll be just fine without you."

"I doubt that," came the voice of a familiar little gray haired woman, glowing with a tawny brown haze in my passenger seat.

"Ahhh!" I yanked the car to the left thinking that would take me away from who was sitting next to me. Car horns blared as I was head on into oncoming traffic, and I yanked the wheel more until I was making a left into a strip mall, or rather the curb that surrounded the strip mall.

The front wheels barked as they hit the edge, my head went up into the ceiling, and my lower jaw went into my tongue. The back wheels hit, I went over the sidewalk, and I came back down into the seat slamming on the brakes. I was astonished I came to a complete stop perfectly aligned in a parking spot.

The mule sputtered their disapproval and the engine died. Still dazed, I looked over and the seat next to me was empty.

I scanned the area looking for cars that stopped and hoping no cop saw what happened. It was quiet and people went on about their day. One middle aged man in a fedora, who fortunately was far off when I jumped the curb, looked in the window and I gave them a wave to say I was okay. They sneered but kept moving along. When no one further was coming to investigate, I dropped my head to the steering wheel, closed my eyes and sighed.

"Estúpido. Estúpido." The word didn't come out with my usual accent as my tongue still throbbed. With my head resting, I opened my eyes staring blankly to the floorboard. Glinting from a little sunlight shining through the window was Abuelita's necklace next to the center console. I picked it back up by the chain letting it dangle and shimmer in the light.

"You almost got me in a little trouble Tita," I said, shaking a finger at the bauble before dropping it back in my palm.

"You were driving, so don't blame me."

"Ahhh!" I scrambled up the seat like I could miraculously push myself through the roof. As I stared in awe, recollection set in and I saw the face of my abuelita, not much different than when I last saw her a year ago, just more translucent.

"Sebbie. You were always high strung, even as a child," said Tita. "You jumped at everything. Complained about monsters under you bed. Once saying you were chased home from school by a chupacabra."

"Am I dead?"

Abuelita turned toward me, her haze of brown followed a

moment after, and twiddled her fingers in a menacing way as her voice dropped to a gnarled intonation. "I am the ghost of abuelita past! And you, Sebastian Scrooge..." she coughed and cleared herself before talking in her normal voice. "I'm sorry, I couldn't resist, and it was always one of your favorite stories."

"What is happening?"

"Well, you nearly hit poor Jorgé Vázquez as he's going to see his daughter in the hospital." Tita admonished.

"How did you know who the man was? What is going on?" I yelled.

She didn't say a word but just gave me her smile that was like a warm cup of cocoa and Edam and dropped her eyes to my clenched hand. I opened it, and for the first time I actually saw the necklace. The chain was attached to silver wire suspending a brown jasper stone carved with a taino coquí; a tribal image of the small, mottled brown Puerto Rican frog. I grasped the chain pulling the bauble across my palm.

"It took some effort, but I knew I wouldn't be ready to leave when my time was up. You see Sebbie... "

In an instant she slipped away like a light had been turned off leaving a wisp of umber that dissipated to nothing. The necklace spun lazily in a circle above my palm, and I lowered it back down into my hand.

She appeared as quickly as before. "... and I had the necklace sent to..." I lifted it again, and then set it back.

"... because I knew ... who could help me... prideful mother... Sebbie!"

I flinched letting go of the chain and the medallion dropped to my hand.

"That is really annoying. You may find it cute, but each time it feels like you're putting me in a glass jar and I only hear the echo of my own voice."

"Sorry, Abuelita."

"The medallion connects us so we can talk, but only when it touches your skin. That is why I made it a necklace so you could wear the charm," and she pantomimed me putting it on, "and stay connected with me at …"

I grabbed the chain letting the medallion dangle. Tita was gone again, and I placed the necklace over my head letting it rest against my chest. Nothing happened.

"Tita?" I tapped it a few times, looking around the car and into the back seat. "Tita!" As I looked at the medallion I thought about holding it and then realized my mistake and tucked the bauble into my shirt so that it pressed against my skin.

"You're back!" I said, relief filling me. "Tita, can you hear me?" She sat there with arms crossed staring out the front window. "Tita. I can see you, but I can't hear you." I pressed the stone through my shirt thinking I needed to activate it like a walkie-talkie. "Are you there? Over."

"You are right." She let out a deep sigh. "Estúpido."

"I'm sorry, this is all new to me. It's not every day a kid has his grandmother come back to life."

"I'm not the Walking Dead. I'm just a projection into this plane and the necklace is what connects me to this world through a specific host."

"You're… in me?"

"Oh, Dios mío." She lowered her head and squeezed the bridge of her nose between two fingers to stave off what I could only guess was an astral projected migraine as she talked to herself. "When I imagined what this would be like… there was laughing, crying, joyous rapture and even, while improbable, a choir singing Ave Maria. No, no. We're moving past this Juanita."

"Tita?"

She turned, cupping her hands to her chest. "Sebbie, mi cielo. When your mother left with you, I was heartbroken. I knew she would never come back home in my life because pride..."

"Stubbornness," I retorted.

"Boricua pride," she emphasized, "is deep within our family. I had been searching for a way to see her, if not in this life, in my next. She left us before that could happen." Tita crossed herself and murmured a short prayer. "But now I'm back, to be here for you, Gabriela, and" she hesitated, "and for whatever you may need."

"Tita, I love you with all my heart, but what can you do like..." and I gestured to the wispy haze of a fragile grandmother sitting in the passenger side of a 2009 Toyota Corolla.

She didn't say anything, and didn't have to. The warm, confident smile that grew into her hazel eyes told me all I needed.

\* \* \*

"Stop ghost seat driving!" I barked.

"You're going to lose her," Abuelita squawked. In the past few months since she arrived, she has been more vocal with advice. Although, I think she couldn't have cared less about catching up to our current suspect, Yurena Diaz, and was more thrilled with the chase from the frequent whoops and gasps emanating from the passenger seat.

"I know what I'm doing, just hang on." I could see her derision out of the corner of my eye. Not only could her insubstantial form not hold anything, but she was tied to the necklace, so no matter where I went, she was there.

"And we prefer ethereal spirit. Patrick Swayze ruined ghost for us." she huffed, then crossed herself for speaking ill of the dead.

We had been trying to tail Yurena, and we got stuck in

traffic at a light. I drove frantically trying to catch up to her by veering up on the berm a little to pass some cars, and maybe coming a little close to some pedestrians as I burst through the intersection.

"I think that was Mr. Vázquez again," said Tita, as she craned her neck to look back, her aura shifting to amethyst.

"See. Yurena's 4Runner just made a right on San Lorenzo." I stomped on the gas to make up ground and the engine sputtered; I think the mule laughed at me. By the time I made the turn, I could hear sirens in the distance only because the AC went out a week ago and I had to drive with the windows down. I caught up to Yurena but was doing about fifty when she made a left onto Pompei Drive.

I turned the steering wheel hard and the tires chirped as we slid around the corner. I tried to compensate by counter-steering into the turn, but the suspension wasn't built for rally racing. The mule spun in a one-eighty, coughed its own derision, and the engine died. We were perfectly parallel parked along the curb of someone's house, which was becoming a theme with my driving. Osceola's finest, certainly called in by 911 for a reckless driver, with sirens blaring, went racing past the drive without giving a glance to a parked car.

"Tsk, tsk, tsk."

"This is not easy. And I have to work with… no, no. I'm not having this debate again. I love you Tita, but I'm not doing this again."

"Sebbie, darling, you did your best and that is all a good abuela can ask." Wrinkles in her tawny beige smile added to the ooze of her pandering sweetness that only a grandmother could deliver.

I didn't take the bait and waited for the sirens to fade. "There's no finding her now. We should probably head home and maybe I'll get there soon enough to put Isabella to bed."

In the many months that followed since Tita first appeared in my car, there have been some dramatic changes in my life: The obvious, a sarcastic spectral matriarch with a steadfast commitment to be some type of guardian angel; The birth of my beautiful daughter Isabella, which apparently Abuelita knew about before me, and even Gabriela; Me being fired from Tire Emporium for constantly talking to myself and freaking out the customers when draining oil in the pit; Taking on a new job at the local bodega, which was convenient to feed Gabbie's constant craving for alcapurrias during the pregnancy; Oh, and becoming a vigilante crime fighting duo with the spirit of my abuela to serve the people in our community.

It took some coaxing for Gabbie not to divorce me a second time when I told her I was communing with the ghost of my dead grandmother. Apparently, the talisman didn't work for just anybody, only those that had a tight familia connection to the spirit. Tita knew Gabbie's family from the homeland and had some details, and of course a few family secrets that even I didn't know, to help convince Gabbie Tita was there.

What really sold it is when Tita knew Gabbie was pregnant and expecting our little girl. We learned in her omniscient ghost-like state, Tita can not only see people, but see into them, to include their thoughts, desires, and things they may not even know they know. That is how Tita knew that Mr. Vázquez was going to see his daughter in the hospital that first day when I jumped the curb and almost ran him over.

In the beginning I kept the necklace on twenty-four seven so Abuelita could be in our world, looking out for me and the family. But then Gabbie soon insisted I remove the necklace before coming to bed, but not as much as Abuelita insisted. Knowing the mind of others has its disadvantages, like the evening after Gabbie put Izzie to bed, peeked around the living room door and gave me a wink.

Before my simple brain put the pieces together Abuelita started yelling, "Take off the necklace. Take it off."

Gabbie saw the perplexed look on my face, put the pieces together as well, and then I had two women in my life yelling, "Take it off!" It was very confusing.

Gabbie didn't even give me as much as a hug for a week. In time we learned how to internalize some emotions and Tita learned the same, or at least to ignore it.

We started off simple, as we learned how to navigate Tita's telesthesia, or plain old common sense, as she referred to it. She'd let me know when I should wash the dishes without Gabbie having to ask. She'd give some advice on who might be bluffing in a round of brisca during game night at our house. Then, there was the time when Luis didn't want to burden anyone, but his back was hurt one day at work and we were able to help with some Workers' Compensation. When I hinted that maybe our friend's son, Manuel, was getting bullied at school and we gave specific enough examples that the principal took action. Or the day when I suggested Gabbie's cousin, Sophia, might want to see her doctor, and they found a lump just in time.

That is when people went from coming just to hang out with the Ayalas to actually coming over because they thought I was an adivino and could tell their futures. That was also when people stopped coming over just for poker night.

As custom, no Puerto Rican would show up at someone's house without a gift for the host:

"Gabbie, you look wonderful. My wife sent over her famous pastelón. Is Seb around?"

"Buenos dias, Gabbie, I knitted you a new snuggle for Izzie so she doesn't get cold. Is Sebastian home?"

"It sure is a hot day. I had Marcos weed the planter so you don't have to bear the heat. Seen Seb?"

I could not take money from family and friends, and I felt a personal fulfillment being able to help in a world where everyone feels helpless. So, while their courtesies were no windfall, they enabled us to save a little money and satiate the collectors a little from constant harassment.

We found some joy again, and there was even talk of getting remarried.

"Who's the client tonight?" snarked Tita.

"These are not clients; these are my friends." Tita was a giving person, much like me, but being dead I guess she couldn't appreciate the simple happiness she brought to the living as much as I did.

"You seem to have a lot more friends each month."

"Tita!"

"I am sorry, Sebbie." She shrugged and the russet hue dimmed to a more walnut brown. "It is nice we can help these people. I just," and she searched for a word, "I just thought, maybe, we could do a little more."

"More than what?"

"I don't know, like helping the police." Her smile grew proportionately with the brightness of her hue. "We could be private investigators!"

"Oh, like Holmes, Poirot, or Benoit Blanc?"

"No, like Jessica Fletcher." Now her hue glowed iridescent.

"I don't think the police would be willing to call me Jessica."

Her face lowered realizing she would not, could not, be known by the police and all the credit would go to me.

"I'm sorry Tita, it's…" I stammered.

"No, it's not that. I just sometimes forget. Being with you

and the girls is so wonderful that I just sometimes forget that, well, I'm dead."

"I'll get it," came Gabbie's voice from the living room. I was in the kitchen so engrossed with Tita that I didn't even hear the knock at the door.

"Tita, I understand. Maybe we'll get something like a lost dog, or a saucy theft." Tita rolled her eyes and I got up from the table to greet our dinner guests.

When I came into the living room to greet Victor and Mya Rodriguez, something was off. They had no gift.

"He does not look good," came Tita's voice from behind me.

Victor's eyes were the dark of a man who hadn't seen sleep in days and Mya, who normally was the epitome of style and grace, had her hair in a tight ponytail without a brush of makeup. Mya went to school with mom, and they were at our house frequently for dinner when mom was alive. Mya was a successful senior manager at Critcare Medical Devices where she and mom used to work, and Victor was self-employed as a freelance graphic artist. They were an amazing couple that everyone loved.

"Seb," said Victor, his eyes pleading. "We need your help. I think we're being hexed by Yurena Diaz."

I flinched, not from Victor, but from Abuelita's whoop over my shoulder.

* * *

"I THINK they're in the next room," whispered Tita.

"Let's just sit tight and observe for a bit," I whispered back. "You stay over there and watch my back."

"Roger," she whispered, giving me a salute that looked more like she was waving.

"Why are *you* whispering?"

"Because you're whispering."

"Yeah, but why are you whispering?" She gave me a perplexed look and a scrunch of her lip like I was insane. "Never mind. Just let me know if anyone is coming."

Tita and I had been trying to tail Yurena for a week to find out where she goes in the evening. It's not as easy as they make it look on TV. The first time ended up in a spin out on Pompei Drive trying to keep up with her 4Runner in my little Corolla. Several times after that we had trouble because of a low tire, stopped in a crosswalk by a slow, old man in fedora, following the wrong 4Runner, and once for an emergency diaper run following a particularly extensive blow out by Izzie.

We followed her the other night north of Poinciana to a broken-down warehouse near Kissimmee Gateway Airport. We knew this was the place because as little as TV taught us about tailing, we were certain nothing legal ever happens at an old warehouse. There were people standing outside as Yurena pulled up, so we kept driving and decided to come back tonight.

"All clear," said Abuelita.

"Shhh," I instinctively sounded, hearing her voice at normal volume, but still, at least to my ears, echo through the warehouse.

We had arrived before sunset and things were quiet while we staked the place out for a bit. The south loading dock was left up a foot. I was able to shimmy under the gap, covering my shirt and pants in grime and grease. My belt buckle stuck, I watched Tita walk through the dock door.

"You know this side door is unlocked?" she asked.

"No," I said casually, as I continued to contort to free my belt buckle. "Thank you for telling me."

"Work smart, not hard. That's what your abuelo would say. God rest his soul," she said, then crossed herself.

The place was empty when we got in, and we found the area off to the side of the rear door was a little dustier than other places, implying there may not be a lot of foot traffic in this area. We had been hiding near some old crates listening for nearly an hour as the sun dropped, the stifling heat subsiding to just heat.

"They're supposed to drop them off at ten," came the sound of a large man we saw earlier, as his smaller cohort opened the door to the makeshift windowless office set against one wall of the warehouse.

"I swore they dropped them off earlier," the smaller guy said. "I'm going to check before she gets here."

He wandered around the warehouse and in time made his way to my corner. There was scuffling as the small guy stopped right in front of the box I was crouched behind.

"Well look here." The small guard said triumphantly. "Here they are," he said, tapping a label on the box. "Hyperpic fluid monitors."

"Hysteroscopic," guffawed the large man. "I guess we don't have to worry about you taking them and trying to sell them someplace if you can't even pronounce them."

"Screw you, Hector."

The two bantered as I traced my memory trying to remember that word. Mom said stuff like that when she worked with Mya. She was a saleswoman and would travel around to hospitals in south Florida selling equipment.

"Co-kee."

Mya must have learned, or at least guessed, that Yurena had a consigliere at Critcare to pilfer medical supplies. When she started following up on transcripts and bills of lading, odd things started happening to her. Her car wouldn't start. She felt like she was being followed. And one night she felt like she was pushed in front of a bus and was nearly run over. That's when Mya and Victor came to me thinking they were hexed.

"Co-kee."

I looked around the warehouse in what little I could see in the dim light and there were hundreds of boxes in various sizes stacked around the place. Yurena must be working more than medical supplies and has her hand in all sorts of businesses.

"CO-KEE."

I turned back to look at Abuelita, "What are you doing?"

"Hello Sebastian." Yurena appeared as if stepping through fog, materializing as she passed through Abuelita. I did not have time to speak as something black swung from Yurena's hand, and then my vision went just as dark.

* * *

"WHY DIDN'T you tell me she was there?!" I gingerly touched at the side of my head where a substantial goose egg had formed.

"I did! I was being subtle. I made the sound of the coquí to let you know she was behind you."

"Abuela! No one but me can hear you. You should have just said; hey Sebbie, the freaking psycho woman is coming up behind you!"

Juanita Maria Esguerra viuda de Alaya stared up at me tight-lipped and so still that even her aura didn't waver. The usual flow, like water along the shore, was stagnant, and the color took on a deep reddish-brown hue like dried blood.

I stood a head over her, but I felt like I was eight again caught in the kitchen with her standing over me and my hand in the cookie jar. "I'm sorry, Abuelita."

"That's better." Tita's warm smile returned, her hue softened and gentle ripples flowed again. "Now how do we get you out of here?"

It looked like we were in a janitor's closet with just a single bulb dangling from the ceiling above us. Shelves lined the walls with various bottles and sundries with only a single door.

"Blocked," I said, after testing the knob.

"Of course it's locked. Did you think they would just let you walk out?"

"No, it's blocked. There's no lock on the door, but there's something keeping it closed." I stepped back into the room looking at the door through Abuelita trying to figure out my next step.

"Maybe you try running at it with your shoulder and knock it open?"

I smiled looking at Tita and just started walking toward her slowly.

"What are you doing?" In that moment, the pendant that connected me to Abuela also held her at a minimum distance from me. When I got close enough there was the sensation of thick fog as Tita was pushed backward like a spring was between us.

"Sebbie, what are you doing?" The last word was muffled by the door as Abuelita was standing on the other side. "Ohh," she said. "I guess I could have just moved out here on my own, you didn't have to push me."

"Sorry Tita. What do you see?"

She scoffed, "Amateurs." She made her way back through the door. "They put a chair under the doorknob."

"I think we need to Jessica Fletcher this problem," I said, and Tita grinned like a Cheshire cat.

I found a slim broom and slid the handle under the door until I found one of the legs of the chair. Two quick bumps, the slow scratch of wood on metal and the chair fell to the floor.

"Let's get out of here," I said as I pushed open the door. Yurena and her two goons were standing there to greet us and she casually tapped the blackjack to her palm.

"Ready for another dose?" Yurena asked.

"You could have told me they were standing out there," I said to Tita.

"And ruin your surprise as you opened the door," said Yurena.

"Kick her in the monkey Sebbie!" Yelled Tita.

I let out a slight laugh.

"You think this is funny Sebastian? I'm no one to be trifled with and your little shenanigans have put me in a precarious place."

"Yurena, no one knows I'm here or about this place. You can just let me leave. It's just your word against mine so nothing will ever come of it."

"Thank you." An evil grin curled on her thin lips. "That's exactly what I needed to know."

"Oh Sebbie, this is not good. We need to go," pleaded Tita. "I can see it now. So much hate. She the devil."

"Yurena, don't take this to a place you can't come back from."

"But my dear Sebbie, we're already there." She gave a nod to the large man who produced a gun from the small of his back.

I could feel the blood drain from my face. "Wait, what are you doing?" I started to back away, but there was nowhere to go, other than back in the closet.

"Always with the questions. You're just as curious as your mother."

"What do you mean, my mother?" My ears pounded as the heat rose seeing Yurena's coy smile.

"Oh Sebastian, is it really that perplexing? Your mother took care of sales and got a little too curious when her invoices didn't align just right."

"No, she had a heart attack on a hot day in the parking garage," I stammered.

"Of course. It's not like I could get a hold of clarithromycin, or something that a local coroner wouldn't notice, or other mamaos might think was a hex."

I stared at Yurena in shock as a flurry of emotions were matched by the low growl of Tita behind me.

"I'll admit I was surprised to see you here, but yours will be much easier to explain. A divorcée thief broke into a warehouse to get money. A deadbeat father trying to get back into his daughter's good graces—is tragically shot by a security guard." As she said the words, the big guy took the cue and leveled the gun at my chest. "It's just so tragic."

"Leave my nieto alone you bruja!"

My ears rung with the banshee-like yell of Tita, and the cold shiver of feeling her pass through me and the medallion. I could see the shock of the three as an old woman, with what I could only imagine was a rictus of vengeance, materialized in front of them.

They backed up in unison, with matching faces of terror. I saw the faint line of the large man through Tita as he raised his gun, and I dropped to the ground as he fired off his entire clip at Tita in quick succession. I watched the shots ripple as they passed through her, and one giant ripple as the desperate man threw his empty gun. They backed up adding their own screams to the echo of Tita's unwavering howl as she forced them to retreat into the office, yanking the door closed behind them.

Tita dropped down to the ground, exhausted, "Sebbie, the door."

I jumped to my feet and snatched up the same wooden

chair that had kept me captive earlier and wedged it under the office doorknob. I scrambled and slid over one of the larger crates to help brace the chair in case they too had a broom in the office.

"Tita, that was amazing. I didn't know you could do that."

"I didn't either," she said, her voice had a breathy, strangled sound as she sat on the floor bracing herself with a single arm.

Thumps came from the office and the slight squeak of the wedged chair against the concrete floor. "Harder you morons," came the muffled voice of Yurena, urging her brutes. The fear must have passed and they were resolved to finish what they started.

I pushed over another crate and shouldered it against the first. "We need to get out of here," I said. As I moved away from Abuelita, she stayed in the same place, no longer tethered to the necklace.

"I can't," she said, her voice sounding hollow and far away.

"What do you mean?"

"The shaman said never… interact with others." She took a long breath every few words. "It takes… so much… too much." Tita turned translucent and her vibrant aura faded to a dull beige like the drifting of sand across a beach.

"Abuelita, what's happening?"

"Sebbie my darling… I need to go."

"Abuelita, no."

"I'm sorry… I wasn't here… to help your mother."

"Tita, you can't go."

"It's okay." Her appearance thinned, and I could barely pick out her features like a face in fog.

"Tita?" I pulled the coquí out of my shirt squeezing it between my palms. "Tita, don't leave me too!"

"Give Izzie a kiss… from her bisabuela."

Her soft brown haze thinned and diminished like a waft of smoke on the wind.

* * *

AFTER THE ATTACK, I had parked my car in the shadows down the street watching the warehouse as the cops arrived. I wasn't concerned about Yurena, part of me just hoped I might catch a glimpse of Tita.

The next morning I drove back to the warehouse, circling from a distance, but by then, the news media and more cops infested the area like gnats.

That evening I had gone back to the parking lot where I first saw Tita so many months ago. The music played softly on the stereo, with very little treble from the old speakers. Long hours I gripped the medallion so tightly it would leave an impression on my palm. The phone rang and the screen showed an old selfie of me and Gabbie in her long dark curls when we went to Universal on that water ride. She was soaked and making one of those silly duck faces. I pressed the button for speaker.

"Corazón." She paused, giving me a moment to speak, but I didn't have the words. "Be grateful for the time you had," said Gabbie. She was trying so hard to be supportive, but having never been able to see Tita, she didn't have the connection that we developed. "She probably just needs time to rest. She'll be back." Another pause, waiting for a response. "There's someone here who wants to say hi."

The speaker crackled and a nom-nom sound as Izzie gummed the phone, followed by the occasional ba-ba over the speaker.

My heart melted. "I'm on my way home, preciosura."

* * *

THE FOLLOWING NIGHT, three days since Tita left, I fell in my favorite recliner on the couch enjoying a breather from crawling around the floor. Izzie bounced in her walker in front of the TV, still not tired from playtime. Gabbie sang along to a song in the kitchen. The news had glommed onto the story with a continuing segment as the investigation unfolded.

The anchor talked about an anonymous caller the other night after locals heard shots fired in the warehouse district by the airport. When police arrived and found Yurena Diaz with two other persons locked in a room, they also discovered a slew of stolen items. The depth of Yurena's criminal network grew from discovery of the first warehouse, to multiple locations across south Florida.

"We did it Tita," I said to myself, patting the coquí under my shirt.

"Serves her right," said Abuelita, appearing on the couch next to me.

"Ahh!" I kicked frantically, spilling my Captain and Coke down my front, then teetered over the arm of the chair onto the floor with a loud thump.

"Sebbie. You really need to work on being less jumpy." Abuelita watched the TV like nothing was wrong.

I scrambled to my knees looking over the arm of the couch. "I thought you died."

"Sebbie, I was already dead." She glanced over at me shaking her head before turning back to the TV. "It would be a rather cruel world if a person could die multiple times."

"Seb, what's going on?" A panicked Gabbie ran into the living room in dish gloves brandishing a frying pan with both hands.

"Tita is back!"

"Oh," said Gabbie, dropping the pan to her side. "I thought it was something serious."

"Tita— is— back— from the dead," I emphasized.

"Yeah, she told you she had to go. And she wasn't dead, well not again, she was just tired," said Gabbie.

"You're a lucky man. She's much smarter than you," said Abuelita, still transfixed on the news.

"No one is shocked by this?" I asked, pleading to the room.

Gabbie rolled her eyes, "Tell her I said hi," and went back to the kitchen. Izzie giggled and bounced in her walker. I slumped back into the couch next to Tita, still trying to recover my faculties as she continued watching the rest of the broadcast like it was any other night.

I started to say something a few times, but I already knew the answer I would get. Eventually I just smiled. I had my Tita back.

"I'm sorry," said Abuelita. She patted my knee, or made the motion of doing it since she passed through everything.

I changed my shirt and then settled back in for the night. Tita was home, I had revenge for my mother that I hadn't known I needed until the other night, and the monster plaguing our community was behind bars. No one really knew what I, we, had done, and that was okay by me.

Aerial film clips of the various warehouses rented by Yurena were shown on the screen with speculation of locations outside of Florida. The news clip cut to a reporter running with the camera man as they caught a shot at the side of the Osceola County Courthouse where Yurena was leaving in handcuffs by women in navy blue FBI windbreakers.

"She looks pretty scared," I said.

"Más jincho que nalga de monja," said Abuelita.

I gasped and choked out a chuckle at some of the things that can come out of my sweet abuela's mouth. There was a gentle knock at the front. Abuelita perked up and her aura shifted toward bright amethyst as I went to the door and opened it.

Mr. Vázquez took off his fedora, and balanced a casserole dish covered with aluminum foil in the other.

"Hola, Mr. Ayala. My wife made you her pastelón." Mr. Vázquez extended the dish, and I had to grab it for fear it might drop between us.

"Thank you, um, would you like to come in?" I asked.

"El es lindo. You should definitely invite him in," came Tita's sultry voice peeking over the top of my shoulder.

I took a step back to give him room to enter, but more to push Tita into the hall closet behind me.

"Thank you, but it is late, and I don't want to impose," he said, now holding his hat to his chest by the brim with both hands.

"I understand, but I don't know what I did to deserve such a thoughtful gift."

"Cristina, our daughter, is much better and home from the hospital." He dropped his eyes. "She worked at Critcare before the accident. Your mother got her the job. Yurena..." his voice trailed off, "but we know what you have done."

"Mr. Vázquez, I..."

He shook his head softly as he raised his eyes that told me I didn't need to deny, or even explain. He stood tall, put his hat back on, and smoothed the brim, "Buenas noches." Then turned and walked into the night.

I watched him go down our block for a moment before going back inside.

"Who was that?" Called Gabbie, finishing the dishes in the kitchen.

"El guapo," said Abuelita, accompanied by the sound of someone enjoying a tasty bite.

"He's married," I chided.

"Until death they do part," she said like a cat purring.

"Abuela!"

"I may be dead Sebbie, but your abuela is still a woman that needs…" In a wisp, she was gone from sight.

I let the pendant rest on the outside of my shirt as the shiver finished the journey. "Uh, it was Mr. Vázquez." I called back to Gabbie. "He dropped off some dinner."

"Perhaps he's an adivino too and knew I didn't want to cook tonight," said Gabbie. "Bring it in here and I'll get it ready while you put Izzie down."

I was greeted in the kitchen by a proud and bouncing Izzie, who managed to move her walker from the living room. I set the casserole on the counter and knelt down to pick her up.

"How did you get in here?" She giggled and squealed as I lifted her above my head and blew raspberries on her belly. "We're going to need Tita to make a charm that works for you so I can keep you connected to me too."

Izzie and I went through our nighttime routine of cuddling in the rocker as I finished her favorite story, "Three little bears running fast. Home again. Safe at last." I set her down in the crib and bent over to give her a kiss on her forehead. "Sweet dreams, Mija."

The coquí pendant dangled from my neck glittering from the Timmy Time night light. Izzie's eyes lit up as her tiny hand reached and grabbed the little frog.

* * *

ISABELLA COOED and kicked her feet as her bisabuela appeared in a soft haze, the shade of a warm mug of cocoa.

"Sweet dreams Nieta," said Tita. "I foresee us doing wonderful things when you grow up," and she leaned over, placing a kiss on her forehead. "But don't tell your papi just yet."

. . .

*Tim Lewis manages rocket programs by day, and collects hobbies by night. Writing has been the longest running hobby, going back to middle school and first place in a Halloween story contest. He took creative writing at Purdue, but his public works have all been scholastic and technical. Tim leans toward Sci Fi, Urban Fantasy and Noir, where each contain an element of humor from a life spent as a smart ass. He published his first fiction work, Switch, in 2019 and followed with short stories in notable anthologies as distractions from finishing his novel.*

*For more on Tim go to* www.lewisventure.com.

# ETHAN'S BRAND

## IAN ALEXANDER TASH

*E*than sat in his bedroom in complete silence, occasionally glancing back up at the screen from time to time to see if anyone was in the waiting room. The summer was slow, incredibly slow. So slow, in fact, that he was the only one not moved off the night shift. Usually, the school employed about four people at any given time that the writing center was open, but since it seemed the rush to get papers done, and done well, wasn't as strong as in the Fall or Spring, especially at night, Ethan was the only one left. He needed to be present. That was his only job requirement at this point: be present and prepared to get work done whenever someone presented him with papers to proofread. Ethan was mostly just happy to be paid to do things he liked.

The doodling he did at his desk was more than just mindless sketching. He was practicing. He was putting together the best portfolio he could. He knew that if he was going to be an artist, he needed a portfolio in order to attract people and convince them to do commissions. His brand could not survive without this. If he wanted to touch the souls of others, burn his image into their soul forever, then he needed to practice and put in his 10,000 hours. Being a writing consultant might as well have been a side hustle with how much he pursued his art every day. At the time, he was making a pencil sketch of a mockingbird in a tree filled with masks, each of which were unique, based off the faces of his coworkers. Right now he couldn't afford to get sucked into the black void with just his name on it, staring with absolute boredom as he knew that no one would be coming in to get help.

Ding-Ding.

Ethan looked up. In the waiting room was a name: "Lucy D. Vell". He sighed and placed the pencil down on the table. He switched on his customer service smile before switching on the camera, and likewise his customer service voice before the microphone. Then he admitted Lucy into the meeting.

"Good evening. Welcome to the NHU Virtual Writing Lab. My name is Ethan. Are you here to work with a writing consultant?"

A pause. The screen was still mostly black, but this time with a new name scrawled across the screen in white. A voice piped up from the other side of the screen. It was low and slow, but somewhat enticing to Ethan. "Hello," Lucy said. "I'm here to work with you, yes."

"Excellent," Ethan responded enthusiastically. "What's your student ID number."

A slight delay. "It's 616216666."

Ethan wrote that down and read it back to her. She confirmed that he had written it down correctly. "Excellent. So, what are we working on today?"

"I need help articulating my thoughts, to help me explore my options."

"Okay. What can I do to help you with that?"

"I don't have a paper yet," she admitted, "but I want to

work through my argument with someone else, a captive audience that can help me develop this further."

"Excellent. I can definitely help with that. What's the question?"

A long pause.

"Hello?" Ethan asked. "Are you—"

"Is there such a thing as an unforgivable sin?"

Ethan stared at his computer monitor in confusion. "Um, what class is this for?"

"Does that matter?"

"Well, I do normally have to report what class this is for, anyway, just in case the professor asks us to see whether you've seen us or not. Is this like for a religious studies class?"

"Yes. You could say that. Do you know the meaning of death?"

Ethan assumed that this was the Meaning of Death class he had taken last semester as part of his GE, one of his upper division themes he had to complete.

"Yes," he responded. "I do."

"Good. Then you'll understand the importance of this. Is there such a thing as an unforgivable sin?"

"Is this a new paper that's been assigned? I didn't have to write on that."

"I was given a personal choice."

"Oh, a free topic for your paper. Cool, cool. So, what made you choose that question if you got to decide what question you would write on?"

"Some questions are ones that we search out. Others find you, and they won't leave you alone."

"I guess I can understand that."

"Okay. So is there any such thing as an unforgivable sin?"

"Do you have a position?"

"I want to hear your position."

"Well…" Ethan paused for a minute to think. "Well, I

think that there is no such thing as God or anything like that, so I would say that there are no such things as unforgivable sins. After all, an unforgivable sin means that you'd be kept out of heaven for it, so therefore we must not have unforgivable sins because no one needs to be forgiven if none of that stuff is real. What do you think?"

Seconds passed. "I think that there is such a thing as unforgivable sin."

"So you now happen to believe in a position after I said the opposite of it?"

"Call me a devil's advocate."

"Touché. Okay. So what is you reasoning for the presence of unforgivable sin?"

"Well Ethan, I simply believe that there is a God, and he judges you when you die."

The light burned out in the bedroom.

"Power outage?"

"No," Ethan responded. "I can see that the hall light is still on. I guess I just need to change the lightbulb."

"But you'll still be here with me for now, right?"

"Well, I would... Yes." Ethan knew that he could survive a call in the dark for now. After all, this student sounded like she really needed help and the sessions were only 30 minutes anyway.

"You can go and open the door if you need to, Ethan. I'll be waiting right here for you."

"Okay... Thank you." Ethan got up and opened the door that led out into the hallway. He looked left and right to see if anyone was there. He was still home alone, just as he thought. When he got back to the computer, Lucy resumed the conversation as if nothing had happened.

"Now, what would you say to that, Ethan?"

"What would I say to what?"

"That there is a God who judges you when you die?"

"Oh, right. That. Well, I would have to say that I don't

believe in a God, so that means that I couldn't believe what you believe. There is nothing more to say on the matter."

"Oh. So you won't even entertain the potential existence of the Divine?"

Suddenly, the hall light started to flicker. However, at some points Ethan felt like he was seeing lights that were brighter than what the hall light was generally used to.

"Having some power problems today, huh Ethan?"

"Yeah, I guess so. Do you mind if I —"

"I would rather you stay here with me for now."

"Oh. Okay."

"But Ethan," Lucy continued. "I would argue that even without a God, there would still be such a thing as unforgivable sin."

"Why's that?"

"It's simple, really. Does God need to exist in order for sin to do so?"

"Well, if God does not exist, then there is no universal standard, no absolute truth."

"Does that then mean there is no morality?"

"Well…"

"Does that mean that I could kill you and it wouldn't matter?"

"Well, that's a bit of an extreme."

"You're right. I'm sorry about that."

Ethan could swear that he heard something. It sounded like rustling, but ever so faint. It was as if it was coming from something that was downstairs, that he could hear it only because his door was open.

"Something spook you?" Lucy seemed amused.

"Listen, I am getting a bit uncomfortable with this. Maybe we should—"

"You're right. After all, you're home all alone. This topic probably doesn't make you feel safe."

"Yeah, I... How do you know that I'm home alone?" Ethan then looked to his door. He could still hear the rustling, and it began to get louder.

"Well, no one else is responding to the power issues. Your door is wide open and yet there isn't a single sound interrupting our conversation. I'd say it's safe to assume that no one is home with you. You're all alone."

"Well Lucy," Ethan spoke more quietly now, "it has been great talking with you, but I am going to suggest that you take some time to write your paper and then come back to talk with me for the edits."

"We don't have that kind of time left."

"When is your paper due?"

"Think about it, Ethan," Lucy continued. "We have to acknowledge that morality is real. Even if there is no God, we would generally agree on ideas that are right and push away ideas that are wrong; that are sinful. Right? We have so many moral philosophies that are separate from religion that still push a standard by which we are to live our lives. And therefore, we see that people need to be able to live by some kind of moral code. But why? What makes morality necessary?"

"Look, here, I really got to go. I need to call the...."

When Ethan turned back to his computer, he saw that Lucy had turned on her camera. But Ethan did not see the face of a college girl, nor did he see the face of anyone at all. All he saw was a top step of a set of stairs, a hallway filled with doors, with one door open in particular next to a flickering light. Ethan began to slowly turn his head.

"Don't. You. Move." Ethan heard Lucy's voice through the computer, but he heard some sort of chittering coming from in the hallway simultaneously. "I won't come closer if you don't look away. Let's finish talking about that paper, Ethan."

Ethan sat there in complete silence for what felt like

hours, just looking at the screen. When Ethan finally blinked, he heard the words, "That counts." He shot open his eyes to see that the perspective had shifted ever so slightly. He now no longer saw the top step, just the hallway.

"Okay, okay. Let's talk about your paper. We've got some time left for that, right?"

"You're right." Some chuckling could be heard in both directions. "Now, where were we, Ethan? Oh, that's right. I asked you a question. Assuming that there is no God, why would you discount the existence of sin if atheistic morality systems still exist?"

Ethan kept his eyes as wide open as possible, fixed on the screen in front of him. "Well, we don't live in a vacuum. We live in a society, so you must have rules on what you can and cannot do to live in a society. Otherwise, everything falls apart."

"What if society does not forgive you? What if an individual docs not forgive you?"

That's when a new voice whispered into Ethan's ear, a new voice, but a familiar one. "What if I don't forgive you?"

Ethan turned around in his swivel chair as fast as he could. No one was there. Just the flickering hallway light.

"Did you hear something?" Lucy's laughter mixed with the rustling and Ethan's racing heart. He quickly turned back to his computer. The display now showed his door on the right side of the screen, exposing the corner of his desk. What also terrified Ethan was the realization that his camera was still on, and he did not see anyone else in the room with him when he heard the noise, turning purely on fear and instinct.

"Okay. What is this? Who are you? Who put you up to this? How many of you are in my house?"

"So, what do you think of my argument? I mean, if

someone never forgives you, and this life is all there is, with no hereafter, then does that not mean that these things are technically unforgivable sins?"

"That is a rather compelling argument." Ethan picked up his phone, making sure that he wasn't looking away from the screen. If he could just call the police and tell them that someone was in his house, he could get through this. But as he touched the screen, it lit up, he noticed it was being erratic. Sometimes it would flash on and off repeatedly. Sometimes it would scramble the numbers on the pin pad. Sometimes it would show random images; art, faces, all of which seemed familiar to his brain and yet seemed wrong to see.

"So why are you the only one on tonight?"

"Huh?"

BLINK

The door was now closer to the center of the frame.

The light from the hall went completely black.

"I mean, why are there no other tutors on here?" Ethan had to strain to hear her properly because the chittering was now so close to his bedroom door. "Normally when someone comes in they may see a person, or perhaps multiple people, but they are always assigned to a smaller room in the online meeting. You, however, didn't need to put me into a smaller room. You just let me into the big meeting and that's where we stayed. It's big and empty with no fear that someone is going to intrude on what we are doing together."

"Well, if you'd prefer, I can—"

"No, no. I like it. It's nice to have the house all to ourselves instead of being confined to one room. I was just curious why no one else is here."

"Well, due to how little work is done at this time of night and the limited budget, they could only afford to keep one staff member on for this shift, and so that's why I'm the only one here."

"You seem calmer."

"Excuse me?"

"You seem calmer answering that question. It's almost as if you had rehearsed that line before."

"Why does that matter?"

"Are you used to rehearsing lines?"

"No." He could barely get the whisper out.

"So why is it really you on the night shift? Did they fire everyone else?"

"No." He suddenly couldn't control his breathing.

"Did they move everyone else to other shifts?"

Tears started to feel up in his eyes. "Yes."

"So why did they stick you in this shift all by yourself?" The noises from the hallway were close.

"I don't know."

"You don't know?"

"Probably because I'm the most willing to work this shift, so they left it in my hands. It probably also has to do with the trust that they have in me."

"Is that what you really think?"

"Excuse me?"

"You think that you're on this shift because they all think so highly of you? You're the star employee, so they gave you the shift that would require you to work with as few people as possible, where your coworkers and supervisors would rarely have to see you?"

"Hey now, that's a bit—"

"They don't like you. Nobody you work with likes you. If you could hear the things they say about you, you would know that. You wouldn't be in such denial about it."

He began to move his mouse to her name in the participants list so that he could exorcise her from the meeting.

"I didn't mean to be rude. After all, it isn't your fault. You can't help the way your brain is wired. You can't help your brain chemistry. You can't affect the hormones and chromosomes that stewed around in the womb. You are just you, and yet they can't seem to forgive you for it. So, funny enough, wouldn't that mean that your entire existence is an unforgivable sin to them?"

BLINK

His door was now fully centered in the frame. He froze.

"You've got some really nice art on your desk, Ethan."

He couldn't stop the tears. As his eyes shut, he could hear the floorboards creak behind him, the chittering getting louder and louder.

"What exactly did you draw, Ethan? Hmm?"

No response. He just held his head in his hands, allowing the snot and tears to coat them.

"I'm waiting."

"It's for my portfolio."

"That isn't what I asked, Ethan."

"It's… It's a pencil sketch of a bird in a tree."

"What's it called, Ethan?"

"Look, I'm sorry. Please, I am sorry. Please, don't hurt me. I didn't do anything wrong. I swear."

"You know what's funny, Ethan?"

"What?" He choked on it, gasping as it came out.

"You're so scared that I am going to hurt you, but—"

He heard the next part in his ear alone: "I can't even touch you."

There was nothing else in the room with him on his camera, but he saw the back of his head centered in Lucy's However, Lucy disappeared from the call with a chime. As soon as Ethan's camera took up the entire screen, he saw it. Right behind his shoulder he noticed a second face, a woman's face, dead and lifeless. Her eyes were rolled up and her mouth was agape. Horror was permanently frozen on this face. But there was more than just a woman's face that concerned him, for along the face was a large, black silhouette, and underneath the woman's chin was another mouth, one with big, sharp, white teeth. Ethan couldn't even scream.

"Go on," the monster said in a voice that sounded like thousands. "Touch me. See if I could even hurt you."

After a few seconds of paralysis, Ethan waved his hand through where the monster would be, but felt nothing, not even a warm or cold spot that could tell him this thing was here.

"Good. Now look at me." When Ethan didn't move, it shouted, "Look at me!"

He looked. There was nothing there. He panted and relaxed before he heard the voices again.

"See. It's like I'm not even there."

Ethan jumped out of his seat and saw nothing, only catching it in the camera again, now sitting in his computer chair.

"Yeah," it continued, "really limited ways you can sense me."

"This is not possible. It's not possible, it's not—"

"Possible? Yeah, you would think. And yet, here we are. And we still have about half of our session, Ethan."

"But… But…" He felt like he was about to faint.

"Like I said, there are some questions that won't leave us alone, and I asked you my question, my itch I have yet to scratch. And I need your help to find that answer."

"What do you want?"

"A deal."

"A deal?"

"Yes. A deal."

"I don't understand this at all."

"Good. It's easier that way. I just need you to agree to

help me."

"I don't—What is this?"

"Okay. I guess some context is needed. I have dedicated my entire existence to figuring out what cannot be forgiven by anything or anyone. I need this answer, for it is the intellectual itch of my being. And you, well, look at you. We both know that nobody likes you. You need all the friends you can get."

"So what? You want to be friends? You want to do this big research project together, huh?"

"Oh, absolutely not. Even I don't want to be your friend. But we do need each other."

"How so?"

"You have a body. I have power."

"Excuse me?"

"I can't touch anything. I can't feel anything. I can't do anything that will test the boundaries. But you do. You have all the physicality I need."

"So, you want my body?"

"Well, not forever. I just need to wear you for a moment, like Lucy here." It took off the mask. "She's safe at home as we speak. I can't wear the same outfit more than once, you see, and I tend to change clothes daily. But I need you to agree. I am only allowed in with consent."

"Why would I ever let you in?"

"Because if I get to experiment with your body, I'll give you the power to be well liked."

He stood there, shocked.

"Think about it. You're all alone in every way you can think. So why not accept this trade? You lose a day, but you gain a lifetime of happiness afterwards."

"But what happens if you succeed?"

"Then you're locked out of heaven, which you don't

believe in anyway, so you were already going to be locked out. So, what do you think?"

"No! I can't! This is—"

"Don't you want to create?"

"Huh?"

"Gatekeeping is real, you know. I can help you make your big break."

Ethan took a deep breath before responding. "So how do we do this?"

"Do you accept the deal? I get your body for the next day, and you get a lifetime supply of power?"

"Yes. I d—"

Before he could finish, he felt an intense pain. He felt as if he had been hit by a train. However, instead of being dead upon impact, he felt as if he were alive and conscious, feeling every bit of excruciating pain as he flew through the air, hit the ground, and then was run over by said train, which he then felt in excruciating detail as well. When he regained consciousness, he was back at his desk. He trembled as he looked down at his body. Everything was intact, but he was covered in so much blood.

"What the hell ha—"

"Oh, nothing much, really." The voices rang inside his head. "Nothing important enough to matter at least. Nothing that severed the bonds of grace from you or me permanently. So sadly, this was a failure. But don't worry. A deal is a deal. I'll be going, and leaving behind my gift as well."

He felt his hand move without his will behind it and start dialing a number in his phone. He placed the phone up to his ear and heard it ring.

"Hello! You've reached the 24 Hour Hawthorne Mart on the corner of Scarlet and Veil. We're here for all of your pharmacy, photo, and phase of life needs. How can I help you today?"

"Hi!" The words came out of Ethan's mouth involuntarily. "I'm so glad that someone is there. I made an order with you guys and I was wondering if it was ready to be picked up yet." As he spoke, a black mist departed from his mouth and into the phone.

"I can check that right now, sir. What's the name?"

"It's Ethan. Ethan D. Vell." Every second felt horrendous, like he was slowly dying.

"I'm sorry, sir. The system is running a bit slowly right now. You're welcome to call again later when the internet is perhaps a bit better."

"Well, are you needing to help anyone?" He felt as if a fire-brand had been pushed deeply into his soul.

"No, sir. Not right now."

"Then, if it's okay with you, I would feel better if I could stay on the line with you. This is a bit urgent for me. I work really weird hours, but also don't want to waste gas, you know." He wished he could vomit out the rest of this evil spirit, but all he could do was quake as it slowly left him.

"Okay sir. That's understandable. I'll keep you posted on when it finally loads."

"That's great! While we're waiting, I was wondering if you could help me with something else." His eyes watered. He soon realized that he wasn't even talking anymore. Sounds just formed from the mist with his voice.

"Yes, sir. What can I help you with?"

"Well, I run a small business, or at least I'm trying to, and I work with consulting and art. Fun stuff, honestly. Anyway, I got this project and there's this big overhanging question about it and I just want to bounce some ideas off of someone, you know, for inspiration. You seem rather lovely, like as a person, and so I wanted to see if you could help me out with this." He could feel as if everything that burned within him was his again. He would move his toes and soon his legs without any resistance.

The person on the other end laughed. "Sure thing. What's the question?"

His voice then became much more serious. "Is there such a thing as an unforgivable sin?" The mist rushed the rest of the way out of his body and into the phone. He ended the call, but he wondered if that would stop this monster from getting his next puppet ready. He coughed and he wretched, about to go take a shower, when the rush kicked in. He didn't know what it was, but he felt good, finally good. Finally powerful. Finally like his tongue had been loosened and his mind had been opened, like he could finally do anything.

So what, he then thought to himself, if he could feel the brand of this monster forever in him, these unknown acts forever etched within him. He was about to make his own mark on the world very shortly.

*Ian Alexander Tash is a writer and podcaster from Bakersfield, California. He spent the pandemic not only attaining his Double Major BA in English and Religious Studies from California State University, Bakersfield, ultimately earning the distinction of Most Outstanding Graduate for the School of Arts and Humanities, but also working as a Writing Consultant and Religious Studies Tutor for the school. His love of Nathaniel Hawthorne and hungry ghosts, as well as his many hours of working remotely, helped inspire him to craft "Ethan's Brand" for Inkd Publishing's Noncorporeal Anthology. Ian's other pieces of speculative fiction can be found in Sci Phi Journal and Orpheus, while his essays can be read in Amendo, Writing COVID, Calliope, and the Los Angeles Times. When he isn't working or working on his next project, Ian spends time with his lovely wife, Stephanie, and adorable Yorkshire Terrier, Mini. Ian can always be reached on his social media accounts under @TellingItTash.*

# ERE NIGHT YIELDS

## JOSHUA DYER

*T*he heightened visits from Tallen's ghost confirmed what Vanguard suspected. His soulmate's murderer was somewhere in this town, Grayfall. Vengeance consumed Van's every waking moment, which were numerous. *Just point them out and give me five minutes alone.* Nightmares of Tallen's death haunted him still. Reliving his last moments and watching the life drain from his bright eyes left purple sacks of insomnia under Van's hollow brown stare. He stumbled downstairs with the finesse of a runaway vegetable cart.

The tavern crowd muttered in somber tones. Tendrils of fresh smoke slithered from snuffed torches on the walls. A cleansing breath. *Pull yourself together. Townsfolk can't see you like this.* He dropped into a seat near a front window, spilling the contents of a secret mushroom pouch concealed under his tunic. Van scooped them off his brown trousers and the top of his black boot. Crowns and commoners alike admired him. *Valiant heroes don't need painkillers.*

Mila soon sauntered from the kitchen to his table. She

had her mahogany locks braided at her back today. "Here's breakfast."

Van nodded through a pounding headache. Six frothy tankards last night and still no reasons as to why this world took Tallen from him. He propped his pounding noggin on a hand. Nothing filled the chasm in his shattered heart.

Mila scribbled on her pad. "Have you heard?"

He glanced at her through his fingers.

"Someone was murdered in the night," she said. "There are whispers that it was one of the knights."

Van fumbled for his coin purse. "What do I owe you for the meal?"

Concern for him lingered behind Mila's smile. She had probably seen his withdrawal symptoms in others. "The king says everything's complimentary." She drew a ledger from her soiled apron and set in on his table. "Just a signature is all you owe me."

He eased into his chair and scribbled in her book. "His Highness is most gracious."

Mila turned for the kitchen. "Guess it's the least he could do for your help."

Vanguard gnawed on a morsel of eggs. A fresh murder meant another shot at the serial killer's identity and more expertise from the neighboring town's constable. King Inthos didn't have to summon Van here under official seal. Bringing his love's killer to justice led him into Grayfall, and its castle, regardless. Partway through his fried potatoes, a young girl darted to his tableside, fighting for breath. She wore the wool tunic and crest of the crown. "The---king requests your---presence at once, sir."

Van chewed off the end of his last strip of bacon. "After you, squire."

Her light brown ponytail whipped in the wake of her race to the barracks. Vanguard had to run at a steady clip to keep her pace. A few nosy townsfolk shuffled behind a line of knights ordering them to stay back. The tall guard at the front door gave Van one look and stood aside.

The royal barracks sat just inside the gates of Castle Grayfall. A group of knights huddled around their table in the great room. Some sat and wept into their hands, while others consoled them. The remnants of last night's stew hung in the air. Van trailed the squire up the steps to a waiting group in Sir Fendrel's quarters. Pale daylight drew long shadows of three men across the dusty floorboards in the hallway. King Inthos, Sir Jornis, and Constable Alden conferred at the threshold of the crime scene. The king's hawkish stare studied the constable. Uneasy tension simmered between them. Van's heart skipped a beat when Tallen's vaporous form coalesced beside the three men.

Short, brown hair. A gray tunic pocked with bloody gashes and cinched with a belt. Sculpted arms and a torso absent Tallen's lively tan color. Soiled green leggings, conforming to muscled thighs and calves. Vanguard peered into Tallen's eyes, his spirit grasping at the straws of a failed love.

Inthos's blond bangs hung over a troubled brow. "Terrible news."

Van followed his lover's vaporous form as it strode to the king's back. No one else saw it. "I caught wind of it at breakfast, sire."

Jornis joined them. "Strangled to death with a rope. The killer got in via the loft access." The towering man scratched his long mustache. "He was one of our veterans." His words trembled. "Fendrel was like a brother."

Inthos led Van into the room. "We hope you can help decipher the mystery."

"I shall do my best," Van said.

Fendrel's body lay face down on the mattress. Flies

hummed around his head and landed on an ashen face. The rope draped across his brown mane. An unfolded note sat on his dresser.

"Our serial killer again," Alden said. "Same signature." He leaned his lanky frame over the dresser. Blond strands hung about his skeletal features. "Signed, Scarlet. Strange cryptic message this time, though."

Van felt inside his blue jerkin for the mushroom pouch. Not the time to have it spill again. "Oh?"

Tallen's essence moved next to the constable as he read the letter. "Three pillars will meet the same fate they built." His glare found Van. "Mean much to you?" Color drained from the faces of Inthos and Jornis.

"No." Van shuttered at the sudden rush of cold air.

Tallen's apparition pointed a translucent finger at Alden. Van whispered into Alden's ear. "Not many places in all of Phelos to get rope like that."

Alden rubbed the nape of his neck. "The armory likely has it."

Vanguard glared through his greasy black bangs at Alden and the king. "So do people who make nooses."

* * *

VAN SWIRLED the dregs of his ale. A heavy cloud hung over the tavern. The few locals in attendance peered into the amber contents of their cups in contemplative silence. Sir Fendrel's murder didn't lessen the other two prior, but a knight? Van's mind churned through the information, but the message made little sense. *Three pillars?* Alden had a role in it. Tallen had been clear in that. Proof was the problem.

Vanguard drank the last of his ale and slid off the barstool. Neither drink, potion, nor punishment could numb his pain. His head swam. Van reached for the fazing tankard handle and fumbled it across the bar. He snagged his spent container and slammed it on the polished wood, startling the others. "Enough's enough!"

Van listed up the stairs, a ship adrift in a storm of his own design. He reached for the trunk at the end of his bed, but toppled to his knees. He slammed the side of his head into the bedpost, earning a knot for his poor choices. Van went to curse the post and himself, but the weight of the last few months broke him. He hugged the chest and wept. It all found its way out. Tallen, his love for him. Masks of death haunted him, pushing Van to sanity's precipice.

"Why you?" Gooseflesh raced up Van's arms as Tallen's ghost knelt at his side. "We never did anything to anyone."

Vanguard drew his rapier from its sheath hanging on a bedpost. He turned its point on his sternum. His chest hitched through more sorrow. "A lifetime apart is too long."

The spirit stood over Van and rested its hands on his. Warmth calmed Van's suffering. Vanguard pinched some cured mushroom from his pouch and tucked it in his jaw. Their earthy flavor soothed his nerves. Numbing calm blanketed his battered body. Vanguard's slender nose detected an impossible scent this late at night. "Cinnamon rolls?" A chuckle. "You were a hound for those things." His weapon hit the wooden floor. "How can we bring him to justice with no evidence?"

Tallen floated backward through the wall, curling a finger for him to follow. Van secured his husband's sword and wiped his tears on a sleeve. He had to hustle out the door before the narcotic took full effect. Tallen led him along a rutted road parallel to the mountain range beyond the reaches of Grayfall proper. Frogs and bugs offered their nocturne in honor of the crisp evening. His husband's phantom veered off the road into a flat field. Copses of birch and elm dotted the swaying grain.

Tallen angled toward a faint light in the distance. Vanguard ducked close to the whispering oats and followed. The moon hung on the horizon, rippling in the inebriation of his mushrooms. Its oversized distortion illuminated the countryside in a milky yellow hue. *Where are you taking me?*

Van paused at the first glade to scout the cottage and surrounding farm. Lanterns twinkled on the back porch. Stoic horses swung their tails in the paddock behind the barn. The masonry and pipework for a tar kiln sat on the far side. A silver tendril of smoke slithered from a chimney on the stone cottage. He lowered his voice. "He's here?"

Tallen drifted at the field's edge near the barn and pointed toward its doors. Vanguard scampered through the grain away from a hooting owl to the ghost. "What do you want me to do?"

Tallen grinned and strode through the wall of the barn. An unwound length of twine dangled from the right door handle. Van tugged on it and padded inside. The pungent odor of hay and manure hit him in the face. Tallen hovered beside an oaken barrel and sacks of straw near the back wall. Glistening black lines soiled the barrel's façade, trapping a thin golden strand of hair. Van leaned in and plucked the blond hair from the congealed tar. "Alden."

Tallen's gaze fell to the dirt.

"Why the tar and straw? Whose home is this?" He followed the thin lines of tar from the barn out toward the cottage.

A drizzled trail snaked across the yard to the home's chimney. Tallen gestured to the stack's narrow portion. The smoke had ceased.

"What has he done?" He scanned the premises for any intruders. Nothing stirred, save the whispering oats at his back.

Van crept to the chimney, a hand extended. A thunderous

explosion left his ears ringing. Heavy debris pelted his arms and back. Menacing flames belched from the hole in the side of the home. Feminine yelps indoors crescendoed to full-on screaming terror.

He raced to the front of the cottage, the lawn tilted back and forth. The lady of the house staggered outside carrying a limp boy in her arms. Ravenous fires devoured the interior of the cottage. Orange tongues lapped at the ceiling trusses. Black smoke belched through the hollow entrance to the home. A male voice pleaded for mercy from a god who refused to listen. Vanguard teetered to the engulfed front doorway. *He never answers my prayers either.*

The woman lay her child in the grass and turned to her home. "Jorni!" She ran for the door.

Van waved her back. "It's too late." He dragged her under his muscular arm away from the inferno. "Focus on your boy." He flopped into the grass and listened to the child's chest and mouth. Neither beat nor breath sounded. His moistened stare found hers. "I'm sorry."

She sank to the grass and cradled her son's body. "Why? Why!"

Vanguard's strength was no match for his emotional torrent. Tears came. Raw loss chewed on him as fresh as the day he found Tallen. Vanguard stammered away at the emergence of the boy's ghost. It walked to the waiting soul of Sir Jornis at the road into their property. The boy clung to his dad's ethereal hand and the pair disintegrated.

* * *

A BLAZING sun dominated the clear blue skies the following morning. Wisps of smoke curled off charred posts and support beams. Van combed the rubble and remains of Sir Jornis's property with the constable.

Alden knelt over the lifeless body of the child in the yard. "No signs of burns or bodily injury."

Van inched closer. "Suffocation by smoke."

Alden glared at him. "The lone survivor placed you on the scene during this tragedy." He rose and strode over blackened stone and smoldering wood to the chimney's remnants. "Looks like a clog built up heat and pressure and it exploded."

"A tragic accident." Vanguard fondled the blond hair in his hand. Daylight stabbed his tired eyes like glowing hot daggers.

The constable studied the inside of the chimney with a discerning eye. "Looks that way." He eyed the pouch poking from Van's jerkin.

"But looks can deceive," Van said.

An accusatory vice squeezed Alden's blue eyes wider. "In what way?"

Vanguard led him to the paddock where the horses grazed oblivious to the carnage. "Interesting detail I discovered on the killer's note left for Fendrel."

Alden propped a boot on the lowest rung of the split-rail fence. "That being?"

"Several of Scarlet's strokes in the letter bear a striking resemblance to those in your signature in Garin's ledgers at the inn and tavern."

A nervous scoff from the constable. "I think you're looking too hard for something that doesn't exist."

"Perhaps I am." Van held up the blond strand. "Regardless, I took the liberty of advising the king to evacuate at his earliest convenience." Van paused for eye contact. "I'm sure you'd agree."

Alden gritted his teeth. "Of course." His glare fell to Van's pouch again. "Not much room for error."

\* \* \*

THE MORNING'S investigation left Vanguard with a redoubled sense of urgency. If Alden struck again, chances are it would happen soon. Tallen must have sensed it as well. As soon as he resurfaced, the ghost led Van out of Grayfall and beyond the borders of the forest of Blindwood to a secluded lake. The apparition stopped at the water and stared out over the sparkling waves.

Vanguard studied it. "Are you out there somewhere?" He propped himself against a tree as a black wave of misery swelled. "I'm so sorry, love. They dragged you away so fast. I couldn't catch up."

Tallen's spirit nodded. It turned and wandered into the forests away from the water. Shafts of daylight punctured Blindwood's dense canopy and obscured Tallen's form.

"Wait." Van shuffled around a protruding root. "Where are we going?"

They walked through the shaded wood and emerged near a cottage surrounded by barren fields of baked earth. Brittle pieces crunched underfoot as he followed his soulmate to the door of the thatch home. Tallen pointed to the door.

"I should knock?"

His lover grinned.

Vanguard rapped on the crooked door. A soiled old woman answered in a frustrated huff. Blonde curls hung around her oval face. Soot and dirt streaked her leathery cheeks and button nose. Her icy blue glare pierced him. "I have no interest in travelin' salesmen today, good sir."

He stopped the shutting door with his hand. "I'm not here to peddle anything." The weight of the door surrendered.

"What, then?" She bobbed her head toward the fire in her hearth. "I've got stew that needs stirred and loaves a-risin'."

"Just a question," Van said, "then I'll leave you be."

She cocked a hip out. "Blabber swift-like."

"Did you know a young man who died around these parts?"

A sharp, "No." The woman went to shut her door again. "Good day to you---"

"Just a moment." He held the door ajar. "It's hard to explain. His name was Tallen."

The woman froze.

"I believe he was from around here."

Tallen nodded. He drifted to a towering pine in the yard.

"If you'll come with me, I'll try to make sense of it." Van went to the pine where he found a name scored into its trunk. "Tallen." He passed a hand over the letters in the sticky bark.

The woman broke down. "He..." She waited for her sobs to subside. "Tallen was one of my sons."

"One?"

The old woman blotted her nose on her dishrag. "My other boy was taken from me when he was eight."

"For what?"

"His father..." She couldn't complete the thought.

Van eyed her gray-streaked curls. "Who took him?" The knights?"

Tallen's spirit hovered beside his mother.

"As he got older," the woman said, "more and more people noticed that they looked alike. So, he had Alden sent to another town far away."

"Alden resembled who? Jornis?"

She giggled. "Hardly. King Inthos." She wiped a nostril on her rag. "Ain't proud of it. We were both much younger then." She watched a passing cumulus cloud sail north. "No. Jornis and a stout brown-haired companion of his took my boy."

"My god." The pieces to Van's puzzle came together. "He's

picking them off one by one." He turned to leave. "Please pardon my intrusion, madam."

"Wait." She grabbed his hand. "Have you talked to him? Tallen, I mean?"

"Not so much talked." Van strode toward the forest.

"Please," she said. "Next time you see him, tell him I love him." She choked back tears. "So much."

Tallen wrapped his mother's terrestrial chest in a hug.

Vanguard smiled. "He already knows." He bowed. "Again, pardon my intrusion."

He ran through the woods, ducking and leaping branches and roots. He slowed at the water's edge. The lake possessed as many undulations as Van's stomach. "We need to stop the king's murder."

* * *

GRAYFALL CASTLE STIRRED with frantic activity. Servants packed and loaded travel trunks onto the royal carriage. Squires tended the horse team and double-checked their jingling harnesses. Vanguard sat perched on a boulder a short distance from the castle's front steps. Feathery painted cirrus clouds formed a rutted road toward the final hint of daylight. With no sign of Alden on the road, he hopped down and strode through partial spirals of wildflowers ornamenting the main gates. "Looks like the queen's homecoming had been cancelled."

Dozens of candles and torches brightened the main dining hall. Servants hurried about finalizing His Highness's emergency departure. Van wove among the staff in the foyer searching for Inthos. "Where's the king?"

The servants stared at him with blank expressions amid the castle's whirlwinds of commotion.

"The old man in a crown." Vanguard shook a young man. "Have you seen him?"

"Last I saw," the servant said, "he was up in his bedroom, packing clothes for the next several weeks, sir."

Van released his prey and bounded up the stone steps to the second level. The upstairs corridors stood devoid of any other human being. He leaned on the marble bannister and shouted into the buzzing hive below. "Where are the guards? The knights?"

A woman from the kitchen staff answered as she waddled beneath him. "Heard tell he sent the knights ahead to scout the roads. The guards were ordered to patrol the town."

"Then, who's protecting him?"

She shrugged her meaty shoulders. "Constable's here. He felt the king didn't need all that watchin' for one man."

"Your Highness?" Vanguard hoped for a response, but none came. He spun on a heel and sprinted down the corridor.

Tallen materialized at the intersection of a perpendicular hallway and sailed to the left. Steel sang in the right-hand length of the hall. Vanguard swiveled with his rapier drawn and raced along the hallway. A servant pocketed his dagger and flint strike with a gulp. His sagging jowls puffed on the torch, bringing it to life. Van raced past the old man and chased Tallen down this long corridor. A set of ornate oaken doors embossed with the royal seal signaled the end of the line. Torchlight reflected on their polished surfaces.

"Highness?" Van rapped on the door.

He leaned an ear closer to the carved stags and shields. A muffled struggle unfolded behind closed doors. Van thrust a shoulder into the door until it relinquished its hold. Alden had King Inthos in a choke hold with his sword in hand. Van stood face to face with Tallen's killer. The damaged part of his soul begged Van to unleash its furies. *More than vengeance now hangs in the balance.*

"I wouldn't go through with it." Vanguard shuffled toward them.

"Not another step!" Alden laid the blade of his short sword at Inthos's Adam's apple. "Or father dearest lets like the pig he is."

Van obeyed. "Your mother told me everything. How Fendrel and Jornis took you away."

Alden hissed. "You know nothing!"

Inthos staggered with Alden toward his balcony. "They told me they left you for dead."

Alden tightened his blade against the king's throat. "That they did, but I keep coming back like a fungus." His maniacal glare found Vanguard. "Isn't that so?"

"I know you murdered your brother," Van said.

Alden inched into the doorway onto the balcony over-looking the courtyard. "He had everything. A father. Mother's pride. You."

Van crept closer. "You stole everything that mattered to me from this world."

Alden snagged a green drape as it fell over his shoulder. "You've waited long for vengeance, Vanguard, but you may have to hold a bit longer. I've seen the real you. Had a bit of nature's biscuit myself. Hell of a ride, isn't it?" He wrapped the drape around Inthos's neck and tied it off. The tandem shimmied to the balcony's edge. "What will it be? Uphold your valiant heroic name and save our king?" Alden pushed the old man over the edge. "Or scratch the itch of your personal obsession?" He grabbed the other drape and repelled into the courtyard.

\* \* \*

A WANING MOON poked through the trees and turned the water sprouting from the fountain into molten silver. Inthos gagged and swung by the fabric that choked the life from him. Van hacked at the drape with his sword as Alden raced among the courtyard's shadows. For a fleeting instant, Tallen's ghost appeared in the moonlight, then vanished into the darkness in pursuit of his brother.

"Inthos?" Van hacked through the curtain with strike after strike.

Inthos's face was turning blue. Van's blade sliced halfway through the fabric before the king's girth did the rest. Inthos hit the stone courtyard and choked on inhalations of fresh air.

Vanguard grabbed the other drape and slid to the ground.

A yelp echoed from the far end of the sprawling court-yard. Alden backpedaled into the moonlight and tumbled onto his rump. Color drained from his face. Alden's blade scraped across the uneven stonework.

"Stay away from me!" Alden was a spider entangled in his own web, and the crow descended for its meal.

Several spirits drifted into the light. Some disfigured by fire and beheading, others showing signs of rot and decay. The sounds of the insects ceased. A deathly silence filled the yard. A sudden chill dried the sweat to Van's arms.

The constable had found his invitation to Hell. "Leave me be."

Van held up a boot heel and waited for Alden to scoot into it. "To truly cure an itch, you have to rid the carcass of its fleas."

His boot connected with Alden's head as the man turned to stand. Alden rubbed his cheek and unsheathed his short sword. Van pulled his rapier and forced him back against a large boulder in the yard. Van swung for his shoulder. Alden flattened against the boulder, avoiding the swipe by the hair on a chipmunk's ear. Steel clashed with steel. The force of the constable's blade pushed Vanguard's rapier back, nearly knocking it from his grip.

The short sword's point lunged for Vanguard's face, slicing a gash lengthwise into his cheek. Warm blood oozed from the searing sting.

Alden took another hack at his left arm. "Not even the dead will sway me."

King Inthos hobbled back into his castle. "Guards!"

Van tested his opponent's weak side with a couple of jabs. "Time's running out."

Alden took a swing at his neck. Vanguard countered the assault and shoved his adversary away. Blades collided again, singing under the gibbous moon. Alden pursued him around the yard, leaping onto a low stone wall and driving Vanguard back against the boulder. Alden brought his weapon around in both hands. Van whipped up his rapier to parry, but the short sword cut through it. A few quick blows knocked the busted weapon from his hand and left gashes in Vanguard's arm and side. Alden's boot found his gut, sinking Van to the ground.

"My brother's sword had a weak spine much like himself." Alden spat in the direction of the broken rapier. "Time for you to join him."

Fading moonlight glinted on the ornate hilt and hand-guard of his once glorious weapon. Everything lay in ruin. Broken futures. Shattered dreams.

"Did they know?" Alden lowered the tip of his sword to Van's nose. "About your little pouch of mysteries?"

The sword's edge cut the corner of Van's mouth. A rivulet of blood dripped onto the granite.

"No matter," Alden said. Armored boots resounded from the castle halls. "You can take your secrets to the grave."

Vanguard rolled toward his sword as Alden swung downward. He grabbed his hilt and sprang like a viper. His jagged blade plunged through the constable's throat. Alden shrieked.

Van met him nose to nose. "Never speak ill of my late husband in my sight."

Alden crumpled to the stones as a crowd formed around them. Servants and knights alike gasped at the skewered lawman.

A brawny knight hustled to the scene. His astonished expression locked onto Van. "What is the meaning of this?"

Van held up an open hand. "He confessed to the killings and attempted to murder the king." His exhausted body collapsed against the cool boulder.

A group of gleaming spirits arose and strode into the rising sun. Tallen floated to Van and caressed his cheek with a ghostly hand. After one last smile, he walked with the others and disappeared into the daylight.

Van reached for his pouch, then thought better of it. "It's over."

*JOSHUA DYER WRITES in several different genres and styles including fantasy, science fiction, and horror. Several of his works have won awards in L. Ron Hubbard's Writers of the Future competition. Previously, he wrote for the Los Angeles Times where his fiction won their "Reader's Choice Award" for best story of the year. When he's not writing, Dyer likes to read, study languages, play video games, and bake.*

# THE CURSED DARK

## ROSEMARY WILLIAMS

*T*he car's radio faded out as the engine shivered to a halt, leaving Sephie in an appropriate silence in which to ponder her life choices. The particular choice that had brought her here had clearly been a doozy. She turned to the driver. "An abandoned mental hospital? Really?"

Thalia nodded, a bright smile spread across her face. "Spooky, right?"

Sephie pursed her lips in a frown, then smoothed it as soon as she realized how transparent her emotions were. "That is definitely a word for it." *Other words might include tired, stereotyped, and overdone.*

"C'mon." Thalia said, seeming to take Sephie's skepticism in stride. "We're a new group, and this is our first *big* ghost hunt. We wanted to go for something special."

"Okay," said Sephie, her mouth twisting into a wry half-smile. "But if we run into a couple of overly handsome men whose names happen to rhyme with *jam* and *spleen* we are packing up and getting the hell out of here."

Thalia chuckled. "That's a deal."

The women unpacked their gear. They didn't have much,

just Thalia's audio recording equipment and Sephie's backpack and cane. There was a comfortable security to the feel of the handle in her grip, the soft thump of its end on gravel. The familiar weight of the cane soothed her anxiety.

It wasn't that she was anxious about any potential ghost encounters. The dead she could deal with—it was the living that tended to throw Sephie for a loop. She'd been chatting with Thalia online for several weeks, but this would be her first time meeting the other two members of this little crew.

Sephie took a cleansing breath and turned her face to bask in the last few rays of the setting sun. Massachusetts winter would come all too soon, with its wretched cold and heaps of snow, but for now the air was crisp with early autumn. She still missed the Keys, but this…this was nice.

Thalia clicked the button on her key fob to lock the doors. She wrinkled her nose at the hatchback she had parked next to. "I'd hoped the boys would wait for us, but I guess not. No worries, though! I know the way in." She led Sephie onto the unkempt grounds.

The waning day still cast enough light to see, but the calf-length grass could be hiding molehills and holes, so Sephie stepped cautiously. She dodged past a clump of prickly thistles and made a mental note to check herself for ticks when she got home.

They squeezed through a thicket of brush that hugged the institution walls to one of its many large, low windows. The glass was long gone, but rusty iron bars blocked their ingress. "That doesn't look like a way in," said Sephie.

"Oh, ye of little faith." Thalia grabbed the bottom of one of the bars and pulled. The entire apparatus lifted away from the brick, leaving enough room to squeeze through. Thalia held it for Sephie, then clambered in after her.

Their passage stirred up dust, and Sephie sneezed. The place smelled of mold and old antiseptic. Their sneakers crunched on bits of detritus. As they moved deeper into the dim building, Sephie clicked on the flashlight embedded in her cane handle.

"We came in a few weeks ago during the day," Thalia said as she led Sephie down a mint green hallway stained with years of grime. "To get the lay of the place when it's light. It's a lot spookier now." She turned long enough to waggle her eyebrows at her companion, then continued onward. "This place is like a rite of passage for local ghost hunting groups."

Sephie allowed herself an amused eyeroll. Thalia was enthusiastic, which wasn't necessarily a bad thing, though the inexperience of her team could get them into trouble. But that was part of why Sephie was connecting with them; she had abilities the average person didn't. If they—or any of the other ghost hunting groups they knew—ever ran into something truly nasty, they could contact Sephie for help.

And Sephie wouldn't have to stretch herself so thin *looking* for all of the spirits only she had the tools to deal with.

First, though, she needed to get through one or more nights of essentially babysitting the group on the bunny slope. *This place will work as well as anything, I suppose.* The classic horror trope vibe of the old hospital aside, there *were* ghosts here. Sephie didn't need to quest out far with her spirit-sense to pick up on them, but they felt…odd. Muted.

*Hm. Ghost hunters aside, I imagine they don't get many visitors out here. They're probably barely aware of the living world anymore. I doubt the hunters will get much out of them.* That suited Sephie just fine. For once, she was there to connect with the living, not the dead.

They found the other half of the group in what had once been the hospital's lobby, setting up various pieces of equipment.

"About time," grumbled a blond man with handsome, chiseled features. "We were supposed to meet at five-thirty."

"You knew I couldn't get here that early because I was picking up our fourth," said Thalia. "You should've waited for us before going in."

The blond shot a sour glance at Sephie. "I thought I told you not to bring her."

The second person, a lanky young Black man with a ready smile chimed in. "You'll have to excuse Aaron, he sometimes forgets he has social skills." He stood up and offered a hand. "I'm Kyle."

"Sephie." She switched her cane to her left hand to accept the handshake. "It's a pleasure to meet you."

Aaron scoffed.

*Apparently politeness is not an immediate way into this man's good graces.*

Kyle offered Sephie a conspiratorial eyeroll. "Aaron. *Honey.* You were literally complaining not two minutes ago that we didn't have enough people to split into two teams. Now we do. We can cover more ground this way."

"Fine." Aaron straightened up, crossing his arms. "Thalia, you brought her, you get to partner with her."

Thalia shook her head. "Oh, no. Last time you and Kyle paired off, you two spent way more energy on making googly eyes at each other than the actual hunt."

"But—"

"I caught you making out, like, *six* times. I mean, it's adorable, but pick better moments."

Aaron flushed bright red.

Kyle just laughed. "That's a fair shot. Okay, Thalia, you should go with Aaron, then."

Thalia shook her head. "Nope."

Alarmed, Sephie tried to catch Thalia's attention, to no avail.

Aaron tried to protest, but Thalia cut him off, channeling some sort of mom vibes. "Uh-uh. You're being rude, and Sephie's a sweetheart. Go. Act like a reasonable adult, or no brownies during footage review tomorrow."

"Fine." Aaron crossed his arms, a petulant glare on his face.

"Oh-kay." Kyle glanced back and forth between the two, then shot Sephie an apologetic look. "Thalia and I will take the east wing." He walked up to Aaron, took his head in his hands, and kissed his forehead. "You take the west with Sephie. And be *nice.*"

*Oh, this is not going to go well.*

Two-and-a-half hours into the evening, Aaron hadn't gotten any chattier. They had explored enough to get the general layout of the wing, and then Aaron had picked a spot to set up. The camera perched on a tripod, its view covering most of the room, and an electronic voice recorder sat running on an old table. He kept hold of a device that measured electromagnetic frequencies, believed to be capable of detecting ghosts.

Sephie had been looking forward to seeing if that actually worked, but so far, no ghosts had made an appearance. She could sense them still, along with that nagging sensation that something wasn't quite right. Despite focusing her attention on it for over an hour, she couldn't identify what it was.

She needed a break, both from the problem and the silent treatment. In a few breaths, she lifted her psychic shields into place and turned her focus toward her companion. "So, are you this prickly with everyone you meet, or am I just special?"

Aaron shifted on the old stool he perched on. His mouth

twisted, as though he was trying to find something palatable to say. "I don't like grifters."

A flash of heat rushed through Sephie's chest and up to her face. Shock melted into anger, which she shoved aside. "Wow." She let the word hang between them, inviting riposte.

He took the opportunity to dig the hole deeper. "I mean, that's what you are. You can admit that to yourself at least, right?" Aaron stood, pacing with a restless energy. "I knew you'd be trouble the instant Thalia told me about you, but she doesn't get it. You hippie-dippy types are all the same—faking powers to make a score. This is a science! And it's people like you who make it so that people like us aren't taken seriously."

Sephie's shoulders arched into a defensive posture under the diatribe. A thousand things to say jumped into her head, each one more pointless than the last. This man had clearly already made up his mind about her. "Well," she said, biting off the words, each leaving a sour taste in her mouth. "That is certainly a take." She might have said more, but movement caught her eye from the hall behind Aaron.

She sucked in a breath. Her stomach flipped over, adrenaline pumping molten hot energy through her body, though her limbs froze in terror.

It stood in the doorway. Pallid skin stretched over long, spindly arms and legs, its body cloaked in darkness. Its triangular head tilted slightly, with a pointed chin angling to the left. The deep rictus of a smile sported rows of tiny, pointed teeth. Its face resembled nothing so much as that of a shark when viewed from below and upside down. Its eyes were the only color on it, jade green set in patches of darkness.

Those eyes fixated on Sephie.

Despite never having faced one before, she recognized it for what it was: an entity that fed on emotion, particularly negative ones like anger and fear. Sephie had found plenty of partial matches in mythology, but nothing that fit closely enough for her to attach a definitive label.

Children had a word for it: bogeyman.

"Hey." Aaron squinted at Sephie, then smirked. "Oh, I get it. I call you out, so you decide it's time to put on the theatrics? There's no ghost here. No EMF spikes." He brandished the detector, showing her the dial.

Sephie opened her mouth, but she couldn't manage so much as a squeak. *This is no ghost.*

The bogeyman gently waved its hands in the air, as if wafting some delicious scent toward it. Curved talons clicked and swished as they connected with each other. It appeared to gain substance as it fed, becoming more *real*.

"Okay, seriously." Aaron said, turning to examine the spot that held Sephie's attention. "There's noth— holy *shit!*" He sprang backwards, stumbling into her.

The bogeyman's eyelids drooped. It hissed in something akin to satisfaction as Aaron's fear joined the buffet.

The shock of the impact wrenched Sephie out of her daze. *It may not be a ghost, but this is still my responsibility. Nobody else is equipped to handle this. I have to get a grip.* She grabbed Aaron's arm and pulled him behind her. "Breathe slowly," she croaked. "Try and calm your heart rate. It's feeding on our fear."

Aaron trembled underneath her fingers. "It...it's feeding..."

*I have had enough.* Sephie summoned up annoyance to try to subsume the fear. She took a step forward and smacked the end of her cane onto the floor, the rubber-capped metal making a blunt *thud* when it struck linoleum and concrete. *Challenge. Don't give ground.* "What do you want here?" It didn't come out quite as firmly as she'd intended.

The bogeyman tapped its claws together again. Its head

turned, slowly tilting the chin to the right with a widening grin, as if it were pleased by her boldness.

She snapped her cane down again. *Noise to ground my senses. Now demand its attention. Make it interact on my terms.* "What do you want?" she said again, her voice stronger, tone firmer.

It blinked and shifted its body in an eerily sinuous manner at odds with its sharp angles. Finally, it spoke in a rasping tone that echoed, like someone whispering into a cardboard tube.

*"Sssave them,"* it wheezed.

And then, like a passing thought, it stepped away from the doorway and disappeared.

* * *

"Aaron, I need you to calm down."

"Calm down? You want me to *calm down?*" Aaron didn't pause his frenetic pacing. "Then tell me what the hell that thing was!"

*Well, at least he's progressed past incoherent babbling.* Sephie didn't have time to coddle him through a soft understanding. The creature had fed enough on Sephie to make itself visible to normal humans, which meant that their other two crew members were now vulnerable. If they could see it, they would fear it, and it would get even stronger. "For lack of a better word, call it a bogeyman."

Aaron finally shuffled to a halt and squinted one eye. "Like, hiding in kids' closets and under the beds type of bogeyman?"

"More or less. They feed off emotion, particularly nega-tive emotion like anger or fear. Which is why we can't waste any more time. After what it said—"

"You heard it *speak?*" Urgency replaced fear on Aaron's

face, and he dove for the digital voice recorder. "There'll be EVP. I gotta hear this."

"Aaron, no. We don't have time—"

"Hold your horses, Spooky Girl. This won't take but a few seconds." He grabbed a tablet out of his bag and plugged the recorder into it, bringing up the display in a flash.

Frustrated, Sephie fell silent, restraining the urge to start pacing like Aaron had been moments before. *Why* did *it say to save them? Is it taunting us?* Or was she missing something?

Aaron opened the audio file and skipped ahead to near the end. He nudged the counter through little bursts of sound, and finally found the right place.

*"What do you want,"* said Sephie's tinny voice through the tablet speaker.

And in a whispery roar that bore little resemblance to the creature's actual voice, came the bogeyman's reply: *"Sssave them."*

"Oh, God," said Aaron. "Kyle and Thalia."

"That's what I've been trying to tell you…" Sephie trailed off as Aaron dashed into the hall. She chased after him in as close to a jog as she could manage, but the gap increased quickly. "Aaron! Wait! Slow down!"

He turned, already too far away for a good read on his face, but his voice projected impatience. "Try running and keep up!"

Sephie gritted her teeth and picked her feet up into a lope. She made it a few yards before she misjudged the angle of a step. Her right foot skidded. She tried to stabilize with her cane but overbalanced and, with a sick sense of vertigo, tumbled over with a shriek. She toppled into the wall and the cane slipped from her fingers. She slid down onto the floor, landing on her hip.

Aaron doubled back to where Sephie lay stunned on the

grimy linoleum floor. "Shit! Are you all right? What happened?"

"I'm sorry," gasped Sephie. *Don't mind me, I'm just a living horror movie trope in action.* "I—I'm still getting used to a new prosthetic. I..." She gestured to the rumpled jeans leg that had exposed a couple inches of metal bar where her right shin should have been.

"Oh, shit." Aaron snatched up Sephie's cane and handed it to her, then helped her heave to her feet. "I'm sorry. I—I assumed it was some sort of gimmick to look harmless. I didn't even think."

*Clearly.* Sephie shrugged, uncomfortable with Aaron's embarrassment. "If I had a nickel for every time someone thought I looked too young to be disabled..." *I'd have an entire Scrooge McDuck vault of nickels.*

"I'm *really* sorry."

Sephie nodded. She had neither the time nor the patience to hold a grudge. "Come on. We need to move."

"Right. Find the others, before the bogeyman does."

A distant, faint scream pierced through the echoing hallways.

Sephie's nerves tingled. "Too late."

Aaron set off at another run, this time slower, and with a solid grip on Sephie's elbow. She found it easier to keep pace with him stabilizing her, and she found a rhythm that kept both her feet moving.

A bobbing light appeared ahead, which quickly resolved itself into Thalia running towards them, flashlight clutched in her hand. Everyone tumbled to a halt as she flung herself into Sephie's and Aaron's collective arms.

Thalia sobbed with relief. "There was a ghost! Or a monster. It had horrible needle teeth and creepy long arms and claws and these evil, green eyes—"

"We know," said Sephie. "We've seen it."

Aaron released Sephie's arm as he steadied the other woman. "It has *claws*? Oh, God. Thalia, where is Kyle?"

"Kyle?" Thalia brushed a strand of hair out of her face with a visibly shaky hand. "I don't know. We ran when the monster showed up. We must've gone in different directions."

"Shit!" Aaron shivered with the energy of a caged animal. "We've gotta find him."

"It's getting stronger. Feeding on our fear." Sephie leaned on her cane to take some of the weight off her sore hip. "The less we fear, the better. Deep breaths, in through your nose, out through your mouth."

Thalia gulped down a whimper and nodded.

"You don't understand," Aaron choked through a sob. "Kyle gets nightmares. Really vivid ones. Sometimes he'll wake up in the middle of the night crying, and I'll be the only thing that can calm him down. He's gonna be filet mignon to this thing!"

Sephie caught Aaron's gaze with her own, projecting a calm confidence she didn't feel. "We're going to find him. It'll be okay."

Aaron scrubbed his fingers through his hair. "Will it?"

"Yes." Sephie's throat felt dry and scratchy, and her blood pulsed in her ears. *It's stuck out here—it needs us. We're a limited resource. It won't squander that.* Kyle would remain unharmed, relatively speaking. "It's safe to assume that the bogeyman has zeroed in on Kyle. That will make him easier to find. Thalia, take us to where you last left him. We'll search from there."

There must have been some genuine authority in Sephie's voice, as Thalia led the way with no more protest than a nervous swallow. She didn't even question the word "bogeyman."

The three of them didn't have to travel far to reach the

room where Thalia and Kyle had set up their equipment. Dusty chairs and tables lay strewn around the space, and an old checkerboard with a few stray game pieces lay in a cobwebbed corner.

There was also a ghost.

A young woman in a faded patient smock drifted slowly across the room. She hummed to herself, lost in some kind of fugue state. She didn't even seem to notice when she passed straight through Aaron.

He shivered, but didn't seem to see her. "Where to now?"

Sephie held up a quelling hand. "Give me a moment."

The ghost floated further, and Sephie frowned, studying her. Something wasn't quite right, but she couldn't put her finger on what it was. Then the ghost reached her and, instead of wafting through like she had Aaron, bounced off.

Sephie felt the usual, airy pressure she experienced whenever she touched a ghost. She was solid to them, and they to her, though that contact didn't carry the same sort of physical sensations that touching a person did. There was no warmth, more of a static tingle. Her shields blocked most of the charge, sending it back into the ghost.

The zap jerked the ghost out of her reverie, eyes wide. "Oh!"

"Did either of you hear someone say 'oh'?" asked Thalia.

Sephie twisted her lips into a frown. *Is Thalia a little bit spirit-sensitive?* That was an interesting wrinkle.

Her trajectory rolled around Sephie, and the ghost kept going in more or less the same direction she had been, almost as if she were being pulled along by some kind of current. But now her attention was focused. "How strange," she murmured, swiveling her head to stare at Sephie until the mysterious force pulled her through the wall and out of sight.

"A ghost came through," Sephie said finally. "I startled her.

It was...odd. I'm missing something obvious." She shook her head to try to clear it. "When you were in here earlier, did you hear anything else?"

Thalia shrugged. "I thought someone whispered, 'Eddie,' into my ear several times. Maybe it's the monster's name?"

Humor caught the edge of Sephie's tumble of emotions. "I don't know. He doesn't really look like an Eddie to me."

"Seriously? Kyle's still out there alone, and you're making jokes?" Some of Aaron's sourness returned.

Sephie lifted her hand again. "I'm about to make myself vulnerable in order to locate an entity that is *attracted* to negative emotions. Damn right I'm taking the edge off my fear." She closed her eyes and folded both hands over her cane handle. Then, cautiously, she cracked open her shields.

Sephie had always been able to see ghosts, for as far back as she could remember. As a child, she hadn't been able to tell the dead from the living, or indeed even known that she was seeing ghosts at all. She had pieced the truth together throughout childhood, coming to a hesitant acceptance as a teen, just in time for adolescence to turn everything upside down again with the opening of her spirit-sense.

Plenty of people had spirit-sense to one degree or another. Sephie's seemed to be stronger than most, though most of that seemed to come with the practice she had put into developing it. But she had never heard of anyone else who could see—or touch—noncorporeal entities the way she could.

Her spirit-sense was the proverbial double-edged sword. It allowed her to feel ghosts and their proximity, yes, but it also lit her up like a sports stadium. Her psychic shields blinded her, but also cloaked her power. They didn't block her Sight—she wasn't sure that *anything* could block that— but they did provide her a layer of physical protection.

Without those shields, the bogeyman's claws could rip right through her skin.

The first ghost Sephie sensed was the one that had just come through, receding slowly away on a curving trajectory. More popped up on the same arc, some in front of the first ghost, and others behind, approaching. It was almost like they were orbiting something.

Sephie reached out further and found the bogeyman: a smudge of darkness further east. But even as she located it, she found more—a trail, almost like that of a comet, that led outside behind the building. *No, a cord.* It connected the monster to...its twin? But even as she thought that, she knew it wasn't true. *An echo. An anchor, and it's tethered to it.*

The bogeyman wasn't just stranded. It had been deliberately *imprisoned.*

Sephie fluttered her eyes open and slammed her shields back down. "Someone lured this thing out here and trapped it. It's been starving to death."

Aaron straightened. "Wait, what did you just—"

"I found it. Follow me." Sephie led them through a door to the south that led into the surgical area of the building. She suppressed a shudder at the thought of the kinds of surgeries that would have happened at an asylum.

"Kyle!" the others called as they traipsed through hallways and scrub rooms.

Sephie didn't need to call; she knew exactly where to go.

Sure enough, as they approached an operating room, a strangled voice cried out, "Aaron?" from inside.

They burst through, and found Kyle cowering under a battered metal table. The bogeyman loomed over him, claws curled, eyes half-lidded as it fed. It looked more substantial now, less spindly, and its eyes had brightened. Almost healthy, if that could be said about such a creature. It turned and grinned at them as they entered, arms folded like a praying mantis while clicking its claws together.

Aaron and Thalia both drew up short and took a step back.

Sephie couldn't afford to let herself be trapped in fear, too. She slammed the end of her cane down on the floor again, letting the noise ground her senses, while she dredged up a memory from her dad's obsession with old sketch comedy shows. "Back off, Candygram," she snapped.

A hysterical giggle slipped out of Kyle.

The bogeyman's smile faded as it shifted sinuously, putting a little more space between it and Kyle. With a small flourish, it offered Sephie a respectful bow.

Her mouth opened in an "o" of surprise.

"Stronger now," the bogeyman hissed. "But speech... hard. Meet me...in the center." Its jade eyes bored into Sephie and it evidently let loose on the effort to pull on its tether. "Please," it said, disappearing into the wall. "*Save* them."

"Wh—what the *hell?*" squeaked Thalia.

* * *

THE FOUR GHOST hunters regrouped in the former patient common room. Aaron cuddled Kyle, stroking his back, though the latter seemed to be recovering surprisingly well. Thalia walked in circles around the camera.

Two more ghosts drifted through the room on their path, unseen by all but Sephie.

"What did it mean, '*save them?*'" asked Thalia.

"It said that before, when we first saw it," said Aaron. "We got it on EVP and everything."

"It means the ghosts. It has to," muttered Sephie. "I—" She cut off. Finally, she *saw* it. "They're transparent!"

"Well, sure?" said Kyle. "We can't even see them at all. They're *ghosts*. They're supposed to be."

Sephie shook her head. "Not to me. If I'm not paying attention, I can even mistake them for the living. But here, they're...faded." She reached out and caught the arm of one of the floating ghosts, arresting his movement. "What happened to you?"

The man gasped and shivered. "The eddy," he whispered. "We're stuck. He's tried so hard. So hard..." He trailed off, staring into nothing.

Sephie released him. "Oh, I'm an *idiot*." She pulled her backpack off and thumped it onto the ground, riffling through it. "Thalia, you were half-right. 'Eddie' isn't a person, it's a *thing*." She pulled a folded mass of paper out of her bag and unfolded it, revealing a heavily annotated map of the greater Boston area. "Give me some light."

More ghosts glided into the room. One, a gentleman in pajamas and a top hat, whirled and giggled as he passed through. Two more, arm in arm, floated horizontally, like passengers on a water park's lazy river.

Aaron clicked on his flashlight, then cursed as it sputtered out. "Damn ghosts." Kyle and Thalia had similar results.

Sephie clicked on the flashlight embedded in her cane and tucked it under her arm, trying to aim the glow properly at the map as she spread it out onto a dusty old table.

"Why is *your* light working?" asked Thalia.

"Lithium-ion batteries," said Sephie. "Don't ask me why it makes a difference. I have no idea. It just does. Try one of your phones' flashlights."

Kyle obliged, lifting his phone to give the map proper illumination.

Sephie set her cane down and gestured to the map. "Now, these are the region's ley lines, as near as I've been able to map them. And these points..." She hesitated as she regarded the colored dots scattered all over the map. They denoted places where mystical glyphs had been hidden in the shape of the roads' intersections, effectively dispersing and interfering with the natural flow of magical energy. Explaining the history and reasoning behind what kept Boston mostly free of true magic would likely be too much for the others. "Well, these are spots that mess with the flow of magic. Noncorporeals like ghosts and bogeymen don't directly interact with magic, but they can be affected by it. With me so far?"

Three heads nodded, though the boys looked perplexed.

"Right, so the magic would flow like this," she waved her hand around a space on the west side of the city, the side closest to their location. "But it can't, so it sort of disperses and then picks back up like this. And like water, it forms an eddy."

Thalia's eyes widened, her mouth dropping open.

Sephie nodded. "Exactly. Ghosts wouldn't normally be affected by that flow, unless their tether was broken."

"Tether?" asked Aaron.

"The emotional tie that keeps them clinging to their old life," explained Sephie. "Without that, they *should* move on to whatever afterlife awaits. But these ones aren't."

"They're caught in the eddy," said Thalia.

"Exactly." Sephie sighed and rubbed at her forehead. "It's not a perfect theory. We're not near enough to the middle of that eddy for it to completely explain their movements. It's more like…the eddy current is keeping them moving, but they're still somehow tied to the thing in the center."

"And that is?" asked Aaron.

Kyle groaned. "She means the bogeyman."

Sephie steeled herself. "You don't have to go with me." The crack in her voice marred her attempt at bravery. "I should be able to handle this on my own."

"No way," said Aaron.

Thalia frowned. "Is it dangerous?"

"Yes," admitted Sephie. *More for me than for you.*

"Then I agree with Aaron," said Thalia. "You can't go by yourself."

"I'm in, too," said Kyle.

Aaron slipped an arm around Kyle's shoulders. "You don't have to, babe."

Kyle shook him off. "Stop coddling me, Aaron. You know better."

"But—"

"*Enough.*" Kyle twisted his lips, looking mildly exasperated. "I need to face fear, not run from it. It's why I got into this hobby in the first place."

Reluctantly, Aaron nodded.

The four of them managed to find a door on the back of the building that wasn't chained. It was still locked, though, so they propped it open with an old brick. Sephie took a moment to orient herself to the location of the bogeyman, then led the way through what used to be a well-tended garden, now overgrown.

Past shaggy hedges and the skeletal remains of untended rosebushes, they found an old, gnarled redbud tree. In the darkness beneath its twisted branches, a pair of jade eyes glowed.

Sephie swallowed, swinging her cane's flashlight to illuminate the spot.

The patch of shadow devoured the light. What should have been revealed in sharp, crisp lines were instead blurred in darkness, the shape of the bogeyman more amorphous than clear. "Hello," said the bogeyman, its teeth glinting. The voice, instead of strained and raspy, now came out in a mellifluous tenor with a distinct masculine edge.

Sephie tightened the grip on her cane and took another step forward.

Her three companions fell behind.

Sephie pushed through the dread that tried to creep through her bones. *Action predicates emotion. The less fear I show, the less I'll feel, the braver the others will be.* She waved a hand in the general direction of the bogeyman. "Would you just...stop that already? We get it. You're creepy. Save the theatrics for the kids."

"You offend me," murmured the bogeyman. "But I suppose that is your due." The darkness around him faded, his blurred form resolving into clarity. He sat on the ground, elbows on his knees, claws folded together. "I was starting to wonder if you would come at all."

"You seem...better," said Aaron.

"Stretching my bonds to manifest even that short distance was a strain." The bogeyman rose to his feet, pale arms and legs unfolding like a spider. "I suppose you expect an apology for my behavior."

Sephie seized upon the suggestion. "Yeah, that would be nice."

"You won't get one." Despite the permanent grin that shaped his mouth, the bogeyman managed to sneer. "I did what I must to survive."

Kyle half-shrugged, half shivered. "You are what you are, man. I guess."

"What he is, is trapped," said Sephie. "Desperate."

The bogeyman lifted his arms to showcase his bonds, chains of dark smoke that encased his wrists. "The Spirit Seer speaks true, more than any of you fathom. I know not who bound me here, but I do know why." He ended in a growl, his anger almost palpable.

Sephie refused to be cowed. "Then please, enlighten the rest of us."

"Child," said the bogeyman, "do you know what it is to devour a human soul?"

Thalia sucked in an audible breath.

"No," said Sephie, her tongue dry rubber in her mouth. "But it can't be good."

"Indeed not." The bogeyman shuffled, his phantom chains rattling. "To consume the entirety of even one would corrupt me into something...terrible. Irredeemable. *Controllable*, by those with evil in their hearts." He curled his talons in what almost appeared to be a warding gesture. "I have been imprisoned with naught but souls to provide sustenance. Until you."

*Is he...scared?* "That's why you said, 'save them.' You want us to save the ghosts from *you*."

The bogeyman's shoulders sagged. "Yes. Please. Release me. Save them...*and* me."

*Is this wise?* In truth, it probably wasn't. Sephie knew too little about the weird ecosystem that made up the spirit world. She knew ghosts, and she had a vague idea of how the rest of it worked, but her education had holes you could sail a cargo ship through.

But what else could she do? Leave him trapped to slowly devour the ghosts one by one? To become a pawn for some mysterious individual bent on wreaking havoc? *No. I have to. They don't deserve that fate. And neither does he.*

"All right," said Sephie, slinging her bag from her shoulder. "Let's do this."

Aaron sidled next to her. "Are you sure this is a good idea?"

"I'm sure it's a better one than leaving him here." Sephie dug her athame out of her bag and slid it out of its sheath. The consecrated knife was a magical tool and would help direct her focus. "And I'm doing the math. These things run the other way the instant they see me, yet *this* one is begging me for help? My nerves may be shot, but my brain says he's not going to give us any trouble. Are you, Chevy?"

Thalia and Aaron looked perplexed, but Kyle covered a snort of laughter with his hand. "Land shark. Classic."

*At least someone appreciates my humor.*

The bogeyman regarded her in silence. Was it acquiescence? Or defiance?

Sephie lunged forward, injecting aggression into her posture.

And the monster flinched away, pulling his arms up over his face.

"Holy shit," said Thalia.

"I told you," said Sephie. "They avoid me." She didn't understand why, but these monsters feared her. *Her.*

"You have made your point," said the bogeyman as he slowly straightened from his cringe. "I shall have to teach you the ritual. First, you—"

Sephie snorted. "I don't need a ritual. *Shatter*," she murmured, and the athame's hilt grew warm in her hand. She stepped up to the bogeyman and sliced the blade through the first phantom chain. It encountered resistance, but ultimately slid through. The chain disintegrated into black smoke.

"Do you have *any* idea your power potential?" murmured the bogeyman, his voice tight and strained.

"Don't butter me up." Sephie spoke the command word again, then sliced through the second chain. The magic broke with a mighty *snap.* Bright light flashed, swallowing her entire field of vision. A shock wave followed, the world lurched to the side, and something hard smashed into her body. She reached out and felt grass and dirt.

Sephie's ears popped as she fumbled for her equilibrium. She blinked the dazzle from her eyes and found first her cane and its flashlight, then her three companions lying on the ground nearby.

"Well, *this* is embarrassing," said the bogeyman.

Sephie levered herself into a sitting position even as her three companions did the same. "What happened?" she asked.

The bogeyman, like the rest of them, now sat flat on the ground, though he appeared to be somewhat less mobile. "In my desperation to survive, I may have...nibbled a little on the ghosts."

"I figured that much. It's why they're transparent to me," said Sephie.

"Indeed," agreed the bogeyman. "My nature being what it is, I focused on the most nourishing pieces of them—their pain, their fear, their grief. But they are naked souls, without the protections of flesh. Their emotions are a vital part of their *selves*."

Sephie scrubbed her face with her hand as the final pieces fell into place. "And this facility was nothing but a ball of pain, fear, and grief when they were alive. You ate their mortal tethers. *That's* why they're drifting." She propped her chin into the palm of her hand. The ghosts were all there now, still circling, but at a radius no more than twenty feet away from the bogeyman epicenter. "You know, that should have freed them to move on."

"As I had hoped when I made the choice. But the spell-work keeping them here bound their route to the afterlife, too." The bogeyman stroked his claws together thoughtfully. "That may have been a purposeful part of the spell, actually."

"So when I broke it," said Sephie, "I knocked the...road to the light loose, I guess?" She accepted Kyle's outstretched hand and heaved herself to her feet. "And the built-up pressure sucked Chevy here into place. He's not a ghost, just a creature that exists naturally on the same plane, so he can't go through."

Kyle chortled. "Like a ping-pong ball on the nozzle of a vacuum hose."

The bogeyman curled his lip, revealing a second row of needle teeth. "Yes, thank you for that *hilarious* description. Of course, this would not have happened had you unraveled the spell *properly* instead of hacking through it."

Shame flushed hot on Sephie's cheeks. "Oh."

"So that's it?" asked Aaron. "We're back to square one?"

"I can escape this by brute force," said the bogeyman. His green eyes softened to something almost apologetic. "But I will need more strength."

"I think our ability to fear you properly may have flown the coop," said Kyle.

The bogeyman sighed, an almost human sound. "I'm sorry. Even if you did, fear would not be enough. To break this…suction, it will take more than that." He drew his chin up. "This will take pain."

Sephie's stomach recoiled.

"Deep, emotional pain will do, spoken and shared," the bogeyman said. "I doubt it will take more than one of you."

"He's telling the truth," said Thalia. "I…I don't know how I know this. But he's been telling us the truth the entire time."

*Ghost empath,* Sephie realized. *That makes sense.* She nodded to Thalia. "I believe you."

The reality of what one of them would have to do sunk in, and the four exchanged mute looks, each waiting for another to take the lead.

The bogeyman's pale green gaze fixed on Sephie.

*He knows.* She closed her eyes, trying to summon the strength to stop her limbs from quaking. Turmoil roiled inside of her. *He can sense what I've been burying.* Years of holding that pain, not giving it to anyone lest it be a burden, and now she was supposed to just give it to three strangers and a monster?

A ghost caught her eye, the same young woman Sephie had first seen, pulled along through an invisible current. The ghost tried to catch herself on a bush, but her hands passed right through.

*It has to be me. This is my responsibility.* The thought fed fuel to the fire blossoming in her belly. Before she even realized what she was doing, the words poured out. "You know how every kid whose parents divorce think it's their fault? Well, I'm probably the only one it was actually *true* for."

Thalia frowned. "What? No."

Sephie shook her head. "I was seeing ghosts since before I can even remember. I just thought they were people. And I was a chatterbox of a kid, so I'd talk to them. My mom would get weirded out when I talked to nobody. One day, she caught a glimpse of one of the ghosts I'd been talking to. Just long enough to realize what was going on. She freaked out. Absolute *panic*. She couldn't even look at me. So, Dad took me and we left."

"Okay, but you get that's still not your fault, right?" said Kyle. "Just because—"

"Shh." The bogeyman cut off Kyle, and then made a noise that was half-growl, half-purr. "I need the rest."

Resigned, Sephie stumbled on. "Mom didn't try for custody. I didn't even talk to her until after the accident years later. Then at least she started calling me once in a while. So, I thought maybe if I went to college here, maybe things would get better. I even got into Harvard. It felt good for her to say she was proud of me, but..." She trailed off, blinking back tears.

Thalia's arm slid around Sephie's shoulders. "But?"

The warmth in the other woman's tone brought a lump to Sephie's throat. "She tries, you know. She tries really hard to be my mom. But she still has that little spark of fear when she looks at me. The last couple years of college, I just wanted to get it done with so I could move back to the Keys. I—I *hate* this city." The words tumbled out of her faster. "I hate this *stupid* city and its winters and its snow and its crowds. But its spirit world is a mess. There are so many ghosts, and I can't find anyone else who can *do* what I do and—"

A roar of effort from the bogeyman drowned out Sephie's words, and the creature wrenched himself free of the trap with an audible pop. Then, without another word, he blurred into the darkness of the night and disappeared.

In the spot he vacated, light flashed again, initially blinding, but then settling into a brilliant, iridescent glow. As Sephie shielded her eyes, she noted that her companions were doing the same.

The drifting ghosts picked up speed and momentum, their orbit turning into a whirlpool.

Aaron grabbed Kyle with one hand, his other arm wrapping in front of Thalia and Sephie to pull them back a few steps. "Ghosts! They're everywhere."

With a joyous thrum of energy, the lost souls flung themselves into the light.

"The gate is unplugged," said Sephie. "They're going home." *Or wherever it is that souls are supposed to go.*

Thalia smiled, lifting her chin. "It feels so warm."

One ghost moved more slowly, grabbing hold of Sephie's hand as she floated past the group of people "Oh! Ow, there's that zap again. You're tingly."

Thalia squeaked and jumped back. "She's talking!"

"They do that." Sephie gripped the ghost's hand, halting her flow towards the light. "Here. Gotcha."

The ghost's fingers clasped around hers, like air taken

solid form. "I heard everything you said. And I'm sorry you feel stuck. But…you saved us all. Thank you."

Sephie nodded, tears still staining her face. "You're welcome. I wish it hadn't taken releasing a monster, though."

"He isn't a monster," said the ghost, her voice growing soft. "You didn't see how he struggled the months he was here. How he howled with hunger when these three came without you, but didn't have enough fear or anger for him to eat." She gripped Sephie's hand harder. "He *fought* for us, and for himself." Her face spread into a beatific smile. "And he *freed* us. Not everything that's dark is evil. You need to know that, I think."

She released Sephie's hand and disappeared into the light. The last ghost over the threshold, it dimmed into a pinpoint, and then snuffed out.

Sephie sagged, her heart raw and tired despite the haze of euphoria left by the ghosts.

"This isn't over, is it?" Aaron fumbled with his phone, its flashlight cutting through the fresh darkness. "Someone did this. They'll try again."

For a moment, Sephie toyed with the idea of letting it go. *How can I possibly stop them on my own?* Maybe someone else would come along and catch them, and she could rest.

*But if not me, who?* Responsibility laid its pressure on her shoulders, like an imp made of lead. She swallowed down the creeping dread. "I'll have to handle it."

"Hey," said Thalia. "You okay?"

Sephie opened her mouth to lie, but instead the truth spilled out. "No."

Thalia pulled her into an embrace. "You're not doing this alone. You've got us now."

"Group hug!" exclaimed Kyle, wrapping his arms around them both.

Aaron piled on as well, adding, "I'm sorry I'm an ass."

Their warmth sank in from all sides. *I'm not alone?* The constriction in her chest evaporated, the rush of oxygen almost dizzying.

No, Sephie still wasn't okay, but she *would* be. *I have help. I can do this.*

*I'm not alone.*

A SECOND-GENERATION SCI-FI/FANTASY *fan, Rosemary Williams has been on a quest for ultimate nerdity her entire life. After devouring countless genre books, movies, and TV shows, she has finally achieved the very unplanned goal of transforming her mind into an Author Brain, and is currently working on a full-length novel with this story as a jumping-off point. As if that wasn't enough, she's also a costumer, crafter, convention staffer, and podcaster. Rumor has it she may also be a My Little Pony in a human suit. She resides in Olathe, KS, with her husband, 1.5 dachshunds, and half a chihuahua.*

# THE COFFIN MAKER

## FRANCO DISPENZA

*C*edar masks odors of mold and putrefaction. Mahogany shields the sweet aroma of organ decay. But only oak conceals the stench of rotting secrets buried in bones. Mr. Owens failed to grasp all this. Whether it was his ignorance of death, or his lack of compassion for the dying, Mr. Owens had no shame when requesting a wood coffin from a different Owens man—Abner Owens—hours before a physician even pronounced his third wife dead.

The two men stood in Abner's workshop. Planks of lumber leaned against walls, wood beams piled on the ground, and iron tools laid across worktables. The afternoon heat left the workshop warm, damp with the odor of musk, and the air thick enough to slow down any dust from falling to the ground. Perspiration clung to both men's backs.

"Her illness came quickly and violently. Just loose skin and fragile bones," Mr. Owens told Abner. "She didn't deserve any of that."

"No husband should have to watch his wife go through so much sickness," said Abner.

"I'd like for her to be buried in something pretty," Mr. Owens said, "just as long as you can make it quickly."

"Always work fast, sir. Can have it done in three days or so," Abner said, dabbing the day's sweat off his forehead with a handkerchief.

"No," Mr. Owens looked away from Abner. "I'll need it much sooner than that."

A strange request. "Not often I'm asked to make one sooner than three days," Abner said.

Mr. Owens took pause, then turned with a shifty smirk. "Best to have her buried as soon as possible."

"I see." Abner's voice remained soft with sympathy. "Cherry wood then. A fine wood. Fitting for someone delicate as your wife. I can work quickly with it."

Mr. Owens peered out one of the workshop's windows. Outside grew the very trees Abner cut down and used for his carpentry. "We used cherry wood for my last two wives, no? How about the wood from that tree over there?" He pointed at a lone oak surrounded by blades of jade grass.

"Not that one," Abner shook his head.

"Nonsense. I'll pay you double its worth."

"That oak is not for your wife."

"You're a cruel man to refuse a grieving widow's request."

"The oak belongs to someone else." Abner gave a polite smile.

Mr. Owens was not accustomed to rejection. He turned toward the window again. His eyes glinting in the afternoon sunlight. "Would you believe that field outside and all those trees on it had belonged to my granddaddy? Once part of the Owens legacy. He had every inch of it plowed, growing, and bountiful. He probably even planted that oak when this was all his."

Abner cleared his throat and offered a slight amendment.

"Certain it was my granddaddy who did most of the plowing and planting on these fields."

The air between them turned stale. Although the two men shared a name, Mr. Owens never cared to acknowledge their family's matted history. Some things were better left unsaid. Mr. Owens said nothing, until Abner broke the silence. "If not cherry wood, then pine. I can make it quickly, as you wanted."

The two men shook hands and agreed on the arrangements. Mr. Owens flashed a peculiar grin as he left the workshop—almost shining as he stepped inside his Cadillac Sixteen. Abner kept his eyes on him from the porch, quivering from a chill that slunk down his damp back.

* * *

Like the generations of enslaved and freed fathers before him—all carpenters, all Owens—Abner crafted and delivered a beautiful coffin. Savannahians attending Mrs. Owens's funeral service found it shameful to bury something so exquisite inside the chambers of Bonaventure Cemetery. Unfortunately, those attending the service did not have long to admire the coffin's delicate finishes. Mr. Owens had five of his men—laborers from his railway and port companies who assisted him with all his personal affairs—position the coffin in the family mausoleum soon after services were over.

However, Abner's coffin may not have been beautiful enough for the dead Mrs. Owens. In her death, she refused to lie in it. She rose from its soft interior linings, ran her dead fingertips across the polished panels, and stared at the intricate carvings. The dead Mrs. Owens became enraged with her coffin and unleashed a deluge of wrath, scorn, and assault on the living husband who put her in it.

Mr. Owens could never have suspected an assault. Not that night. Not as he entertained socialites and military officers serving in President Roosevelt's war. Hosting a party on his estate was already shameful enough, and so soon after burying his late wife. Yet shame had a way of never infiltrating his white skin, his bonnie blue eyes, or his endowed southern blood. Mr. Owens was almost shame*less*.

His guests never noticed Mrs. Owens's menacing presence lurking outside the gates, either. Not that they could have seen or heard her. Her spirit wavered quietly behind palm blades, cutting through the sultry air, before edging up the Corinthian columns and entering the home through the Palladian windows.

Full of disdain, Mrs. Owens punched her husband in the stomach. She punched him repeatedly, each time leaving him to writhe in pain. She then hurled a kick to his chest and sent him to the ground grunting. But it was the hot wound she seared on his face with the golden band around her finger that delighted her most. Fumes of crackling charred skin ascended the air as Mr. Owens poured ice gin on his cheeks to ease the burning.

"Make this stop," Mr. Owens yelled out into the crowd.

No one did anything. They gawked and suspected he had too much brandy and gin and turned rabid in his drunk stupor. When his "fits" continued, they scattered like palmetto bugs in the Georgia heat, leaving Mr. Owens behind, beaten and bruised.

When Mrs. Owens grew tired of striking Mr. Owens, she turned her wrath toward the house. Floorboards and tiles cracked, glasses and plates shattered on all the shelves, and clothes were torn and strung up on the ceilings and chandeliers of every room. Although he could not see her, or make out the scent of her sandalwood perfume, Mr. Owens had no doubts his wife had come back to haunt him. Hurt him, even.

By the third day of attacks, Mr. Owens sent his men to retrieve Sister Trina, a powerful root worker.

Mr. Owens only trusted Sister Trina to quell the disturbance, and for good reason. She spoke the diction of death. A daughter of Geechee healers and root doctors, her blood possessed the strength to work against unseen malevolence. But Mr. Owens had another reason to call on Sister Trina. She had nursed him as a child in that home. She would not deny his plea for help.

When she arrived, Sister Trina lit fires around the estate and prayed to plumes of burning sweetgrass. Sister Trina's cries of lamentation left enough silence to perceive the spite and agitation Mrs. Owens left inside the home.

"Go to the coffin maker who lives and works in the fields that once belonged to your grandfather," Sister Trina said. "Demand he make you a new coffin. More beautiful than the last."

"Why him?" Mr. Owens asked.

"Only his hands can keep the dead in their coffins."

Sister Trina was never wrong about the dead, and Mr. Owens heeded her counsel. Flushed and weak, he mustered whatever energy he had to charge down to the coffin maker. He slammed his fists on the workshop door when he arrived. Abner opened it. The stench of fermented corn and barley seeped from Mr. Owens's battered body.

"How much you been drinking?" Abner asked.

"Some bourbon and whiskey," Mr. Owens smiled.

"Widow's drink of choice," said Abner.

"Firsthand knowledge?" Mr. Owens tittered, staggering through the door.

"No stranger to it."

"I am," Mr. Owens released a nervous laugh.

Abner gave a look of concern. "Don't get many visitors this late in the night. What brings you here?"

Mr. Owens stumbled over a chair, flinching from the soreness and pain all over his body. "I—I," he started before closing his mouth to a long silence.

"Maybe you should be getting back home, Mr. Owens. You don't look well."

"No! I can't go home. I need you to help me."

"Got no help to offer, sir. Coffins can't help drunk men."

"Yes, they can," Mr. Owens cut Abner off. "You make the finest coffins in all of Georgia. The finest in the country. Heck, you must be living in high cotton from all the coffins I ask you to make." He gave another nervous laugh.

Abner's brows twisted with irritation. "Best you be going."

"I'm not leaving." His obstinance was sharp and cutting. "I'm being attacked, and you know who it is."

"Don't know anyone who'd attack you, sir. You should go to the police."

"I can't do that. They can't help me. No one can, except you. Someone you know told me you'd understand my predicament."

"Don't got people to know," Abner said.

"A woman said you could help me get rid of her. You see, *she's* angry with me. She's figured something out and won't leave me alone. Won't give me any peace."

"Who's *she?*"

"My wife."

Drunk talk of a bereft widow. "Your wife's dead. You buried her already."

"Not really," Mr. Owens shook his head. "She hasn't really left at all, and I want her to leave me and my house alone. I need you to build another coffin for my wife."

"Why?"

"She doesn't like it." Mr. Owens frowned.

Abner was no stranger to the torment of widows. Yet he

also never encountered the relentless demands of a man's grief-induced delusions. "Building her another coffin isn't going to make anything different. She's dead. Accept it."

"I'm not broken by the misery of her passing," Mr. Owens scoffed. "My wife doesn't like the coffin she's in. She needs to be in a different one."

"How you know that?"

"Because she told me." His voice battered the air. "She's been telling me in her own way. So, I need you to build another coffin that'll keep her happy and inside it for good." Mr. Owens curled his fingers into a fist and beat the sides of his legs before releasing another frantic laugh.

Abner found Mr. Owens to be a strange and unfortunate man. The rich were never any less pitiful in their grief. However, the revulsion of pity was not lost on Abner. The memory of his own dead wife often detached his heart from the rest of the beating world. A corroding pain crafted from sorrow and fury, burning a hollowness down his own throat and lungs. Although he tempered his fury during the midnight hours—shaved and sanded it down like the wood in his workshop—it was the morning sorrow he struggled to stomach. The bitter acidity of copper rising, coating his throat and tongue, making him so sick he suffered to lay in the same bed that once cradled his wife's dreams.

"I'll build you another coffin," Abner said.

"More beautiful than the last," Mr. Owens held his breath.

"I'll use cedar."

Mr. Owens sighed with relief.

Moonlight filtered through the workshop windows as Abner began building the coffin. The moon's beams pressed through the grains of cedar, enchanting the wood's fibers with a luminous glow. It was as if the cedar still possessed a glimmer of life buried inside its core. As Abner measured, leveled, and shaved down the beams, hammered the wood moldings, and polished the finishes, he took in the cedar's camphor and resin. The cool aroma clouded his focus, and he became possessed by memories of his own wife.

By the early midnight hours, wet dirt and sour bile infiltrated the air. Abner suspected the stench came from the wood, but no amount of rot could release something so foul and uncanny. The odor moved around him, seeping into his lungs, before numbing his hands and limbs. A pile of dust flew up into the air and death stood in front of him. A decaying body with pale loose skin, swathed in mold—eyes inflamed like the color of red poppies.

*Mrs. Owens.*

"What? Not possible," Abner stumbled through his words. "Why are you here?" He almost screamed but doubted if the apparition was real.

It was all real.

Mrs. Owens reached inside her chest, pulled out her heart, and offered it to Abner. He backed away, knocking over a table of wood and iron tools, before falling to the ground. He wanted to scream, but Mrs. Owens dissolved before any sound left his mouth. Trembling, Abner now knew Mr. Owens had not gone mad with bereavement. Not at all. Mr. Owens had done something to make her come back.

A CEASE-FIRE FELL over the house soon after Mr. Owens reburied his wife in the new coffin. Nothing more cracked or shattered; punches, kicks, and slaps came to a halt. However, Mr. Owens developed an incessant spasm that churned under his breastbone. No doctor could diagnose or heal it. On an afternoon stroll, when Mr. Owens was not far from Wright Square, the spasm moved into his shoulders, spine, and legs. Mr. Owens stood wedged between the church and the old county courthouse, solid and unable to move like a stone pillar. When his knees buckled from the intense strain on his back and legs, he fell to the ground like a guilty penitent before judgement.

But Mr. Owens had little capacity for guilt. This is perhaps why Mrs. Owens resurged her attacks. In her death, she wandered through the city squares, discovering her husband's shame and deceit buried in the tiniest recesses and fissures of Savannah's antebellum cobblestones. She followed him through the park squares and all the way home. Her menacing presence scaled up the ornamental railings, wrapped around the veranda, entered through the double doors, and corrupted every room in the house. Windows refused to open, doors remained shut tight, and no human strength could unlatch the handles of any faucet, cabinet, desk drawer, or icebox. Worse, bottle tops of cognac, gin, and scotch did not twist open. In his attempt to open the bourbon, the glass bottle shattered in his hands and lacerated his left palm. Both blood and bourbon rushed to the ground, vanishing beneath the cracks of the floorboards.

Mr. Owens suffered for days—unkempt, unwashed, unable to eat, drink, or sleep. His left hand could not heal, bleeding through all the gauzes and bandages. Mrs. Owens had laid siege on him and the house at the cost of her own eternal repose, attempting to destroy her living husband from the inside out.

Again, Mr. Owens called for Sister Trina. Much like when she had been his childhood nurse, Sister Trina was left with the burden of easing his fretful nature. Her voice and hands were the only likeness to a mother's affection Mr. Owens had ever known; his own mother taken to the grave from influenza before he turned six.

"What have you done, boy?" she whispered.

"She won't leave me or this house," he murmured. "I don't know what to do."

"We must listen," she said before smudging each room with herbs. She recited psalms from Solomon and scattered grains of harvested rice around the home. She pressed her ears against the floors and walls, only to arrive at the same solution. "Go back to the coffin maker. Demand he build you a new coffin. Larger, grander, than the two before."

Mr. Owens did not equivocate. Desperate, he reappeared at Abner's front door, begging, "I need you to build another coffin."

"Made you two already. Got others to build for folks," said Abner.

"I haven't slept or eaten in days. She's infected my house. She's still mad at me." Mr. Owens strained to speak.

"Can't build you no more coffins."

"She's tormenting me. You're the only one who can help."

"No," Abner shook his head. "No need for me to be a part of this. Not you or your dead wife."

"I'll pay you triple for another coffin. The largest and finest you can make."

Abner picked up a hammer and chisel to carve some details on a small plank of wood. "Money doesn't always pay for a peaceful afterlife, even if you are the richest man in Georgia."

"I just want her to be in peace."

"You want to be left in peace." Abner paused and raised an eyebrow, breathing in fumes of friction and dust. "What you do to her—what you do to make her come back?"

"Nothing."

"You did something to make her come back and attack you. She even came here the night you asked me to build you another coffin."

Mr. Owens eyes widened. "You saw her?"

"Standing right where you are now. Looking at me like a pitiful, pathetic mess."

"Don't you dare talk about my wife like that!" Mr. Owens slammed his fists against his chest. "I loved my wife."

"Did you? Dead wives don't come back because you loved them. You must've done something real messed up to her if she keeps coming back for you."

"I did nothing wrong."

Abner tilted his head. "The dead do funny things to us, don't they? And the funny things that some do, others don't do."

"I don't understand you."

"My wife's been dead and gone for years. Never come back to attack me. Never even come back to see me. And yet yours came back. Hell, continues to come back."

A temper, fast and scalding, arose in Mr. Owens's throat. "And here I thought I was the only widow suffering and tormented. I didn't realize I was in such good company with the coffin maker. Maybe you enjoy living in your torment. I don't care if you do. Do what you want with it. I refuse to be stuck with this torment."

"This isn't torment."

"You can't lie for shit. We both know this is torment. Your wife haunts you just as much as mine haunts me. Doesn't she?" Mr. Owens demanded.

Abner didn't speak.

"You think I don't know what happened to your wife?" Mr. Owens continued. "The domestics all around Savannah talked about it for weeks. Whispering in kitchens and laundry rooms about her abduction. All the failed searches along the Georgia coastline. They ran around this city talking about your wife like she was some character from an Agatha Christie novel."

Abner scowled. He moved to say something but then kept

his silence. He turned to face a workstation, passing his hands over a small mound of wood dust.

"And when they found those two men who confessed to severing and scattering—" Mr. Owens started.

"No more!" Abner's voice rumbled.

"You were hopeful she was alive and that she'd come back that whole time." Mr. Owens flashed a set of wicked white teeth.

Abner stared out the window at the oak tree. Its trunk and limbs glowing in the enchantment of the moonlight. He began humming a soft melody as he stared at it. His wife had been a specter in his memories for so long he didn't remember what it was like not to be haunted by her. He didn't want to talk about his wife to Mr. Owens, but then words poured out his mouth.

"I thought maybe she fell on her way back home from work. Bumped her head on some rock somewhere and forgot who she was. Or maybe she wandered away by accident. Hoped they'd find her alive somewhere and bring her back. All she had to do was look at my face and remember she belonged with me." Humming again, he took a hand plane to a wood panel and shaved down its surface. "No policeman in this city was going look for the missing wife of some Black coffin maker."

"I knew there was torment in you." Mr. Owens was almost pleased with himself.

"Owens men *from these parts* are all born with this curse of outliving our wives. Nothing stops us from placing them in their graves. I never got that chance. Always thought I'd get to bury my own wife in a coffin I made for her. But those men took her. They stole her body, and I never got her back. I never got to bury my own wife. No cradle to take her soul back home. You at least got to bury yours."

"Then for the sake of your wife, help me put mine at peace."

Again, Abner glanced out the window at the oak tree. Catching the moon with his eyes, something inside him softened. He turned to Mr. Owens, and said, "I'll build you another."

Abner selected the finest mahogany. The rich, sweet spice of the wood's grain imbued his nostrils, intoxicating his memories of her. The suppleness of her face, the softness of her voice, the soul in her eyes took possession of his course hands as he measured, remeasured, cut, leveled, and sanded each beam, panel, strip, and molding. He pushed his dead wife into the wood with each gesture, carving memories of her into delicate details.

But a rancid sourness filled the air by the early midnight hours. Mrs. Owens had returned and stood behind Abner. Her rotting breath skimmed down the back of his neck. As Abner hammered, chiseled, sanded, stained, and assembled the mahogany coffin, the air filled with the aroma of sweet decay. He refused to turn and look at Mrs. Owens standing behind him. He refused to be haunted by another man's dead wife. Instead, he wanted to be left alone with the haunting memories of his own dead wife.

* * *

MR. OWENS HAD his men reseal the family mausoleum with thicker cement sealant and new locks after he reburied Mrs. Owens. After, all drawers, windows, closets, doors, cabinets, and liquor bottles released their tight grips. The laceration on his palm healed, and the chest spasms stopped.

Avoiding the squares and parks, Mr. Owens took to walking paths along the Savannah River. One morning, he made a peculiar observation as he surveyed the war ships sailing under the bridge. Savannah was silent. Too silent. People's feet didn't shuffle across the ground. Voices didn't rise and rustle through the leaves of treetops. No river wind slipped by his ears, no swoosh of passing vehicles, no birds cooing in puddles. Nothing made a sound. Just absolute silence.

His dead wife had come for him again. This time with an infuriating silence that subjected him to the piercing volume of his own racing thoughts. The silence weakened his defenses, forcing him to listen to the secrets he imprisoned deep in his bones.

"She knows what I've done," he said to himself.

Mr. Owens went for the bourbon, whiskey, and wine to drown out his thoughts. When he emptied each of the bottles, he turned to food. Devoured whole cooked chickens and roast lambs, potatoes and dumplings, biscuits and breads, sweets and pies. When all food and drink inside the house were gone, he pulled and ate the fruits and flowers hanging in his garden. His hunger and thirst were insatiable amid his silent afflictions. Only when he stripped the trees and shrubs bare of all its foliage did Mr. Owens regain some capacity to hear.

"She knows what I've done," he muttered over and over, trembling in the garden.

Dread fermented inside his stomach, spilling into the muggy Savannah air. The awful sourness permeated throughout the city, eventually making its way to Sister Trina's tongue. She recognized its taste and immediately went to Mr. Owens.

"You've become consumed," said Sister Trina.

"How do I stop all of this?" Mr. Owens asked sprawled on the ground.

Sister Trina tossed a pile of bones across the garden's flagstones, divining a message from their scattered placement. "Peace begets peace, and only the strongest cage will contain a loose spirit," she said.

"Speak plainly."

She looked away from him and gazed into the setting dusk.

"Tell me," Mr. Owens shouted.

"The coffins have all been weak," Sister Trina said.

"How's that possible?" Misery seeped from his voice, and in the very moment, all his afflictions reemerged. Blood seeped from his cheek and hand. Patches of skin turned purple and blue, and the spasm under his breastbone stretched across his chest. "She wants me dead." He shrieked in pain.

Sister Trina did not flinch in his agony. She stared through him like glass. "Go back to the coffin maker and demand a stronger coffin. The wood is weak. He needs to make the coffin from the wood of a stronger tree. A stronger cage to contain the spirit."

Anger jolted inside him. "I'll take care of it," he mumbled, then wiped the blood from his face with his hands. "I'll take what should've been mine from the beginning."

Mr. Owens gathered his five men and drove to Abner's fields early the next morning.

A trail of sunlight broke through the morning haze and cleared a path to the oak tree Mr. Owens had originally wanted. He instructed the men to cut it down. All five of them assaulted the tree's trunk with brute force and chainsaw blades.

The violent brattle of men's voices and cutting steel scattered through the field. It made its way into Abner's workshop.

Confused by the harsh sounds outside his workshop, Abner looked out a window, and then hurried out the door. "No. No. Don't! Not that tree!"

"Stop him," Mr. Owens commanded the men.

Two of the men rushed up to Abner and held him back. Abner struggled to push them off. They eventually rammed Abner down to his knees, hovered over him, and forced him to watch the other men sever the oak from its trunk. Abner pleaded with them to stop, but no one could hear his voice over the chainsaw blades.

Just as the tree fell to the ground, the morning sun flashed in Abner's face, and blinded his sight. The tree no longer stood, and Abner had no air in his lungs. No beating in his chest. A hollow ache rose in his throat, and his words came out like gravel. "That was my wife's tree. Now you've taken that away from me."

"I'm taking what should've been mine from the beginning. You've put every ounce of anger and jealousy into those other coffins—letting it seep all the way into my wife's dead body, infecting her." His breathing was heavy. Blood dribbled from his face and hand. "Your coffins have made my wife spiteful, petty, and full of hate."

"You did that to her. Not me." Abner's voice rolled into a growl. "Just let me go. Do what you want with the tree."

Mr. Owens signaled for his two men to release Abner.

Abner stood up and tramped back into his workshop. Mr. Owens followed behind him, leaving his five men behind to finish with the oak.

Mr. Owens barged into the workshop, "I'm not going anywhere until this is fixed. Until this is all done."

"Get off my land," Abner shouted.

"Your land? All this belonged to my family. Every tree, blade of grass, and speck of clay dirt here. Would've all been mine, still."

"None of this belongs to you. Never again. Now get out."

Mr. Owens curled his hands into a fist and punched Abner across the face. He plunged forward, trying to shove

Abner to the ground. Abner pivoted, and Mr. Owens fumbled instead. Abner picked up a hammer, lifted it into the air, and threatened to strike Mr. Owens.

"Do it!" Mr. Owens yelled. "Do it!"

Abner moved in closer.

"Strike, damnit!"

Abner waved the hammer higher, preparing to slam it down on Mr. Owens face. Then he stopped. "What you do to make her come back?"

"Doesn't matter what I did. It won't ever bring back your wife." Blood seeped out from Mr. Owens's face.

"Tell me what you did to her," Abner lifted the hammer even higher.

"Only if you strike." Mr. Owens wanted Abner to deliver a fatal blow. A sure way of ending all this.

Abner did not flinch or look away. Mr. Owens took it as promise and released his secret with one breath. "I did to her what I've done do all my wives. *I loved them all to death.*"

In matrimony, Mr. Owens doomed his three wives to ill-fated promises sealed with gold. Each wife vowed to love and honor him, in sickness and in death. In return he loved them the only way he knew how. He committed them to their sickness, to their death, and to their own coffins.

"You were right about Owens men," Mr. Owens said. "We're all cursed. Destined to bury our wives long before we ever die. My grandfather buried all his wives, just as my father buried my mother. Best to get it over with and place our wives in their graves early."

"You're an evil man," Abner said.

"Then hit me in the skull. I know you want to. Put me out of this torment."

"Life's been served to you on gold plates since the day you were born. I won't make death just as easy." Abner dropped the hammer to the ground. "Your death will be yours. Not from my doing."

"You're cruel."

"The world is cruel. I never had any choice but to live in it."

"I had no more choice than you," Mr. Owens retorted.

"Bullshit. You've had all the choices. The world demands a high ransom for everything you've taken from it. And what have you given back? Nothing. It's time to give over your own pound of flesh as payment."

Abner was right. The world had catered to all Mr. Owens's whims, fed him all his indulgences, and never once did Mr. Owens share his gratitude. Mr. Owens consumed and swallowed every blessing and kindness carelessly, irresponsibly, and violently. He expelled all the excess like bodily waste, leaving it to the rest of the world to clean. The hour had arrived when Mr. Owens had to clean his own filth and pay retributions.

Mr. Owens laid sitting on the floor for some time before speaking. "I need one last coffin," he said to Abner.

"All the coffins in the world won't fix what you've done," Abner said. "You deserve what your wife has done to you. Just as much as I deserve what mine's done to me."

"A simple box is all I need."

"No."

"Just this last time."

Abner shook his head.

"Please," Mr. Owens uttered.

Perhaps it was the resignation on Mr. Owens's face, or the remorse that flickered through Mr. Owens's blue eyes, but Abner agreed to build one last coffin. Abner promised to have it completed by morning.

Later that evening, as he assembled the coffin, Abner's dead wife slipped into his mind with the softness of velvet.

Her face gleamed in his memories, much brighter than he had remembered. Even the wood glowed as Abner measured, leveled, sanded, and hammered. The wood's dust enchanted the air with its earthy bittersweet moss, thinning the rage that always festered inside him. Abner gave the coffin no ornate fixtures, carvings, or shiny gloss. No soft linings, or pillows encased the interior. No brass handles accented the exterior. Just a simple coffin made of wood.

Mrs. Owens never emerged in the workshop that night. No mold, decay, or rot saturated the air. Only Abner's wife consumed his thoughts. Only the memory of her face haunted him that evening, and every evening thereafter.

By sunrise, Mr. Owens's men picked up, delivered, and positioned the new coffin next to his dead wife's casket. He instructed them to return after nightfall, reseal the mausoleum's entrance, and to never look inside. In the hours between sunrise and nightfall, he returned to the family mausoleum.

Mr. Owens placed himself inside the new coffin and closed the lid. Burning, chills, and shallowed breathing were his first signs of dying. As he drifted further into his death, bittersweet moss became the last scent he took in from the coffin's wood. Just as his heart gave its last beat in the darkness, Mr. Owens lost all sensation in his feet, legs, arms, and hands. He could no longer move, hear, or emit a sound. Finally, a coffin that could cage a loose spirit—a coffin capable of cradling all the shame, guilt, and remorse he never consumed in his life. A coffin that could hide the secrets buried in his bones. A coffin made of oak.

*FRANCO DISPENZA IS A WRITER, scholar, and psychologist living in Atlanta, GA. He has a penchant for speculative, mythological, fantasy, horror, and literary fiction. This is his first short story published in an anthology.*

# TAP-TAP-TAPPING

## PAIGE VEST

The sounds of slamming car doors and laughing children on the street outside had easily penetrated the thin walls of Bethany's small trailer. She had exhausted her candy stash and turned off the porch light nearly an hour ago, but hopeful children seeking sweets had knocked on her door several times since. They usually moved on after a few moments when she didn't answer. They knew the drill. At least the older ones did. The younger ones could be heard complaining in high-pitched voices as their parents called them back to the sidewalk to try the next house.

After closing the trick-or-treat shop and taking a hot shower, Bethany curled up in her favorite chair with a book, a glass of wine, and a reserved handful of candy on the table beside her. Thor—the notch-eared cat the color of dirty snow who had come with the house and adopted her when she'd moved in a few months ago—lounged on the back of the chair behind Bethany's shoulder. He was grungy looking but had pretty, pale golden eyes that flashed in the light. He was friendly enough and often rubbed against her legs, though he never purred and didn't tolerate being touched beyond a few scratches behind his ears. The old tom was decidedly odd, but he was a companion of sorts and she had sorely missed the company in the years since Braxton had left for school.

By her third glass of wine, Bethany was relaxed and slightly tipsy as she enjoyed a scary-but-not-really-scary Koontz novel. She glanced at the phone as if willing it to ring and display her favorite picture of Brax at his college graduation last year. His dad had left when Brax was five, and the boy had always confided in her. They'd always been close, perhaps drawn together even more than would be normal by his father's rejection of both of them. She looked forward to hearing about Brax's most recent first date, this one at a Halloween costume party.

The last knock on the door by a hopeful trick-or-treater had been at least a glass of wine ago, so when another knock came, she jerked with surprise. Her movement startled Thor, who hissed and abandoned the chair via her lap, his claws piercing her thighs through her flannel PJs. She cursed and glanced at the clock as she rubbed her legs to reduce the sting. It was past eleven, and the regular candy-grubbing crowd should be tucked into bed, or at least at home, wired on chocolate and flavored sugar, driving their parents insane. Perhaps the knock, really just a couple of soft taps, was older kids hoping for leftover candy or, more likely, pulling pranks.

Bethany watched the door, waiting for another knock, but none came. There was absolute silence but for the ticking of the second hand as it made its monotonous journey around the face of the clock. The urge to get up and peek through the blinds was difficult to resist until her study of the door was interrupted by the jingle of her cell phone.

She retrieved the phone from the coffee table and saw

that the number was restricted, so she rejected the call and moved to return the phone to the table. It rang again while still in her hand, and she frowned as she saw that this call was also restricted. The phone continued to jingle long after it should have gone to voicemail and Bethany heard an odd noise that, after a moment, she identified as herself moaning softly. She stopped, wondering what was wrong with her. It was probably just another prank and she was letting it get the best of her.

But that didn't explain why the call wasn't going to voice-mail. How was it still ringing?

She tapped the touchscreen and held the phone to her ear with a shaking hand. "Hello?" Nobody replied, but she heard a faint rustling sound on the other end of the line. "Hello, who is this?" Nothing. She tapped the phone to hang up.

It rang again immediately, and she felt hot as a stab of fear seared through her belly. The phone fell silent as abruptly as it had started, and she dropped it on the table as if it had grown hot.

Bethany swallowed the remainder of the wine in her glass before she stood and turned toward the kitchen. In moments, she had a full glass and unceremoniously gulped a third of it. As she topped off the glass again, she took a surreptitious peek through the kitchen window.

The darkness of a new moon cloaked the branches of the tree outside as they swayed in the breeze. Too many leaves still clung to the branches; the warmth of an Indian summer had prevented most of them from falling just yet. Perhaps a branch had brushed the side of the house, and she'd mistaken it for a tap at the door. She stuck out her tongue at her reflection in the window, then turned her back on it and returned to the front room. She set her glass carefully on the side table, retrieved her book, and folded herself into her chair.

As she flipped through the book, looking for the page she'd been reading when the tapping sound had startled her, she noticed Thor sitting on his haunches before the front door. The cat was staring directly ahead, as if he could see through the door to the porch outside. His only movement was a slow twitch of his tail.

"Thor," Bethany said, and Thor flicked an ear toward her without turning. "What are you doing, crazy cat?"

She watched him for a moment and then shook her head and flipped through the book again. As she found her page and reached for her wine glass, she saw the cat move and glanced over to find him staring at *her*. The creepy stare seemed to be his default expression, but it was no less unsettling for its familiarity. Light from the lamp beside Bethany's chair made the cat's golden eyes shine, which increased the creep factor a fair bit. Her hand twitched and bumped the wine glass as she reached for it, causing it to wobble.

"Dammit!"

The sounds, the odd phone calls, and the cat's stranger-than-usual behavior had spooked her, and her fear spiked when Thor whipped his head back around to face the door seconds before the tapping noise came again. Bethany's eyes widened as they flicked from the cat to the doorknob. Holding her breath, she listened for any sound beyond that of the clock's second hand, ticking loudly in the silence. She half expected the knob to jiggle slightly as an unknown someone, 'Or some*thing!*' she thought hysterically, tried to open the door.

Bethany let out her breath slowly, then jerked as the phone rang again. Restricted. With anger born from fear, she snatched the phone from the table and answered, her voice pitched too high.

"*Hello!* Who is this? What do you want?"

Again, she got no reply but a rustling sound, barely

audible over the sound of her pounding heart. Bethany ended the call again and was staring at the phone in her hand with trepidation when Thor sneezed, prompting a surprised squeal that she could scarcely believe had come from her. She glowered with a nauseating mixture of fear, irritation, and chagrin, as the cat abandoned his vigil at the door and trotted toward the kitchen and, presumably, his kibble dish. She set the phone back on the table, waiting for it to ring again.

As the tapping came a third time, she growled deep in her throat, stood, and strode to the front door. She tore a finger-nail as she twisted the deadbolt too hard and jerked the door open.

The porch was empty.

Panting, her body thrumming with a rush of adrenaline, Bethany stepped out onto the porch and gazed into the night, squinting her eyes as if that would allow her to see better. The wind rose, rustling the dried leaves clinging stubbornly to the branches of the big tree which did not, she realized, come close to touching the side of the house. The wind died as quickly as it had come, and after the sound of rattling leaves, the sudden quiet felt as if it carried physical weight.

Her arms erupted into gooseflesh and she felt uneasy, wondering if she was being watched. Movement in the tree attracted her attention and she squinted again, eyes straining to penetrate the darkness between the branches. With a sharp snap of wings, a group of ravens burst suddenly from the tree, croaking hoarsely as they flew past Bethany close enough to make her duck.

"Are you kidding me right now?" Her voice shook but hearing herself speak calmed her somewhat. "Halloween night, wind, spooky tapping at the door, and a scene straight out of a goddamn Hitchcock movie?"

She laughed, the sound too shrill, too loud, and rubbed

her shaking hands together. Thor was sitting in the doorway giving himself a post-snack bath, and she nearly tripped over him as she turned to reenter the house.

"Dude," Bethany said, remembering his claws puncturing her thighs, "I should lock your creepy ass outside for the rest of the night."

He finished his grooming and turned to walk away, stopping just inside the door. Still irritated with the gnarled cat, she stepped past him and swung the door closed. Her hands still shaking, she inspected her torn fingernail as she dropped heavily into her chair.

She started as Thor jumped onto the coffee table and sat beside her cell phone, wrapping his tail neatly around his feet. He gazed at her with unblinking eyes, the shining gold reduced to a ring around his dilated pupils. Feeling bad for her anger at the cat, she leaned forward to scratch behind his ears in apology. Arm outstretched, she paused as she saw movement reflected in the cat's shining eyes; he wasn't looking *at* her, he was looking *past* her.

Gooseflesh erupted on her arms and her stomach roiled with renewed fear. She heard the rustle of feathers and recognized it as the sound she had heard during the restricted calls. The sound grew louder, and she thought it would drive her mad. She turned slowly to find an enormous raven perched on the back of the chair, where Thor usually napped. Another low moan escaped her tightening throat as wings blacker than a moonless night spread wide, making the bird appear larger than it should be, larger than was possible. The wings reached for her and obstructed her view of the room. Petrified by terror, unable to move, unable to scream for help, Bethany watched the bird grow larger, its black eyes swallowing light as huge wings enveloped her, swallowed her, absorbed her.

From his seat on the coffee table, the cat—who was not

actually a cat and whose name was not Thor—watched a single black feather spinning in the air as the sound of flapping wings faded into the night through the now open door. He jumped into the empty chair and swiped a paw at the feather until the jingling of Bethany's phone distracted him. With a hiss, he reached to bat the phone from the table and it landed face down, hiding the image of a smiling young man on the screen.

The creature sniffed the air and turned toward the door. Beckoned by the night and a return to freedom, he jumped to the floor and padded through the open door. As the leaves in the tree again rustled in the breeze, he disappeared into the darkness, content to roam as he waited until it was time to seek a new soul to mark. That soul would need to have deep wounds. It would need to be vulnerable and content to take the creature in, as had so many unfortunate others. One could be found easily. Such people were everywhere.

*PAIGE VEST HAS BEEN TELLING stories since childhood, when she visited Middle Earth and Narnia in her spectacular imagination. She continues telling stories today in hopes of appeasing the myriad voices in her head. At work on the third novel of a YA trilogy, Paige is published in* Sensorially Challenged Volume 1, Writings to Stem Your Existential Dread anthology, Volume 3 of 72 Hours of Insanity, *and* Fiction War Magazine, Volume 3, *all of which can be found online. Her article work related to the fantasy of Brandon Sanderson can be found at https://www.tor. com/author/paige-vest. Become a patron by visiting www. patreon.com/paigevest.*

# DOWN TO SIZE

## MARK BEARD

*S*omething had entered the network. He reached toward the anomaly a second time and found it, an entity with a mind of its own. It was impossible.

Dr. Jason Calderus perceived his environment in a different way while inside the processor. It might be more correct to say immersive interfacing. Their minds were literally inside of it. He knew that the two other doctors were there with him. He could sense each, more as a presence than anything else. He sent out tendrils of attention toward them. He assured himself they were there.

Dr. Lucile Colorado and Dr. Grant Canere, both possessed expertise of remarkable value. He had done the calculations and, on his own, he would have spent two decades developing what they had brought to the table in less than two years. He wished for the hundredth time that he had remained alone on the project. While the advancements they had achieved together thrilled him, the clash of their personalities did not.

The additional entity still hovered, a presence that

emoted ill favor, if not a threat. With the other two doctors accounted for, what was the additional presence?

Their minds hovered inside something akin to a computer. Dr. Colorado had invented it and she called it the Hydro-Synthetic Quantum Neural Processor, or HSQNP for short, at least on paper. Verbally, they had changed it to HaSQNaP, with the Q going silent for a simple sounding 'hasnap.'

A floor above the HaSQNaP, Jason's body reclined in an expensive and comfortable chair. A long curving desk console provided room for the other two doctors alongside him.

The device, similar in concept to a computer, could not interface with one not designed to do so. In fact, there was only one HaSQNaP on Earth and Grant Canere had built the only interfacing computer program in existence.

No one should have been able to enter the HaSQNaP with them. Only the three of them had access to their building. Jason might have shuddered, if still in his body. Of a sort, he did, the reaction causing eddies in the liquid channels of the processor near him.

His reaction occurred at the thought of their lab. To avoid detection, they had purchased a building in a depressed section of the city. It had three floors above ground and two below. The first basement had provided a perfect location for Dr. Lucile Colorado's Hydro-Synthetic Quantum Neural Processor. Jason's more controversial contribution to their project was hidden in the lower basement.

For all the security they had installed, the neighborhood writhed with drug dealers and violent crime. What if someone had made it past their locks?

They had tested Grant's interface for months before they had dared to enter the HaSQNaP at the same time, leaving no one behind if things went wrong.

Jason pinged his two conspirators and they responded. He sensed them arrive closer to him. Their minds traveled through Lucile's not-yet-patented liquid circuitry. Practice had honed their skills. It seemed human thought traveled through liquid far better than metal wiring. They huddled together, facing the intruding entity.

Jason attempted to communicate a warning to his two teammates. Their reactions aggravated him, simple impulses in the neural liquid. Surely they could read his intention better than he could read their poor attempts. Despite their brilliance, he still considered himself their superior in intellect. And why not? He'd met a rare few in his lifetime who could challenge him.

He wanted to warn them that the intruding presence might be someone after their work, or more specifically, his work. His was the most illegal and unethical part of their project. He had gained the aid of Lucile and Grant by offering them something no one else could. Immortality.

On the lowest floor of the building, three clones created from their DNA floated in tanks. They were far from ready, being the equivalent of two-year-olds. By the time they matured, the three doctors would be in their seventies. Dr. Lucile Colorado's HaSQNaP had been designed to allow them to transfer their minds into their newer, younger bodies when the time came.

They had no official sponsors because they were breaking rules, important rules. Some nations called them laws. The standard peer groups had little tolerance or understanding of such ventures.

The money came from the royalties of a military application created by Lucile, and a patented genome technique by Jason. Grant sometimes mentioned his lack of financial participation. He played a crucial role, however, and he knew it. Computer work like Grant's had few competitors.

Jason wondered if one of the clones had somehow become self-aware and entered the system with them. The three infant bodies floated in the oxygen-and-electrolyte-rich tanks, kept at even temperatures with thermal jumpsuits that also prevented muscle atrophy by simulating the muscles.

Jason moved toward the intruding entity, leading the others. Lucile and Grant kept pace. The entity retreated and the three followed, navigating the electro-liquid landscape.

An imagined fall always precipitated returning to their bodies. When that odd sensation struck without warning, Jason perceived the other two doctors falling with him. What had just happened? This tumble downward drew him toward something unknown.

The comfort of the HaSQNaP disappeared, and an explosion of emotions racked him. Hate. Despair. Anguish. Guilt. Amid it he also sensed loss. However, the most powerful sensation was that of agonizing need, and surrounding it, an aching physical pain. The sensations stunned him, overwhelmed him. Images swirled and memories that did not belong to him invaded his thoughts. He wanted to scream in horror.

Jason fled back the way he had come. His escape felt like a desperate climb up a slope with no purchase. The horrible mind he had entered attempted to pull him back.

When he found the soft, welcoming liquid environment of the HaSQNaP again, he fled. After a sprint of unmeasurable distance, he stopped and huddled, regathering his wits.

His thoughts flitted past the clones in the basement. Could an unconscious infant have such emotions? He discounted the thought at once. No. They could not have harbored such internal strife. He considered his companions next. Had Grant and Lucile escaped with him? Had they escaped at all?

He calmed as the moments passed, although time had no true index while inside. When the shock subsided, he revisited the moment. He recalled pain and the confined space. The sensations were wretched and tortured. While he searched his recall of the event, a sense-memory flitted past, so faint he almost missed it.

Taste.

That confirmed it. They had, indeed, entered a body.

Jason drew the memory forward to examine it. The clones would have salinated water in their mouths. Instead, the flavor was bitter and dry. It tasted like chemicals and smoke.

He understood what the taste was, and he knew where he recalled it from. It was methamphetamine street drugs. The smell of it often hung in the air at the back of their building, in a haze so thick he had indeed tasted it. Fear blasted Jason a second time. Had one of the addicts who roamed their neighborhood managed to gain access to their building? Once the intruder breached the outer door security, the rest of the upper floors had scant security, including their lab.

The grimy neighborhood had a handful of suspects, but one stood out from the rest. An angry young woman lived much of her life near the dumpster at the back of their building. When they took their trash out, she enjoyed railing against them. Her accusations knew no bounds and she was certain that they were cooking up meth inside their building.

Her name was Adel Furo. They had learned her name from Grant, who, for reasons beyond Jason's understanding, had chosen to have more than one conversation with her. Grant believed all the neighborhood's grisly characters deserved second chances. Jason believed they had already had them. Adel Furo had terrified Lucile on one occasion by trying to follow her into the building after Lucile had dropped off trash at the dumpster. Furo had demanded to see the inside, insisting, once again, that their building secretly housed a meth lab.

What if Furo had broken in? She would have the run of the building while they lay there with their minds elsewhere.

A new convulsion of terror rocked Jason when he realized that to put on a headset, she would have had to take it off one of their heads. She would be in the room with their unconscious bodies.

Jason wanted to cry out, to contact the other two doctors. Panicking, he shot across the breadth of the space, realizing how vast it truly was. Lucile had explained that, in some respects, the interior of the HaSQNaP might have elements of infinite space.

He wandered until the thought occurred to him that the automatic retrieval system had never before given him so much time. Had the intruder removed *his* headset?

Jason had to find the other two doctors. He needed to master the HaSQNaP to a higher degree. He spread a host of fibrous tendrils, feeling and touching. The experience awed him. Could physical human brains do that? He smiled inwardly. If he didn't know, who would? He continued his exercise, reaching and retreating, attaining a greater control each time. The water around him moved with greater swiftness. He did not yet recognize the effect, but he would soon enough.

When he snapped out of his musings, a tingling of dread traveled through him. Why had the system not recalled him to his body? His heightened emotions might have excited the neural systems of the processor and the hours he imagined passing might have only been minutes. Had the other two doctors awakened from the HaSQNaP without him?

Jason searched for them again. He only succeeded at finding new areas inside the network. When he tired of the search, he played with the liquid circuitry again.

He realized, after a short while, that his efforts changed the terrain of the HaSQNaP. His touch caused the liquids to swirl and withdrawing from it caused it to slow. Awed, he administered the effect with greater force.

He watched a section of circuitry wall wither.

Had he somehow destroyed a piece of the HaSQNaP? Jason, at last, understood. The effect he had learned to control was *heat*. The outer linings of Lucile's quantum liquid system did not react well to it.

On his next search for his companions, he found what he determined to be a trace of heat left behind by one of the others. Using his newfound thermal sensing ability, he tracked his companions. In a quadrant of the expansive HaSQNaP, he located Dr. Grant Canere.

Grant occupied a space where a number of control circuits met. To Jason's wonder, Grant worked at something that Jason had difficulty perceiving. Grant reached out with the same wispy tendrils of energy that Jason had learned to use. Instead of producing heat, everything that Grant touched was vibrating. Jason could feel it rattling through the liquid around him.

Grant noticed Jason and ceased the vibrations. The two of them approached one another, but when Jason reached out a tendril in an electronic handshake, Grant withdrew.

Of course.

Grant often avoided contact with them. He showed every sign of having been bullied. He didn't want to be around people. On a few occasions when things hadn't gone his way, he had lashed out with a brief intensity that had shocked Jason. Jason had ignored the shortcomings for the sake of Grant's brilliance.

They attempted to communicate with one another, but Jason received only the same urgency he felt.

They set off searching for Lucile. Although they could not

use speech, the agreement that they search for Dr. Colorado needed no words.

When they found her some while later, Jason and Grant stopped to watch in awe. The processor liquid around her glowed with energy. Were they witnessing the HaSQNaP equivalent of lights?

When Lucile discovered them nearby, she expressed a rare warmth. Jason knew it irked her that she worked among peers like them rather than minions at her command. To deepen her discontent, the establishment had sent her on her way due to her over-daring innovation. That slight had given Lucile something to prove to a degree that made working with her difficult.

She came in close and touched them with extended energy. Grant withdrew for only a moment. It was enough, however, for Lucile to throw up her wall of defensiveness toward them again.

They traveled together from that moment forward. The feeling that they had spent too much time away from their bodies nagged at Jason. With an intruder loose in their building, getting out of the processor had dire importance.

Jason practiced his newfound heat-creation skills when they rested. The others practiced their peculiar skills too. Oddly, Jason could not master Grant's vibrations of the HaSQNaP liquid or Lucile's ability of illumination, nor they his heat creation.

On yet another search through the HaSQNaP, Jason at last perceived something familiar, the sensation of several curiously pleasant impending drops in front of him.

The memory of falling into the mind of the intruder still stung. Yet, excitement from the three of them pulsed through the electronic liquid environment. Jason realized that the third drop off had a pleasant, welcoming aura.

While the other two watched, he allowed the beckoning

descent to swallow him, offering no resistance to the familiar pulses and energies.

The expansiveness of the HaSQNaP receded while he slipped into the comforting sensations of a human mind. No thoughts of pain or foreign memories disturbed him. He had found his body again.

He waited for the system to wake him. While he did so, he spread his consciousness through his body, feeling his arms and legs and sensing the muscles stretch when he moved or smiled. It reminded him of reaching out tendrils of energy within the HaSQNaP.

The system would automatically disconnect them after a short time. After all, they should only have been inside for less than a day, despite the exaggerated perception of time.

He stretched, waiting for his back muscles to push against his chair with a familiar ache, but they did not. Instead, the movement was easy and smooth. His muscles felt good, strong but somehow soft. The thought made him smile. The taste of saline washed over the back of his tongue.

His body did not sit in a chair in the lab, it hung suspended in liquid in the bottom-level basement.

The shock flipped his eyelids up. The blurry vision showed him the familiar tank designed to grow their clones. Outside, life support equipment lined harsh concrete walls. Jason's surge of adrenaline must have overridden the mild drugs used to keep the clone asleep.

IV wires ran into the front of the thermal suit, puncturing his chest. Why had he not considered that a problem? His arms and legs convulsed, panic overwhelming him.

He shut his eyes, struggling to escape back into the HaSQNaP. The water temperature warmed. He ceased struggling and opened his eyes again. Without the interface or a headset, returning to the processor might be impossible. The water in the tank heated and swirled.

A movement in the room beyond his tank caught his attention. He found Grant's child body suspended in liquid, dressed in the one-piece suit. Soft, child fingers rubbed against the glass as Grant writhed.

Beyond Grant, Lucile struggled as well. Her tank glowed with dim light, one Jason had not installed. The light started low but grew in intensity, as if the tank held a light bulb filament rather than Lucile's two-year-old clone. Jason's newly opened eyes went wider.

A sound entered the room, harsh and buzzing. In concert with the sound, the water in Grant's tank trembled. Lucile's tank grew brighter.

Jason's panic rose further. If the containment systems failed, they would die. The water in Jason's tank heated to an uncomfortable temperature, so hot he wondered if his skin might burn. The nearby sound increased, changing to a shriek. Overtop of Lucile's tank, the wires sprayed sparks across the room.

In unison, the metal stands holding up the glass cylinders retreated into the floor. Whatever had attacked the system, it had triggered an emergency safety protocol Jason had installed. When the bottom of the glass cylinders reached the level of the floor, the glass lifted away.

Thick water washed outward, and the three babies spilled onto the floor with it. Jason's fatty flesh slapped the floor, and his skull struck the concrete-backed linoleum. His IV-line tore from the jumpsuit. A burning sting emanated from his chest.

He tried to scream but instead he vomited the oxygenated water that his clone had been breathing since birth. Horrible, dry air entered, cold and harsh. His lungs might as well have been on fire.

The light coming from Lucile's tank had disappeared, the

intense sound gone, while steam rose from the water surrounding Jason.

He flipped to his belly, his soft baby hands sliding amid the thick liquid. He drew one struggling breath after another until he coughed out the last of the oxygenated liquid. Physical sensations of his small body radiated through him. The flesh had so much more vitality than his middle aged one which slept in a room above. Every inch of his skin tingled. His small heart raced. Beyond all those sensations waited another he did not anticipate—emotion. The horror of his situation rushed from his mind out into his body, and when it struck the fresh nerves, it filled his head with a rush of hormones and autonomic reactions.

His mouth opened wide and he wailed, tears flowing. The other two needed no more to break them. They burst forth with blubbering of their own.

When the tears ended, Jason tried to wipe his eyes but managed to smack himself in the face instead. While the clone had the same neural network as his adult body, he had just arrived inside of it. He watched while Grant and Lucile flailed about on the floor nearby, just as helpless. Whimpering and grunts echoed off the painted concrete walls.

A full hour passed before Jason's hands moved to the places he intended. Perhaps another before he could at last rise to his hands and knees.

With tears welling, he inwardly gawked at his weakness. Why could he not retain an adult emotional composure? Did the raw neural wiring of a two-year-old expose him to the unfiltered effect?

A lengthy struggle ended with the awkward and unreliable ability to crawl. He crossed the linoleum toward the other two. They responded by meeting him in the middle of the floor, their movements just as unsteady. They managed to sit up and face one another. Lucile was the first to attempt words. The garbled utterance brought her chubby hands up to her cheeks, one finger entering her mouth and another her eye. She squealed with dismay.

Jason did not try speaking. He grunted at them and crawled toward the door. He knew the protocols had also unlatched the door. It was a preventative measure to allow access to the clones should a true catastrophe occur. He pouted at the thought. A true catastrophe had.

Together they approached the massive door. To their fortune, it provided enough space for them to crawl out into the hallway.

They traveled the cold hallway to the stairs. They had barely learned to crawl, and a two-flight climb separated them from their adult bodies and a return to their normal lives. Grant sat back on his haunches and attempted to cross his arms. Failing, he clutched his arms to his chest and pouted, resentment on his features. Jason wondered if he looked upon a scene played out in Grant's true childhood.

Jason touched the spot of blood on his chest where the IVs had pulled out. Their toddler forms would need food, and probably quite soon. The kitchen waited on the ground floor as well. Jason crawled past Grant and his colleague abandoned his display.

Drawing a breath of air into his fresh and raw lungs, Jason placed his hands on the first step and climbed. The other two would have to follow his example. The flight drew more energy from him than he imagined it would. Had the muscle stimulation he designed been subpar? He did not dare show weakness in front of the other two doctors. When they mastered speech again, he would not mention the short-coming of his design.

While he sat whimpering at the top of the first flight, the other two arrived. When he pushed the emotions of failure away, an unsolicited grunt issued from him. He forged up the second set of stairs before they could witness more. They followed close behind.

The wide hallway led off a considerable distance toward the lab in one direction, but a much closer doorway opened into the kitchen.

"Muh." Jason babbled, pointing a hand at the door.

The room held one table, a long counter with cabinets and a dishwasher along one wall, and a refrigerator. At the rear, a walk-in closet held a washer and dryer. The refrigerator door's magnet proved too powerful for their weak muscles and slight weight. A low-level drawer held cookies, crackers, and puddings with infinite shelf lives. A terrible struggle with the pudding lids ensued. Jason could not make his fingers grip the tab with any useful amount of strength. Lucile hissed at hers and Grant threw his unopened cup across the floor in a fit. In the end, they dined on more readily accessible cookies. Wafers that would otherwise have chewed easily, forced them to suck on the edges until they softened.

Lucile tried speaking again, her mouth covered with cookie crumbs. Her gibberish sounded a bit more like words. When she pointed to the lab, Jason sighed. Of course, they were going to the lab. Why did she always think she was leading him?

They headed off at a crawl, their locomotion far more assured than before. When they arrived, the lab door hung ajar. A disquieting sensation swept Jason's fresh set of nerves. That door should have been closed. Would the intruder still lurk inside? The three crawled through the opening.

A curving desk console wrapped the area where the three chairs held their adult forms. A single headset hung over the front edge. Their short stature blocked their view of anything else. The three shuffled their way further into the room until, at long last, they could see.

Nothing could have prepared Jason for the sight.

Their bodies still reclined in their chairs. The skin on their faces and hands had dried and darkened. Flaking pools rested under each chair, and dark stains marred the seats. Skeletal teeth grinned. Jason sucked in a breath, eyes wide. Lucile screamed. Grant grunted and rolled onto his back.

The two other headsets lay discarded atop the console in positions only possible if someone had removed them.

In the far recesses of Jason's mind, a dispassionate part of him analyzed. He knew the phases corpses passed through. Their bodies had been dead for months.

"No," screeched Grant, his first word. "No, no, no, no." He shook his arms at his sides with force while he still lay on his back.

Jason turned away. Lucile blubbered in a low volume. Jason could not help but join in a display of distress. Silent tears streamed down his cheeks. He imagined the other two doctors as true babies for a moment, and wondered if he should comfort them. He then remembered who they truly were and stopped himself. Instead, he wrapped his arms around his own chest. Separated by only a few feet, each of them suffered in solitude. They grieved until weariness over-took them.

They had outfitted the building with private bedrooms which they had used quite often. They retreated together to the first bedroom along the hall, which happened to belong to Lucile. The bed rose too high and so they curled together on her bean bag chair. Under a blanket, their combined heat lulled them fast toward sleep.

Before he drifted away, Jason reconsidered their time inside the HaSQNaP. He touched his chest and came away with no blood. The IV wound had already partially healed. He had found comfort within the HaSQNaP and eventually learned to control portions of it. He considered their awakening and the strange lights from Lucile's tank, the sounds and vibrations from Grant's tank, and the odd heat within his own. Where had those phenomena come from?

His thoughts then arrived upon the intruder. Their deaths were the fault of that intruder. That person had disconnected their minds from their bodies. He guessed that they had simply starved. He whimpered, mourning his own death. Among the other problems they would have to solve, he established the goal of finding their killer among the highest of priorities.

Jason awoke to the sound of Grant giggling. Realizing he slept alone under the blanket, he popped his head out to find Lucile at the side of the bed. She gripped it, her body swaying back and forth, a wide smile on her face. Lucile had learned to stand. Grant sat on the floor behind her, his hands on chubby cheeks.

Jason and Grant joined in on the effort. With their adult minds as pilots of their new bodies, they managed to gain their feet while holding the side rail of the bed. Jason flicked a sidelong look at Lucile. She had learned to stand first, but he would be damned if she would learn to walk ahead of him. He negotiated a turn toward the door, one hand on the bed. He watched Lucile's brows draw down into a competitive frown.

He made only a single step before she followed. Their insistence upon surpassing one another pushed them beyond their limit with their second steps. They fell into one another, baby heads knocking with a clunk, while they tumbled into a pile on the floor. Jason raged out a vocalization of anger. If Lucile hadn't tried to walk with him, they wouldn't have collided. The knocked heads and the slap of the hard floor, however, brought them both to tears.

Still pouting and crying, they crawled to the bed and

stood again. Eyes glaring at one another, they repeated the effort, failed, and tried again.

"Mya nya bla ma," Grant scolded them.

To Jason's vexation, he and Lucile toddled through the door together.

Potty training arrived next. They hadn't spent the last months trying and failing like normal children. The muscles simply weren't ready. Cleaning their jumpsuits arrived as a terrible result of their first meal of cookies. Jason should have known better. Their digestive systems were not ready.

The jumpsuits weren't simple garments, they were high-tech-wear. In the tanks, tubes had carried the waste away. Without that system, it led to terrible messes. They set a footstool beside the toilet in hopes of preventing further disasters. Balancing on the toilet, however, proved its own new challenge.

Before long, they learned to control their tongues, at least to some degree. Jason decided it was the most difficult muscle in the body to master. Their vocalizations were crude and, despite their efforts, often resulted in gibberish.

Lucile soon discovered what had gone wrong with the HaSQNaP.

"Look," Lucile said, not quite pointing. She hadn't learned to retract her fingers with the index extended. "Here." Of course, the word *hear* sounded like it had a L or perhaps a W at the end of it.

She was right. Not only had someone cut a key line, it had been done so that it remained hidden to anyone who didn't understand the system.

"That broke our 'nection?" Jason meant *connection*.

"More." Her hands moved in an absent manner. "It left our bodies with no minds." The word *mind* was barely discernible, but Jason understood. Their pilotless bodies had wasted away.

"Murder," Grant garbled.

"By n'expert." Lucile indicated the cut connection. "Only we know this sys'em."

"Gov'ment?" Grant guessed.

Jason shook his head. No one should have known they were there. "Furo?" Jason shrugged with his palms up.

"Girl at back door?" Lucile managed.

Grant frowned and crossed his arms, the movement still awkward. "Hmph," he pouted.

When they left the lab, they closed the door to separate their corpses from the rest of the building. Jason wondered when they would muster the willingness or even the ability to remove them. They had a mountain of other problems to resolve before facing that awful task anyway.

Their ever-hungry bellies drew them back to the kitchen. On that visit, they used a plastic step stool to raid the silverware drawer. They used butter knives to stab open the pudding cups. Grant cackled like a mad scientist. Jason no longer wanted to attempt the refrigerator. Everything inside of it would be rotten or moldy after so long a time.

While they stood upon their chairs to reach the tabletop, Lucile announced, "We need clothes."

"And diapers," Jason added. None of them had a perfect record of reaching the bathroom.

Grant put palms to his face and hung his head with shame. He had caused more messes than either of the other two. While cleaning up, a monumental task with their lack of dexterity, they had draped one another in simple bath towels, the fabric ample enough to cover them.

"Probabee a good idea," Lucile answered. She was brave for trying to pronounce *probably*.

Grant enunciated with care. "In-ter-net."

Jason's thoughts returned to Adel Furo. He was sure she was responsible, even if Grant was not. He bared his tiny teeth. Masking emotions with a straight face had proven yet another learned behavior they had taken for granted as adults. "I want to see d'news."

"I want to order diapers." Lucile put up her hands to accentuate the obviousness of her statement.

"Why no In-ter-net?" Grant asked again.

Jason shared his guess. "Cut 'puter line, cut Int'net."

"More sab'age." *Sabotage.* Lucile's eyes roved while she considered.

Jason nodded. "Diapers first."

"Wait," Grant said. "I have somethin' to show you."

Jason and Lucile paused.

He raised his hands, placing them on either side of his half empty glass of water. "Watch." The effect started with a humming sound, perhaps like a small motor or a bee's wings. When it grew louder, the water in the glass trembled as if it had been set atop an audio speaker.

"Wow," Lucile gasped.

The sound stopped and he withdrew his hands. The water stilled, but the glass had a hairline crack.

Jason marveled. How could such a thing be? Grant had mastered that skill inside the HaSQNaP. It should not have followed him into the physical world.

Lucile peered between the two of them. "Me too." She raised her hands palms forward. Across the table from her, above the empty seat, the air glowed. It started as dull and faint and grew, a crackling sound accompanying it. It brightened until Jason and Grant winced and turned away. When they did, the light extinguished.

Lucile turned her palms upward. "How?"

"From the hasnap," Jason said.

Grant shrugged. "How's possible?"

"Is not," Jason confirmed.

"You?" Lucile asked.

Jason shrugged. "I never tried."

"Do it," Grant said.

Could he reproduce what he had learned inside the liquid-processor? Why would such abilities translate to a non-mechanical environment? What was it, exactly, that they had learned to do?

Jason set his hand forward, aiming it at the empty chair across the table. A hissing sound rewarded his efforts but, a moment later the back of the plastic cafeteria chair burst into flames. With alarm, he reversed the effect. The fire went out and frosted water particles collected over the area that had burned.

"You dangerous," Lucile said.

Jason eyed the crack in the water glass. "You too."

They dared an arduous retreat to the basement, and there, they practiced their new powers in the confines of concrete walls. Lights, sounds, and withering displays of heat wreaked havoc. When a potty break interrupted, Lucile was unable to climb the stairs in time. As much as Jason hated succoring his disagreeable fellow scientist, he joined with Grant to work the controls of the washing machine in the kitchen closet.

Wrapped in a towel, Lucile spoke with childish anger. "I want diapers, now."

They napped again, not just out of necessity, but also to allow time for the clothes to dry and the sun to set. The three of them had argued their way to a plan. Upon waking, they headed for the back door.

The temperature outside their building had dropped, and when it hit their skin, the three toddlers winced. The door thumped closed behind them.

"Our thermals will keep us warm," Jason told them. "I designed them for this."

"For this?" Grant stroked the chest of his form-fitting

jumpsuit.

"Okay," Jason admitted. "Not this exactly."

The three slipped into the night, padding down the alleyway with bobbing steps. A streetlight around a corner lit their way.

"See how big our heads are?" Grant asked. "Our hands hardly meet on top of our heads."

Lucile giggled and the infectious sound spread, Jason and Grant joining her. Jason loved the sensation and still could not decide if he should fight it. No wonder children laughed so much. It felt fantastic and, once he let go of his veneer of control, it was unstoppable. Their high-pitched squeals of humor echoed off the alley walls.

A street interrupted their path. Intermittent cars whipped past, exceeding the speed limit in the dark of the night.

"What if we trip?" Jason asked.

"Be careful," Lucile replied. She still slogged through her L's and R's. They all did.

They waited for a long space between vehicles and padded across to the next alley.

Behind them, a voice raised up. "Did you see that?"

"Run," Grant said.

They fled, although any adult could have caught them with ease. They reached the end of the alley and waited, but no one followed. When they faced forward again, their target glowed with bright lights. The 24 Mart had a rough look. Its small interior offered snacks and assorted supplies, like aspirin and motor oil.

"I'm scared," Lucile said.

"Don't 'dulge it," Jason said. "Be adult."

"I was scared in there as a n'adult," she retorted.

"Stick to the plan," Grant said, pronouncing the word as *pwan*.

"The plan is crazy." Lucile raised her hands in the air.

Grant was right. Her hands didn't go very high above her head. Jason touched his own skull with both hands. The plan *was* crazy. If they had to switch to Plan B, things would get weird. They had argued to a standstill on those subsequent options.

They ran across the street and Jason pushed on the door. The door gave only an inch and advertisements obscured any view of the interior.

"He's too weak," Lucile said. "You do it, Grant."

Jason turned hostile eyes on Lucile. Grant attempted the door and failed.

"Move," Lucile told Grant.

Her push was as ineffective as theirs.

"We have to do it together," Grant said.

Jason exchanged a glowering look with Lucile. Relenting, they joined with Grant against the door. Their combined toddler weight opened the dirty glass entryway. An electronic chime rang.

"Hello?" the clerk asked. "Whatever, don't come in then." The sound of him leaning back in his chair came over the counter.

The cloth footies of their thermal suits made no sound and Jason smiled. Not only practical for cold weather but ideal for stealth operations as well. Giggles threatened to erupt, and he slapped both hands over his mouth. Grant led them to the back of the first aisle, and there sat their prize; a dozen packages of diapers.

Jason pointed to the ones he thought would fit and they each grabbed one. Grant tucked a second under his other arm, but it limited his mobility considerably.

"Let's just leave," Jason whispered.

"Without paying?" Lucile asked. "We agreed no."

*She* had said no.

Jason shrugged. "We can't go to jail."

Grant nodded to Lucile, and she sighed with resignation.

Jason grabbed at soft cookie-like health bars and shoved them inside the collar of his suit. Lucile followed his example, hissing. "Dis is so wong!"

Their revised plan had almost succeeded when the door burst open. A woman and young girl, perhaps seven years old, walked in. The sauntering woman had pushed the door so wide that it latched in the open position. Jason smiled.

"Cigarettes," the woman told the clerk. "Those menthols on the left."

The little girl, however, stared at the three thieves with interest. "Mommy look, babies."

The woman turned, half-interested. When she saw the three toddlers, she did a double take. She craned her neck to search the store. "Where's your mother?" Her eyes narrowed.

Jason pressed his lips closed. The woman was summing them up and they had no hapless shopper to tag as their parent. The open door beckoned.

"Run for it," Grant said.

The three of them dashed. The woman paced two steps toward them, bent, and spread her arms to block their path.

"Plan B," Jason snapped.

His free hand pointed at a box of macaroni near the woman's shoulder. The cardboard burst into flames, a mere foot from her hair.

She screeched out and Grant shouted at her, but instead of a mere infant scream, his voice boomed through the store as if he had used a megaphone. The woman retreated deeper into the store, dragging her daughter with her. When the three toddling bandits reached the door, Lucile dropped the interior of the store into unnatural darkness.

They retreated across the street and into the alley, Grant losing the second diaper pack mid-crossing. Behind them, light returned to the store interior, and they saw the woman running to her car with her daughter.

They re-entered their laboratory panting and laughing. The giggling fit lasted until Jason felt the muscles around his ribs ache. His insides, however, radiated a wonderful sensation.

"Do you feel it?" Lucile rubbed in a circle around her sternum. "Here?"

Their laughter ended.

Jason perceived the lingering energy from his center. "I do feel it." He cocked his head. "It's not the same as my heat abil'ty."

Grant agreed. "Not the same as my sound, either."

Lucile nodded, her hand on her chest. "Me too."

Jason placed his attention on the tingling sensation, using the same technique he did to create hot or cold. His mental fix on the anomaly altered the way it felt. "I can change it," he told them.

"Use it," Lucile urged.

"Do it." Grant hopped. "See what it does."

Both broke into childish smiles.

Jason focused on the phenomenon. When he did, he sensed the energy growing, as if his attention fueled it. A pleasant vibration coursed through him. A moment later he slipped off his feet. He squealed, waiting for the painful slap against the hard floor. It never came. He struggled, attempting to gain his feet, but confusion followed when he could not reach the floor with his hands.

"Jason," Lucile screamed. "You're floating."

When Jason pulled his attention away from the effect, his body thudded to the ground with a soft, painless slap.

"Try it, Lucy, try it." Grant radiated a bright smile.

Jason sat up and witnessed the unbelievable when Grant's feet lifted off the ground first, and Lucile soon followed.

When they retreated to the basement to practice their powers, they no longer had to overcome the stairs as an obstacle, floating down and back up the flights instead.

The following sunset, they were ready for their next venture outside the building.

"There's the break in the cable." Jason pointed across the street.

They had their thermal jumpsuits on, but the winds on the roof were too cold and so they also wore their towels over their heads. They had found their cable box undamaged and so followed the line. Across the street, a telephone pole hugged a building and where the top of the pole arrived even with the neighboring roof, a loose loop of wire hung.

"It was cut," Grant said. "You can see it from here."

"Without glasses." Lucile tittered.

"We'll have to go downstairs and cross the street again." Jason sighed. "The police circled for two hours after last time." His eyes flicked to the bulges of the stolen diapers at Lucile and Grant's midsections. He frowned. It wasn't exactly a cool look.

Grant tied his towel at his neck and lifted off the roof, floating at their shoulders. "We don't need the stweet."

"No," Lucile protested. "What if we're hovering instead of flying. You'll drop."

"No way, Dr. Colorado," Grant said. "I'm flying."

She sighed and motioned toward the cut cable. "Live your fantasy, Dr. Canere. I'm not helping." She set her hands on her hips, her small fists settling atop the rim of her diaper.

Jason crossed his arms. They hadn't used their formal titles since reemerging as children. He missed the respect. He let the energy in his chest surge and rose to float beside Grant.

"You don't know wiring," Lucile scoffed.

"He doesn't have the *destermity* alone." He bared his teeth with frustration. *"Desteripy. Dekterp."* He growled and clenched his pudgy fists.

Grant put his palms over his eyes. "Too many co's'nants." *Consonants.*

Jason's cheeks flushed. He'd have to learn to say *dexterity* all over again.

"Right," Lucile said, wiggling her short fingers in front of her face. She lifted and flew off toward their target without waiting for either of them.

"Lucile," Jason scolded.

The boys followed, their towels flapping at their backs.

Jason watched the street pass below with a thrill.

While Grant needed a bit of help for strength's sake, he was a tech expert, and had brought sleek tools that would virtually mend the wires on their own. His small hands, however, made the work arduous.

"Push on the connectew," Grant garbled.

When their shoulders bumped together, Jason and Lucile scowled at one another.

Jason considered their plight. His and Lucile's competitiveness had impeded them since taking on their smaller bodies. As much as it upset him, he knew half of it was his fault. He tried to sigh but it came out as a grunt. "We might have to help each other a lot."

She eyed him for long, silent seconds. She then exhaled, much of the rigidness in her posture relaxing. "Maybe so."

Shoulders pressed together, Jason and Lucile added their weight and the connector snapped into place.

"Let's go," Grant said. He lifted off straight up and flew in a high arc, far above the street.

"Brave," Lucile commented.

"Good," Jason replied.

They regrouped in Grant's room where he kept one of his laptops.

The Internet connection brought up Grant's home page.

"No passcode," Lucile noted.

"Bypassed," Grant said, "very basic connection."

"Are we safe?" Jason asked.

Grant shrugged. "Not at d'moment."

"Order more diapers," Lucile said. "And pizza."

"No," Jason said. "News."

Grant nodded and clicked a link. The next page showed a headline news story. A woman with an enormous two-handed gun stood in front of a raging fire. A headline ran beneath;

MAD SCIENTRESS STRIKES AGAIN

"Skinny girl for a big gun," Grant said.

"Scientress?" Jason asked.

"Impossible," Lucile said. "That gun. I rec'nize it."

"What is it?" Grant asked.

"My design." Lucile's bottom lip pouted forward. "I never turned it in."

"Someone stole it?" Jason asked.

"No," she touched her temple. "I only 'magined it." She pointed at the screen, "But that's the gun."

Something about the onscreen image bothered Jason. The overly thin woman stood atop the hood of a car, the name of a bank overhead while fire silhouetted her.

Jason gasped. "Adel Furo, the alley woman."

Grant and Lucile leaned forward.

"It is her," Grant said.

Jason balled his fists at his side and bared his teeth.

"Oh no." Lucile slapped her hands to her face. "Oh no."

"What?" urged Grant.

"Do you 'member?" She flapped her arms. "We dropped inside of her mind. I could see her thoughts.

She stole my gun." Lucile's hands gripped the sides of her skull. "From my head."

Jason understood. "She could see our thoughts too."

Grant balled his soft fists in front of his mouth. "What else do you think she stole?"

"It went both ways," Jason admitted, "'cause I know how to cook meth, and where to buy it."

"Me too," Grant said. "I remember what it feels like to be high, and the taste." He flipped his palms upward, "and I don't smoke meff."

Jason shook his head. "She learned how to disconnect the hasnap from our minds."

Lucile's pudgy face curled with a snarl. "I wonder if she knew it would kill us."

"Did you?" Jason asked.

Lucile burst into tears.

Grant scrunched down to appear smaller.

"We have plans to make," Jason said. "Big plans."

* * *

THE THIRTY-YEAR-OLD IMPALA rolled up to the curb and Adel Furo pushed her tongue back and forth inside her bottom lip. She looked at her boyfriend. She didn't need him, really. He'd do well for a fall guy when she needed to get away, perhaps.

She rolled down her window while studying the jewelry store across the street. Winter had passed and a reasonably warm breeze wafted into the car. Streetlights shined under a clear sky. She scanned the door of the shop, evaluating its strength and running the diagram of the jewelry store interior through her head again. She had hacked the information that morning. So easy. Damn, those mental nuggets of wisdom from those three dead scientists were the best thing that had ever happened to her. She understood why they'd been so arrogant, being that much smarter than other people.

The thought caused her to glance up and down her boyfriend's frame again. Yuck. "You need to keep the car running this time, and don't floor it until we hit at least 10 miles an hour."

"Ya, I remember," he said, looking away from her.

"I'm gonna go break some things and steal some stuff."

He turned back to her. "Get me a watch with diamonds on it."

Her lips twisting with disdain. He would wear it, too, and be arrested a day later for his stupidity.

"Four minutes." Her car door groaned open.

"Then we go home and light up?" he asked.

"You know it." She stepped out, leather boots thumping onto the pavement. Torn, tight jeans and a sequined jean jacket completed the ensemble.

A few people were out on the street that night, and a pair of light posts bracketed the area. It didn't matter. Lamps couldn't stop her. A smug smile spread across her face as she dropped into a saunter toward the jewelry shop. "Fish in a barrel."

A powerful boom of thunder exploded above her, causing her to falter backward. Three objects streaked through the sky. When her eyes found them, she gasped. They were people.

The trio dropped straight down, hoods and capes of terrycloth flapped over form fitting jumpsuits. When they landed, electric sparks flew with dazzling light, a rumbling like thunder filled the air, and the temperature around her dropped so that the moisture in the air crystallized and sparkled.

Each of the three had landed in a different pose. The impression struck her with greater awe when she realized how small they were. The three stood from their landing positions. Baby faces peered from under the hoods.

"Dwop the gun, Furo." said one in a little girl's voice.

"Time to pay the pipuh," said a boy next to her.

The third slapped his palms over his eyes. "Too many co's'nants."

Adel Furo's jaw fell slack. "What the hell?"

*MARK BEARD IS A NOVELIST, short story writer, and marketing content writer. He is a resident of Central Florida and enjoys both the cities and the wilds of the Sunshine State. He has contributed to the* Noncorporeal *anthology the story entitled* Down to Size, *a tale in which three scientists with towering egos experience a catastrophe that reduces them to much humbler sizes. Mark Beard has published four heroic fantasy novels which comprise the series entitled* The Jeweler of Tirravon. *His trilogy,* Leviathan Brood, *is scheduled to come out in early 2024. Keep up with Mark Beard publications at:* www.Lanthanor.com

# THE MOUNT OF HAUNTED KRISKO

## BRENDA CARRE

*D*espite the place's antiquity, Bette Terwilliger wasn't impressed as she made her way through the shadows of the fourteenth-century portcullis toward Warrich Castle. Why did they have to hold the National bake-off *here* for heaven's sake? This was supposed to be a serious competition, not a bloody three-ring circus.

There were coloured tents, jugglers and even a pretend pillory. Actors in medieval garb pranced across the white stone pathways sparring with theatrical broadswords. There was even a bloke covered in fake blood, dressed as the legendary ghost, Fulk Greville, said to have been murdered by his manservant in 1628. The false Fulk brandished an oversized cardboard dagger and pointed it toward the kitchens.

Banks of floodlights cast their garish wattage on the gold-gray façade of the chapel, the great hall and the fifteenth-century kitchen wing where the bake-off was to be held. There the crowd was thickest. Talented young cooks mingled with raucous tourists and curious locals wanting to catch a glimpse of Roberta Barnes, presenter for Channel Four's Food-and-Gourmet show.

*Ridiculous* thought Bette, as her ankle twisted on the rough pathway.

A strong arm gripped her. "Careful there, eh?"

Bette forgot her kit was strewn halfway to kippers and her tins of precious mixings lay scattered on the ground. Here was a dark and dishy guy tall enough to make her five-foot-eight feel short. A threadbare canvas knapsack hung from his right shoulder. Beneath his denim jacket he wore a tee shirt that said 'Good cheese is the whey'.

"You ok?" he said, as curious passersby ogled them.

"Yes!"

She awkwardly disengaged herself, acutely conscious she looked gauche in her sensible brogues, mannish slacks and long pale, flyaway ponytail. What a stupid way to begin: by tripping like some manner of fool.

"I'm George Zinkewitz," said her stalwart saviour.

"Bette Terw...Oww!" she gasped as her weight hit her twisted ankle. "Bollocks!"

"Hold on—lean on me while I take a look. I used to be a physio before I decided to do therapy on flour," he said, going down to one knee like he was proposing.

She shivered as he ran his hands over her ankle. His fingers were tender, confident and so warm.

He applied subtle pressure to her ankle and then to her hamstring and something adjusted. The pain went away. Delight spread through her.

"Krikey!"

"Muscle release," he explained. "A strain, not a sprain." A dent appeared in one gamine cheek as he grinned up at her. "No wonder ya' tripped, Goldie. Ya' got a case of the nerves, I think."

"Where *are* you from?" she said, as he rose. His accent

sounded someplace between soft French and drawled Scots. He smelled delicious—like aftershave and cinnamon cookies.

"I'm a Noof, outta Canada," he said scrambling to retrieve her deflated knapsack.

"Anoof?" she said.

"Newfoundland," he explained plucking tins off the cobbles and righting her whole kit adroitly. "You're British, am I right?"

"More than that. I'm Cornish, of good strong-boned Kernow stock," she said proudly reaching for her kit. "I can take that."

"Nope, I got it. You got the ankle," he teased.

He took her kit over his left shoulder and his own on his right. "You could always say the ghost tripped ya'? I hear-tell the Watergate Tower's 'hanted'."

"I don't believe in that nonsense," she said.

"Do I look like a fella spouts nonsense? I tell ya' I got the Sight. I'm still very balanced with my two packsacks and all."

Now she chuckled, giving in to his charm. Her nervousness disappeared.

He *was* balanced and funny and likeable. It felt like she'd known him forever.

The Great kitchen's oaken doors were open wide and looked like two nail-studded pieces from an old 'Robin Hood' movie. The place was a vault. Three tall transom windows cast a flood of unearthly light on everything. Two magnificent fireplaces belched flames, and spits of meat dripped hissing fat. There were women in gowns, men in smocks-and-hose scurrying in and out. A swarm of cooks and apprentices chopped veg at a massive table stretching half the length of the chamber. The place was a riot of echoes and coarse accents. Bette smelled succulent gravies, roast pig, game hen.

"What the?" she gasped, and blinked. The vision was gone.

No, there it was again projected on the ashlar walls. Techs worked everywhere, taping down cords, testing equipment. A flash of fool-the-eye glare had disoriented her, tossed her backward in time in a flash of virtual-seeming reality.

Those three tall windows were still there, catching the sunlight dancing off the Avon River, but now the ancient fireplaces were empty, unusable, cold. This was nothing but a big oak-beamed kitchen, turned into a competition floor. The Buttery was filled with camera equipment, industrial stainless steel and modern lighting. It smelled of petrol cookers and borax.

At least twenty chefs, mainly young males, were causing the noise with their chatter, setting up at marble-topped workstations. She found her own workstation, not far from the entrance. Her name was placarded in medieval script on one of those footed ovals.

George winked at Bette with mischievous brown eyes, picked up the oval placard with the name 'Heather Norris' off the workstation next to hers and took it to his table one over.

"Don't you think they have a list of who goes where?" Bette said.

"No, I don't think they care who goes where," he said, plonking his name placard not far from hers. He nodded at her ankle. "That still painin' ya'?"

"No, it feels wonderful," she assured him and grinned. She'd be vying with him today for Roberta Barnes's cachet to launch a show on Food-and-Gourmet; somehow if he was the winner it wouldn't bother her.

"So, how do you get the 'Sight' with a name like *Zinkewitz*?"

He slung her kit to her counter and his own to the floor. "My mum's maiden name was Buchan—aak!"

He winced at the loud squeal of feedback coming from the dais.

"Someone?" Another squawk as Roberta Barnes stepped up where everyone could see her. She waved her hand mic like a baton. The thing made an angry rattlesnake hiss. "This is bolluxed!"

A tech scurried up and made an adjustment. Roberta tapped the end. The tech winced.

"Don't you wince at me you daftie!" Her strong Glaswegian accent boomed off the walls. "I wanted a lapel mic!"

"I swear, I turned it down," he said.

"Bollocks you did. Fix it now!" she snapped and shoved the mic at him. "Competitors!" she shouted sans mic, rolling her r's like she was marching to Culloden. "You all have thrree hours for your prractice bake. Be prrofessional! Be brrilliant!" She glared at the suffering tech.

"Most of all, don't scrrrew up!"

"Right," Bette said watching the dumpy little woman waddle out waving her arms in the air. It was time to concentrate on folding and working the dough for her test bake.

Even raw, Grannie's dough smelled like buttered bliss. During the heat test she took time to sort and mix her ingredients for the actual contest. Dry ingredients were supplied on shelves at knee height. Wet awaited her in a cute little pink Smeg fridge shared by her station and the affable George's.

When the scent of baked shortbread grew too enticing to ignore, George left off his own test bake and peered through her oven window. "So, how'd ya' get 'em into those little animal shapes, Goldie? Phoenixes and Griffins en't they?"

Bette grinned at his teasing. Phoenixes indeed.

"I'm achin' to try one. Can I?"

At her nod, he folded a tea towel and took out the tray. Bette's grin turned into a gape. Instead of the test lozenges she'd dropped on the bake sheet, here was an edible zoo, courtesy of Edvard Munch.

"Nuttin' wrong with the taste," he said crunching with gusto and nicking another one off the tray. "You'll get the animal crackers crowd dyin' for these."

"All dying aside, I don't know why they did this." She sniffed at her tin of shortening.

"Could be your oven's the problem. Don't trow the dough away just yet. Try my oven, it works just fine," he advised her. "Here, eat while the heat goes down. Ya' look peckish."

She stared with envy at the golden-hued, deep-dish, steak-and-mushroom pie he dolloped into a dish for her. It smelled divine. She was usually way too nervous to eat before competing, but the man knew how to make crust.

\* \* \*

OVER TWENTY MINUTES of mutual anecdotes and two amazing dishes of pie, her second test batch went into his oven. She went back to her preparations, and he to take a quick 'saunter' to 'check out the competition' so he said.

No matter what happened she'd be dreaming of pie crust tonight. That had been the best Steak-and-Guinness she'd ever eaten...

"Oh soddit!" She hissed, as the smoke alarm whooped overhead. White smoke now belched out of *his* oven! Aargh! She grabbed a tea-towel, threw open the door and flapped at the miasma dispersing upwards.

"Well, that's caught it," said a posh voice filled with hostility. "If you'd turned on the rain, I'd have needed to kill you."

This sylph of a woman was garbed in a tweed Dior suit

and expensive slip-on shoes. Her silver-gilt hair fell to her jawbone in a perky geometric bob. So *here* was Heather Norris of the movable placard, complete with title. Behind her, George wheeled in a Vuitton trunk with her name *Lady H. Norris* written in large gilt letters.

George put a finger to his lips and winked.

The smoke alarm cut off. Bette sneezed and the echoes reproached her.

Lady Heather gave a dainty cough and posed for the cameras.

"What's going on over here?" shouted Roberta Barnes emerging from whatever floury corner she'd been lurking in. Her ample frontage was now armed with the desired lapel mic.

She elbowed George out of her way, snapped her fingers for an oven mitt and moved in to take a look. "Mmmm, smells a real treat," murmured a very thin, nervous little bloke leaning past Roberta for a shot with his GoPro.

He got an elbow in his gut for his pains. "Bloody amazin,'" he gasped, avoiding a second gut punch as Roberta slid out the tray. He focused on the shortbread monstrosities spread out on the tray as if they'd scuttled there on their own. They looked hellishly realistic, dotted spotted and tentacled.

Heather leaned past Bette to study her name placard. "Do you plan to ruin this contest, miss—erm—Terwilliger?"

"She meant 'em to look like that," said George. They're called *Grumpits*."

"Astounding," Roberta chimed in. An odd low buzz came from her lapel mic like bees on a warm summer afternoon. "How clever. They smell marvelous and look vicious enough to jump out and bite."

"Yeah, they do," said the helpful George. Truly the man had the gift of the blarney. "But it's us Foodies get to bite them instead. Adult monster crackers. There'd be a big market for these things back home in Canada."

"Grotesque but delicious," said Roberta Banks, sampling a monstrosity that looked like Cthulhu bumping uglies with a unicorn. "Good show, Miss—er..."

"Terwilliger," said Bette. Roberta seized Bette's hand. "Chuffy?"

The thin little bloke wielded his handy device to bring the 'Grumpits' up on the big screen.

"Roberta Banks here, with Miss Terwilliger, and her test bake...Bloody Hell, Chuffy, why arre we not getting sound?"

"You turned it off, Ms. Banks, remember?" said Chuffy.

"I cerrtainly did not!" A shriek of feedback came from the overheads. Everyone winced. Chuffy ran a hand through his thinning hair.

Bette heard a ghostly hiss of amusement.

"Why can we no get sound?" whispered Roberta. The overhead speakers purred back.

"Ach, that's better," she said, subdued. "This is Food-and-Gourmet, Channel Four. Ok ok, can we please have it sound this good laterr?" she told Chuffy and flicked off her lapel mic.

"As for you, Bette my lass, you get back to your station, and write me up this recipe," she said.

"They're a bit tricky," Bette replied. "They vary greatly with the amount of shortening used."

"That's no excuse at all," Roberta retorted striding off with Bette's tray of monsters.

The ponderous kitchen became a frantic zoo. Noisier than rush hour in Euston Station. Contestants bumped elbows, pans clashed, nut grinders whirred, spoons and whisks snapped against porcelain. The air went thick with the rich scents of nutmeg and almond paste.

"Cmon, Goldie, I got a few things I need to say." George touched her elbow.

He had the look of a man on a mission. A mission she couldn't deter with a ten-foot rolling pin. "You don't have a recipe for those things, do you?" he whispered.

Aproned up over her silk blouse and tweed, Lady Heather sent them a sour-milk glare.

They moved out of her hearing, away from all scurry and flurry, over to an open window near the castle garden. The earthy scent from the garden wafted across Bette. An icy breeze ruffled her hair with ghostly hands.

"You're being 'hanted'."

"That's all very well, but I told you already I don't believe in that nonsense. I'm on Roberta's good side and I aim to stay there. No silly talk about ghosts!"

Silly or no, she was cold. Icy cold.

*Kill her!*

"There's an entity in here and it's mad. My senses are fizzing like a can o' wild cola," said George.

"Did you hear that?" she whispered so terrified now her knees felt like spaghetti.

"No, but it's here. I can feel it. We don't stop it quick we're ukered. Look over there."

At her workstation the red plastic lid on her blue-and-white tin of Krisko was rising on one side like a lid venting steam.

It took every bit of strength she could muster to force herself back to her station.

*Revenge. Give me revenge.*

"Stop it!" She pushed on the lid. The white cold mass of goo underneath pushed back, like a tin of snakes trying to get free. The back of her neck hurt like a knife was cutting it. She was freezing…

"There's a skip outside! Help me," she whimpered. "He's

going crazy!"

"He's not gonna stay in the rubbish and you know it. Look at your hands. We gotta settle him down…"

"How?" she quavered. Her hands were slimy and sticky and there were blobs of nasty gunk down the bib of her apron that smelled of mint, marzipan and rot. "Agh!" She tore off her disgusting apron, rubbed her hands clean and hissed. "How!"

*"Eeeww,"* said Heather coming over to see what was wrong. "What have you done now?"

Bette tossed her apron over the haunted tin. She could feel a good roarer of a scream burbling up inside her like cheese fondue.

*"Kill her, Jeannette. Here is your chance."*

"Go away," she pleaded.

"Is she alright?" Heather pursed her lips like she'd just found a dirty hair in her soup.

"She's fine, it's the nerves."

"Very well, I'm going away as commanded. P'raps some tea and a settle down then," Heather sniped.

"Like saying 'settle down' helped Anybody. Ever," muttered Bette once she was gone.

"I'm not sayin' she's right, but if we settle you down, could be the troubled ghost that's botherin' you might leave this contest alone."

"So now it's my fault?"

"No. He's fixed on you. My guess is he lived and worked here and he wants your help."

"He called *me* Jeannette. He told me to kill Heather," she whispered. "I can feel him standing beside us. What do we do with less than an hour before everything begins?"

"We bake. Boil me up a pot of water, Goldie, and let's get busy. Listen up, Fella, whoever you are. Listen and learn. I'm gonna bake up three layers of pure, irresistible, Canadian bliss. They were created for a World's Fair back in 1986. When they're done, I'm gonna feed one to 'Jeannette' here and she's gonna channel the taste back your way. We mean ya' no harm."

"He's interested," said Bette as the air warmed around her.

"Course he is. Like Paris, Nanaimo Bars are always a good idea."

In a glass bowl, over Bette's boiling water, George made a *bain-marie* of melted butter, sugar, egg, rich dark semi-sweet Callebaut chocolate powder and extract of Madagascar bourbon vanilla. To this, he added graham crumbs, shredded coconut and chopped pecans, pressing the whole thing into the pan Bette greased.

"Now comes fifteen minutes of baking heaven," said George. "Time to whip up the layer of creamy delight."

The 'Fella' hovered near, as George mixed softened butter, icing sugar, Bird's custard powder, and milk into layer two.

"Take note. It's gotta be Bird's or nothin' good Sir," George said, spreading the pale custardy mix over the spicy-smelling base layer as easily as he spread his charm.

"Give 'er a taste?" he passed Bette the spatula.

"Oh, my dear word," she sighed. A groan of bliss answered hers. "He thinks so too."

George gave a pleased chuckle. "Trust me, Chum, they're even better cold. Fifteen minutes into the fast freeze to harden the chocolate."

He flipped a glass pot in the air and caught it by the handle and melted Calebaut chocolate and butter. Once the consistency was perfection, he spread it thick over the custard layer, winked at Bette, and ran to the freezer.

*"One cannot absolve a crime with sugar,"* said the voice.

"What crime?" she whispered.

*"They killed me, my sweet Jeannette,"* said the ghost. *"All but*

*you must die. Everywhere in my kitchen are snakes filled with lightning. I control these. You are my voice. Tell them why they must die. I have waited so long for my revenge."*

"Oh, this is not happening," she moaned. She sat at her workstation and bowed her face into her hands and stayed that way until George returned with his bars.

"It didn't work George," she whispered and pointed at the rigging everywhere. "This is why none of the sound is working. *He's* working it, and the lighting and the volts of power. This is a disaster in the making. I'm to tell everybody why he wants us dead. It's too…"

"Late!" cried Roberta.

Echoes rebounded from the walls. "It's now just gone six and time to begin. Your first assignment will be flans! The world is watching."

"It can't be too late," breathed George. "I'm gonna keep trying. Listen up, Fella. You got a bunch of innocent people here. Let us bake for you. Bette—I mean Jeannette here—and me are your friends. Let us be your voices and tell the world what happened. There's a ton of folks thinks you're nonsense, and dousing the room with yards of equipment will only convince them you're bad. Whatever happened, however you died, let us set the world straight?"

*"Bake,"* said the voice. *"I would study your technique. Bake and we'll see."*

* * *

BETTE BAKED as she'd never baked before. There was more than a prize in this for her now. Her flan was a twelve-inch square, which her Great-Gran had aptly named 'The Perfect Square.'

It was topped with a crust of brown sugar and crushed almonds that should caramelize nicely under heat. As she slid her tray into the oven, she tried to ignore 'Chuffy' who invaded her workspace to ask nosy questions.

"Does 'No Stick' make you nervous? Have you ever cooked with peanuts?"

She was almost happy when a *yeep* of horror from Heather sent Chuffy running over there.

"It just appeared!" cried Heather, pointing at what looked like oil on her pale heart-shaped creation.

"It's a smear is all. Here let's…"

She pushed George away. "Don't touch it! Get out of Chuffy's way!"

Heather turned on Bette now, leaving Chuffy to focus on the words 'You Die' written in oily letters on the surface and beneath that a palm print. "I don't know how you did this, but you deliberately ruined my work!"

"I didn't, I swear!" Bette protested.

"You are all on the clock, darlings, why are you all mincing about here?" shouted Roberta reaching them now with the flock of the other competitors trailing her. Her augmented volume boomed through the speakers. A second boom came from Bette's oven.

"A bomb!" shrieked a voice from the back of the crowd.

"Terrorists!" screamed another.

"Not unless they're hiding in Bette's oven!" shouted George, shifting the focus back to Bette's station.

"We have to tell the truth, Goldie," he whispered. "If we have to evacuate the kitchen in mid-contest, I'll take the blame."

"No, you will not. I must prove to him we are not the ones to blame for his death. No more hiding."

*"Speak for me, Jeannette,"* moaned the ghost.

"If you promise to listen to me," she murmured pushing through the crowd of contestants.

"Oh, I say. Blimey," murmured Chuffy. His device brought

236

the wreck of Bette's flan up on the big screen. The caramelized crust had popped off and was now a mask with empty eye-slits, a bit of a nose, a down-turned mouth and even a scruff of a beard.

"How did you do this, Miss Terwilliger? It looks like a sugary death mask," said Roberta.

"Evil! She's an instrument of evil," cried Heather.

*"Please, my dear one. Release me. Tell them the truth. Put on the mask. I will not stop until you do."*

"I'm not an instrument of evil," Bette answered Roberta's question. "Pass me the mask please and I'll tell you what happened."

No turning back now, she took the mask from Roberta.

*"Show them. Put it on, Jeannette,"* said the ghost.

Feeling his desperation, she pressed it to her face. A gasp of awe came from the room as the mask fused on like a second skin. Hers was now the actual face of a bearded man of no more than thirty-and-five. Up there on the big screen was the swarthy face of the chef who haunted this place. A truly mesmerizing vision with a beard that tickled Bette's neck and eyes of a dark, flashing black.

She felt George take her arms and turn her to face him. "Who are ya'?"

"Claude de Calais." The back of her neck hurt terribly from the axe that had ended his life. She knew what had happened. Her voice wasn't hers anymore. Ah, but the need to speak was.

"When were you chef here?" George asked.

"Blessed question. I have waited four hundred years, never heard, never seen, to say I was betrayed, falsely condemned and beheaded for a crime I never did."

"Doesn't *anyone* see this is a well-planned trick? She's in this to win," cried Heather, "Ask her how she got the sugar to do that? It's legerdemain."

"No, it's not," George argued. "You're wrong. There's more than one ghost stuck here in this castle. Just go down into the oubliettes and try to maintain your composure. This poor lad's been waiting like mad to be heard. What is it ya' want, Claude? Why'd ya' write 'die' on Heather's flan? How can we make amends so you can go free and move on?"

"I don't want to be free. You all hated me—the foreigner. I want justice."

"That wasn't us Claude," said George. "You got us pegged wrong."

A spear of anguish struck Bette. "But he doesn't have us pegged wrong." She ripped the mask from her face and dashed it to splinters. She knew everything now down to the minute the poor betrayed chef had laid his innocent head on the block.

She remembered that one glorious day in this very kitchen baking Claude's perfect raisin scones. She had been Jeannette, Claude's nine-year-old daughter. She remembered the taste of the clotted cream, the homemade raspberry jelly —the Spanish Muscat raisins—the recipe they'd dubbed the *Heavenly Claudes*.

She remembered the Earl's twelve-year-old son who'd come to help bake with her that day. The boy's name had been George. He'd called her Goldie.

"We were all here four hundred years ago, all of us. We were spit boys, scullers, butchers and maids. One was even an Earl's son." She choked up.

"More trickery," said Heather.

"You were a chambermaid. You wanted your father to be chef!" Bette pointed at Roberta. "*You* were Claude's sous-chef, Roberta. Your daughter stole money and poisoned the boy she stole it from. Claude was condemned. Everyone in this very kitchen backed her claim that Claude p-poisoned the son of the Earl."

Bette covered her face with her hands. She could not look at George.

"I don't know how to make amends! You were wronged. An innocent boy died and your little daughter became a villain never to be trusted again."

The white apron leaped off Bette's Krisko tin. The red lid blew off. The floodlights on the rigging trembled and buzzed.

*"Here is my vengeance, Jeannette!"*

Chef Claude's ghostly form erupted from the tin and flew at Heather.

With a cry of horror Bette leaped in front of Heather and took Claude's fist full in her face. It was like being hit by a strong blast of wind and it toppled her into George's arms. The air sparkled and a man-shaped nimbus formed. *"Jeannette! Mon Dieu, I didn't mean to hurt you!"*

Bette struggled out of George's arms. "I can't let you hurt these people because of a four-hundred-year-old crime. People grow. They change. I forgive. So must you. Say you'll let this go, Claude."

*"I cannot,"* the ghost wailed in despair. *"You broke my mask. I want to be heard,"*

Roberta's lapel gave an extra loud buzz.

"Blimey, what if you can? Chef Banks, I need your lapel mic for a titch."

"Here," said a sheet-white Roberta.

Bette held out the little device to the nimbus before her. "What may we all do to help you find peace, Chef Claude?"

"Declare I'm an innocent man with an innocent daughter…"

Claude startled as his own voice rolled out loud and clear from every speaker in the cavernous vault. "Is that I? Am I truly heard?"

Bette nodded, unable to speak for the lump in her throat.

"Mon Dieu," he whispered in awe. "I am heard, after so many years. Only one more thing I wish. Could you bake my scones from that one happy day, Jeannette? You know the ones?"

"Of course." She found her voice. "Just know whatever happens, the credit is yours tonight, not mine."

She looked at Roberta. "Do you accept his entry, Chef Banks?" A wash of wonderous warmth filled her now.

"How can I refuse?" said Roberta taking back her lapel mic, clearly struggling to manage her emotion.

"Do these scones have a name," Roberta said swiping her eyes with the back of her hand.

"Heavenly Claudes," replied Bette. At this the ghostly chef vanished, his blue-and-white tin gave one last burble and settled into silence.

"Ach indeed," said Roberta. "Well then, lass. It looks like our next bake is going to be scoones, aye? Contestants! Take your stations. Doon't let a wee ghostie try to beat ya'! I want your best. So does the world."

As the contest continued George seized Bette's hand. "Just out of me bein' curious, what happy day did Claude mean, Goldie?"

"It was one that started happy, George. I can't say the rest right now." She knew her heart was in her eyes as she looked at him.

"Fair enough. Tell me later." He kissed her hand, his own gaze tender. "I got plans for us later, Goldie, after you and Claude make the best scones ever. As for winning on telly, it doesn't matter to me if we win or not. I gotta idea to invent a show called 'Newfie Roamer' complete with more ghosts. We'll go cook in 'hanted' places, including Nanaimo. There's this place on the beach…"

* * *

ONE YEAR after Claude's Heavenly Scones won a posthumous award, George and Bette brought their winning show 'Newfie Roamer' back to the Castle to cook up a Medieval Meal. They even used a bit of shortening out of the famous Krisko tin still mounted in full view where Bette had left it.

"We know that even after last year's happenings, there's still those of you who don't believe in ghosts," said George. "But you do believe in our cookin' and the ghostly hints we give ya'. We can give ya' the recipes. Try them and love them."

Always the showman, he winked at the camera as he scooped out the right amount of shortening from Claude's tin. "Just know what you bake won't be as sweet as we're makin' it here. You can come to the castle and check for yourself. I could say it's because Bette and me are in love, or because of the cold in this kitchen. Truth is, dear viewers, it's because this blessed tin never goes empty."

BRENDA CARRE WRITES *both long and short fiction with a decidedly quirky point of view. Her short fiction hits a variety of genres often in a single work.*

*This story of a ghostly visitation to a British baking competition includes humor and a kiss of romance and was written on a dare from a fellow author, long before the well-known British Bake Off series took reality tv by storm. Brenda's fiction can be found in the Magazine of Fantasy and Science Fiction, Pulphouse Magazine, Pulp Literature Magazine and a variety of anthologies including the* Wizards and Wolves Anthology *celebrating the life of David Farland. Brenda's debut adventure fantasy novel Gret of Roon launches this fall.*

www.brendacarre.com

# THE LADY'S FAVOR

## VINCENT E.M. THORN

$\mathcal{I}$t started, as tragedies often do, with a mistake. One single, solitary mistake. A mistake made repeatedly with forethought, but a mistake nonetheless. Seph had sworn to herself she was done after the first time, but convenience proved the better of her. The seeds were sown, and she feared what would be when it was time to reap.

Wrapped in a thin shawl and wearing her husband's too-large boots, Seph tramped down to the lake through clinging fog that chilled her to the bone. When the whisper of soft grass surrounding her village gave way to the crunch of lake-side gravel, she was near frozen and shivering. With a heart full of reticence, she shed the boots and stepped into the water.

She had awaited this night with dread and a sickness that rivaled her mornings of late. It was oft said by those who knew of local lore that the Lady of the Lake would appear to any girl or woman of the valley should they come to her in great need on a night when all the moons shine full. Since Seph was a girl she had heard tales passed down for genera-tions of the Lady and her gifts of favors granted.

But there is a cost to miracles, and no spirit is guileless.

As the cold lake water threatened to turn Seph's blood to frost, she considered turning back, returning to the warmth of her bed, to the solidity of her husband, and to simply let fate decide if her shame came to light or remained buried. She was unsure how long she waited looking with straining eyes for some sign, all the while losing feeling in her toes.

Turning on her heels, she saw a young girl dressed in a gown sewn from the night sky with an oversized hat broader than her shoulders. Her skin was more luminous than alabaster in moonlight, and midnight hair floated around her as though she were submerged in the lake. She looked up at Seph with eyes dark as night and stars surrounding fathomless white where her irises ought to have been. A mischievous grin played on her pale lips.

"My, my, how the years have changed you," she said, in a voice that was at once heavy and weighed down by experience as an adult's, and yet slight and impish as a child's. "No more the girl who would frolic on my shores, who picked flowers for their beauty and not their usefulness. Where once you braved the future with a smile and a disregard for what had yet to be, now I see your brow knit with fear of what may come. Tell me, old friend, have you come to swim with me as in the summers of old?"

Seph's breath quivered as she let it out slowly. "No," she said, and there was a lament weighing down her words, a lament she hadn't even been aware of before she heard its dour tone in her own words. "Alas, the halcyon days of frivolity have passed me by. Nay, I have come to you with need, *my lady*."

"Alas, indeed," said the child, "that time ravages you so thoroughly, in body, in heart, and in mind. But if it is the Lady you seek, mayhap I best be fit to greet you thus."

She whisked the enormous hat from her head, and with

the flourish of a traveling bard, she swept it in an arc before her. When it passed, the girl was gone, and in her place the spirit appeared as a woman grown, taller than Seph and more beautiful than the stars she wore.

"Tell me, o healer, why have you sought my aid?"

Seph tried to speak, but a lump had formed in her throat. She swallowed it down with difficulty, but still the words were like slugs in her mouth. "I am with child," she managed slowly.

The Lady showed no surprise, though she tilted her head, looking down at Seph with one nebula-filled eye as if suspecting a trap. "As one gifted in the arts of the valley and its myriad blooms and vines, surely you know the brews and concoctions to both prevent a seed from taking root and to dispense of one unwanted."

"'Tis too late for such measures, and t'is not the having that is the problem," Seph blurted out.

The Lady shifted in the air, poised as though sitting upon a stool, but nothing sat beneath her. "You have my interest. Pray, proceed."

"My husband is a man of distinction known across all the villages in the valley, not only for his station as a hunter and protector, but of his guise as well. For his crown is a mane of flame, thick and regal as a lion's and sleek as satin. For any in the valley, or even the next, t'would take a journey of a hundred leagues to find another with that same hue and texture.

"But my troubles, o lady fair, is that of..." her voice dropped precipitously as she said the poisoned words, "my lover. For just as the man I married is a man of singular appearance, so too is the man who might, for the toss of a coin, be the father of the child to come. And should the child not take after my own common appearance, I fear he might be born with tight curls of deep sable that speak far too loudly of my own indiscretions.

"What I ask, Fair Lady, O friend with whom I once shared these shores, is that you please grant me assurance, I beg you make it so, that when the time comes that I must deliver, my child resembles not the man with whom I have dallied, but the husband to whom I have sworn, that none shall question —for even a moment—my fidelity."

The Lady tapped a finger to her lips, and as she appeared to think it over, the mist around her began to swell and churn, and soon her image was swept away, as though she had merely been a trick of the moons playing over the lake in the fog.

"Wait!" Seph reached out for the spirit, but her fingers found nothing. "Please! He is a good man, and my deception would break his heart! He does not deserve such!"

"What you ask is no small thing," the Lady whispered in her ear. Seph could feel her like the very chill threatening to take her feet. "Deception is as poison. Who can say whose cup it shall fill?"

Seph turned to face the Lady, who now stood far out on the lake. "But can it be done?" she called.

Despite standing so far away, Seph heard the spirit's voice as if whispered by the fog around her. "Take from the head of the man you have wed a lock of hair and carry it to a cave on the southern slope of the Dawn Wall." The spirit pointed a long, slender finger to the east, where the mountain loomed just beyond the edge of the lake. "You shall know it for at its mouth in the snow lay the bones of a dragon. Do this and I shall tell you what it is that must be done that your need be satiated. If you are certain of your desire, this is the path you must walk."

The Lady vanished, this time with a sense of finality that Seph could feel in her bones.

The fog lifted shortly after, leaving Seph standing in the lake, plainly visible to anyone should they decide to admire the moonlight on the lake so late at night. She hurried out of the water and tried to prepare her excuses.

She needn't have bothered. Her husband didn't stir when she returned. While she dried her feet vigorously with a towel, his gentle snoring never abated. She loomed over him with a pair of scissors, shivering from both the cold and from anticipation. She was certain her heartbeat would cause him to wake. With trembling fingers, she positioned the blades.

*Snip.*

The sound of steel through hair was as loud as thunder in Seph's ears, and it was his ears that were closer. She clutched the severed locks tightly in her fist, thinking quickly for an excuse why she was cutting his hair in the middle of the night, or worse, looming over him with a pair of scissors.

But even that didn't wake him.

Seph placed the lock of hair in her satchel and slipped into bed.

* * *

As the local herbalist and apothecary, Seph had free reign to venture anywhere in the valley without suspicion. This freedom was what had enabled the illicit trysts that had landed her in her current predicament in the first place. All it took was finding a few useful roots or leaves or berries to create a fine alibi, and she seldom had to lie about her where-abouts, on the rare occurrence that she was asked.

That same freedom would solve the problem it caused.

"I am going up to the mountain today," she idly told her husband at breakfast that morning. "This time of year there should be ice lilies in bloom."

"'Tis the time for it," her husband agreed. "Were I free, I

would join you, but alas I am needed to settle a dispute in another village. Pray, take caution, and be wary of your steps."

"I know the path," Seph said, slapping her husband on the shoulder.

Seph made to leave, but her husband's strong arm landed gently, yet firmly, on her waist. She felt weightless as he lifted her and pulled her into his embrace. A thrill of terror shot through her like iced lightning.

*He knows!* she thought, a frantic edge of terror tapering at the contours of her mind.

He kissed her, and her fear burned away, leaving confusion in its wake, which in turn sloughed away into relief. She melted into that kiss, warm and soft, and returned it with a fervor only partially motivated by guilt. When they broke apart, she found the world was cold, and tears pricked at her eyes unbidden. She turned away, lest he see, and bid him a safe journey before retreating.

By the time she had reached the mountain trail, Seph was already bone weary. The long walk had done much to churn the potent brew of guilt and shame fermenting in her stomach, and that didn't sit well with the sickness of impending motherhood. With legs quivering beneath her, she found the stump of a tree, cut smooth by an axe in the recent past. She brushed aside fallen leaves and sat down heavily.

She checked her satchel—not for the first time—for the phial containing the locks of her husband's hair. It was so strange that her fate could hinge on something so small. But the Lady had been clear in her instruction. If she did this, she could bury her shame and fear and move forward.

So why was she hesitating?

As if sensing her trepidation, the wind picked up. She heard an insistent hiss, subtle and barely distinctive from the leaves brushing over the ground, but for the sharpness in her ear. And with that wind, the patterns in the falling leaves moved with an uncanny synchrony, as if beckoning her onward. With a deep sigh to quell her nerves, she found her feet and trudged on.

The climb proved strenuous as the trail became increasingly steep as the hours wore on. Seph forced each foot forward and up with a will she hadn't known existed within her. Perhaps if she had, lingering glances and stolen kisses might not have led to her climbing a mountain in desperation.

Seph had climbed this mountain before. Never so hurriedly, but she had walked these paths in the past. So, it came as a shock when she came across the cave the Lady bid her seek. The bones of the dragon were laid low and flat to the ground, yet Seph was dwarfed by their glory and magnificent scale. They were a new sight, and yet from the way the earth had settled around the bones with foliage and flowers growing, it seemed to have been resting there for a great many years. Ice lilies—translucent blue flowers with medicinal and poisonous properties—bloomed in the joints between its massive talons.

It struck her as uncannily fortuitous that her alibi should be so readily secured.

Unease filled her as she stood before the tunnel. The dark, vacuous space loomed oppressively, as though the mountain itself were condemning her for seeking this remedy to her plight. A yawning rumble emerged from the emptiness, the sheer weight of it threatening to bowl her over.

She checked again for the locks of hair she had carried and swallowed her unease. She took her first step forward. The second. The third put her on the threshold of that impenetrable dark, and then she was striding in earnest as the shadow subsumed her.

A bright light appeared ahead like a hole bored into a starless sky. The roar she had heard resolved into the sound of churning water, accompanied by the spray and scent of the river. When Seph crossed the threshold of the tunnel she emerged, not along the mountain trails under the sun and sky she knew, but to an enormous cavern with an opening in the ceiling that let in moonlight—which seemed strange, as it had been daylight just moments before. Housed within that chamber was a lake every bit as vast as the one neighboring her village.

Seph approached the edge of the water. Instead of herself, it was the Lady she found reflected in the placid surface looking up at her.

"You have ventured far," the Lady said, though her voice came from the recesses of the chamber, echoing from no fixed place, "and along your journey I trust you have had time to reflect upon the consequences of your decision?"

"I have," said Seph.

"And you still wish to pursue this course of action?"

"I do."

The Lady nodded solemnly. "Give me the stolen locks. This lake feeds the rivers and lakes of the mountain and the surrounding valleys. When you return to your home, simply drink each day from the waters that flow from this source, and your progeny shall wear the mantle of your husband."

Seph retrieved the phial containing her husband's hair without a second's consideration and tapped them out over the water. The flame-colored threads did not land on the lake's surface, but instead continued to fall as if there were no barrier until they landed in the Lady's waiting hand. The Lady closed her delicate fingers around them, and the water rippled. Her image distorted and faded, leaving Seph staring at herself when the surface stilled once more.

Seph's return journey found her heart buoyed and jubilant, as though a weight lifted from her chest. With a satchel filled with herbs, she strode the path with a skip in her step. When she looked back she saw neither sign nor lingering impression of the cave, or the dragon, but instead the same familiar switchbacks and winding paths, but she considered that the disappearance only proved the deed had indeed been done.

The sun was set when she returned to her home, and at once she encountered her husband, also reaching his journey's end. Despite the raw exhaustion leaving her feeling empty and the agony of miles in her steps, Seph ran to her husband and threw her arms around him, tears streaming down her face.

"Ah!" he exclaimed, pulling her tight to him. "Is something wrong, my love?"

"Nay," she said without drawing away. "Nay. Quite the contrary; all is well, now."

* * *

IN THE MONTHS THAT FOLLOWED, Seph endured the trials and tribulations with the trust that she had averted a great disaster. Even through sickness and debilitation, she found solace in the knowledge that all was well and right, even if some shadow of doubt remained.

Her faith was rewarded in the end, when the midwife presented her with a daughter crowned with a patch of hair like a flame.

And if that were the end of it, Seph and her family might have lived happily ever after, with the mistakes of the past blissfully buried and forgotten. But the Lady had given her warnings left unheeded.

The year after the birth of Seph's child proved to be a fertile one. Not only for her village, but for each village in the valley, for it seemed as though every married woman still within her childbearing years had found herself with child. From spring until fall, Seph's days were spent preparing tonics and remedies for expectant mothers far and wide while her husband made similar ventures.

Until one fateful night in fall, while Seph was tending to her family, she heard a dreadful uproar. Outside her window, the tranquil peace of the stars gleaming like diamonds set in a black sky was replaced by the blazing orange of a second dusk. The noise resolved into voices raised in anger.

"Devils' spit, what is going on?" asked Seph's husband, taking hold of his spear and venturing outside. Seph peered out the window, straining her eyes until the shadows came into focus, the silhouettes of a small army of men, armed with torches, pitchforks, bows, sickles, carving knives and more.

A shiver of dread choked Seph and chilled her to her core. She burst into motion, scrabbling to the door. The shouts of the mob were semi-coherent, and she caught cries of, "back-stabber!," "traitor!" and "bastard!"

Her husband stood his ground and slammed the butt of his spear into the dirt. "What is the meaning of this?" he demanded.

"You think you could get away with forcing so many to wear the horns?" shouted a woodsman.

"Did you really think we wouldn't notice?" cried a miller.

There was a scuffle and a shadow barreled forward towards Seph's husband. He hefted his weapon, but it was a slight woman curled helplessly around a bundle of cloth. It was the wife of the baker from here in Seph's own village. A stricken look of terror and confusion marred her face as she presented her burden, unwrapping it with trembling hands.

It was a babe with hair like flame.

The mob shoved another woman forward, and she fell to

her knees but managed to keep a safe hold on her load. She, too, presented an infant with the telltale red hair that could only ever have been bestowed by Seph's husband. A third, a fourth, and so on, until it seemed every woman in the vale was forced to present their shame.

Seph's initial stunned heartbreak melted into horror when understanding dawned on her; *she* had caused this. She had meant only to make assurances for her own child, but it seemed the Lady's solution had been far less discriminating.

Seph's husband's face was a rictus of uncomprehending fear as the undeniable evidence to a crime he did not commit was brought to bear. So pure was his disbelief that he didn't even notice the first attacker until the knife plunged into his chest.

"No!" Seph cried as a deep, resounding horror tore through her. She felt as though *she* had been the one stabbed. Inside, her child began to wail. Seph watched impotently as her husband tried to fight back, but it was in vain.

By the time they finished, not even the gathering crows could recognize what remained.

\* \* \*

Seph sat on the shores of the lake that night, trying hard to scrub the horror from her eyes.

"I never wanted this," she cried into her hands.

The temperature plummeted, and when Seph looked up, dense fog enveloped her. The spirit appeared once more in the guise of a child, sitting on the water's surface opposite Seph. "Deception is as poison," she said. "By your hand, yours was not the cup to bear it." And perhaps in a way, that was true. But to stand as witness as one she loved paid for her very crime writ large tasted of poison, indeed.

But such is the nature of tragedy.

It began, as they often do, with a mistake. Only a single mistake at first, but that first spark ignites a flame, and careless action proves worse than inaction. In time the flame becomes an inferno, heedlessly destroying lives and livelihood without thought to blame or fairness. Seph had started the fire, let it burn, and in her attempts to smother it had only fed it until it had consumed not only her own life, but the lives of everyone in the valley.

"I seek the advice of the Lady," Seph said resolutely, and no sooner than the words escaped her mouth did the spirit appear as such, standing above her as if in judgment.

"Speak your need, O healer."

"Pray, tell me what I must do to account for my transgressions?" Seph pleaded. She had burned herself and so many this way, but it was the only recourse she could see. She owed it to those she had hurt, to the women who had lost their husbands as surely as she had—if not by bloodshed— and to the children who would grow without the love of a father, as surely as her own. She owed it to them to find some way to set it right.

She only hoped she wasn't making another mistake, setting in motion another tragedy.

VINCENT E.M. THORN *is a biracial Japanese American author based out of Atlanta. Inspired by a vast array of works and mediums, from fairytales to massive series spanning five, ten, or fifteen doorstopper books, he hybridizes genres into the epic fantasy mold and made his debut in 2019 with the* Skies of the Empire, *book one of the Dreamscape Voyager Trilogy. When not writing, Thorn enjoys comic books, animation, cinema, musicals, and heavy metal music.*

# FREYA, QUEEN OF THE CATNIP THRONE

## SIENA BUCHANAN

reya twitched her tail, eying her prey as it darted across the floor in front of her. The tiny dot of red light wouldn't escape her this time. She would be victorious.

She took a step forward, and then another one, letting her paw land lightly on the wood floor, trying not to startle her quarry. She was so quiet, so still, she must be invisible. And then, when she judged herself to be close enough, Freya leapt, claws extending in midair as she reached out. She slammed against the wooden floor, only to find empty space beneath her paws where the dot of light had been.

Foiled again. She would do better next time, and finally catch the silly little thing.

"Sorry, Freya, I need to head to work."

Freya gave an indignant meow, staring up at her human. He called himself Jax. Freya obliged by calling him that to his face, though she knew his real name was Her Majesty Freya, Queen of the Catnip Throne's Loyal Food Delivery Service and Personal Janitor.

She wished she could convince him to stay here with her

all of the time, but in the end she had to relent and let him leave the house. After all, he did sometimes bring home new toys and food, which she appreciated. Though he didn't get the tuna paté *nearly* enough to satisfy her desire for it.

Freya followed Jax around the house as he got dressed, trying her best to rub her head on his legs so that any other cats he encountered would be able to smell her and know that he was already taken.

"You can't come with me Freya, I'm sorry."

She meowed. Of course, she couldn't go with him. The few times she had left the house, she had encountered the scary man who poked her with needles. She didn't want a repeat of *that*.

An object in Jax's pocket began to vibrate, and he pulled out his magic mirror, looking at the screen with a faint frown on his face. A moment later, a woman's voice came warbling through the mirror.

"Hey Jax. I know you've needed time to recover and grieve, and I've been trying my best to give you that space. But today is the one-year anniversary of William's death, isn't it? And I thought you might like some company. So please come over to our place tonight... me and your father miss you very dearly, and we would love to see you."

Jax sighed and tucked his phone back into his pocket. "I know she means the best, but I'm still..." He took a deep breath. "See you tonight, Freya," and shut the door behind him as he left.

Freya's ears flicked back and gave another low meow. Jax seemed sad. She didn't like it when he was sad. His cuddles were less enthusiastic, and he had a tendency to forget to feed her on time. She would have to figure out how to make him happy again, before he forgot to clean her litter box. Perhaps she would try her best to find a big spider and bring it to him when he got home. She would have gone for a mouse, but those had cleared out months ago.

In the end though, her mind couldn't focus on Jax's plight, and instead she found her way to her throne—a comfortable chair that was positioned close to the window, allowing her to stare out and watch the birds at the feeder outside.

She dozed off as she watched the birds flutter outside, awakening in the afternoon and padding into the kitchen to find a drink of water from her bowl. As she finished drinking, a few annoying drops dripping off her chin, *something* appeared in the middle of the living room.

It had the vague shape of a human, perhaps a little shorter than Jax was, with short curly hair and wearing a simple shirt and pants.

A human appearing in the middle of Freya's living room was frightening enough. What was even more frightening was the fact that this human was glowing blue and semi-translucent. He didn't seem to have a smell to him, either. Just... nothing. Not even a faint, generic smell of humanity. It was as though he wasn't there at all.

Freya glanced around, trying to find some sort of shelter. The couch was too far away. The kitchen table might offer some protection, but it was also too high up.

Before she could make a decision, the strange human was standing before her, reaching down and picking her up before she could give more than a token protest. His hands were cold, as though made of ice, so unlike the warmth she was used too from Jax.

*"You must be Freya,"* the human said, in a voice that seemed to work its way into Freya's mind and leave icy tracks in its wake, not unlike his touch to begin with. Freya growled, trying to wiggle her way out of his grip, but he maintained on, holding her indignantly like a kitten!

*"At least, that's what Jax always said he would name a cat if he got one. Freya. The goddess in Norse mythology."*

Well, of course she was a goddess. You couldn't get much more perfect then four paws, a tail and claws she kept razor sharp using the scratching post in her room.

Perhaps this strange human wasn't as bad as she assumed. Even if he was holding her far too tight for comfort and refusing to let her down.

As she looked up at the strange human, a thought struck her, and she twisted around, still held tightly in the creature's grip, her eyes finding one of the pictures on the mantle. It was a photo that Freya had knocked over many times, mostly because it didn't have *her* in it. But Jax had always put it back on the mantle, even after he decided to take out the glass entirely. The image was Jax, standing beside a man that Freya had never seen before. But now, she knew. This man was the one holding her now, glowing and see through and altogether not quite real.

*"Oh. He still has that picture of us,"* the man murmured, floating over and reaching out to pick up the picture in his hands.

*"He took this on the trip when he proposed. It was right before I got my diagnosis. But Jax still wanted to go ahead with the wedding. And so, we did."*

He turned the picture over in his hands, revealing a small engraving on the back that read, simply, *"To William and Jax."*

Freya shifted in William's arms. She couldn't imagine Jax falling in love with this strange floating person. No, not at all. Actually, she couldn't really imagine Jax falling in love at all. He was her provider, sent to this flat earth in order to provide and see to her every need. If William and Jax had gotten engaged, and fallen in love, and all of that... where had *she* been for that?

*"Yes, I know, you're probably wondering what I'm doing in your house, aren't you?"*

William began to walk down the hall towards the bedrooms, still cradling Freya tightly in his arms. *"Ghosts have all sorts of rules on when we can visit, you know. We're only allowed to come visit our loved ones on the anniversary of our death. This is my first time coming back. And... it feels strange, but also as though I never left."*

The first room William stopped by was Freya's bedroom, with her scratching post and litter box. *"And I know I'm talking to a cat, and you can't understand me."*

Freya tried her best to respond that she could, in fact, understand him perfectly—It was humans' translation of cat that was the problem, not the other way around. In usual human fashion, however, he ignored her.

Freya might have hoped that a ghost would be more understanding of their feline overlord's language, but well, apparently not.

Instead of paying attention to Freya's litter box, however, William was entranced by the wooden easel in the corner, that Freya had once scratched up the legs of, and the paintings on the wall, the majority of which were paintings of various boats on the open sea.

Boats. Who liked that sort of thing? Freya preferred to stay as far away from water as possible, thank you very much. Water had nothing good in it. After all, it wasn't like people got tuna paté from the ocean. They got it from the supermarket.

*"He didn't take down my paintings,"* William murmured softly, looking up at the nearest of them, a huge ship with big sails on a tumultuous sea.

*"I'm glad that he changed the room at least a little bit. But I wish it was more. I wish that he didn't have to see my artwork every time he comes into this room. Maybe it helps him. I don't know. But clinging onto the past like that... It can't be healthy."*

William moved on to Jax's bedroom, one door over.

*"It hasn't changed much in here, huh? If you told me it had been a month rather than a year, I wouldn't be surprised."*

Freya managed to wiggle out of William's grip as he floated over to Jax's desk, landing lightly on the floor. She hated being held in the best of times, and certainly being held by an unfamiliar ghost was not her favorite, even if it was Jax's former husband.

*"I wonder if his password is still the same,"* William said, flipping open the computer that was always present on Jax's desk. Freya leapt up onto the desk, trying to help him out by lying on top of the keys. William shooed her away, and she settled for sitting on the edge of the desk, watching him, her tail hanging off the end.

*"He should really change it, you know, since I swear that's been the same for the past five years,"* William murmured as he continued staring at the screen.

*"I was afraid to find that he was dating someone else, you know? But I think that this might be even worse. He's been alone. The only people he's talking with are his work colleagues, and even then, he doesn't do anything more than he's required to from work. And of course, his colleagues never knew that we were married. He was too nervous. Scared that they would judge him. Scared that he would lose his job. Afraid, thinking about what has happened to other gay folks. I tried to convince him to be open about it, but in the end, it was his choice. So, he never even told his boss why he took those days off, when I was sick... I imagine none of them knew why. And now, he continues to avoid the topic. Making sure he isn't around anyone who knew me. So, he can avoid the pain. But the only way to ease the pain is to accept it. Face your fears and overcome them."*

William glanced down at Freya, still sitting on Jax's desk. *"Remember that, little one."*

Freya meowed. She didn't need that. She had nothing to

be afraid of. They should be afraid of her, not the other way around.

*"I know you've been trying to help him, Freya, but a cat isn't going to be enough. He needs to interact with other people. And I don't know how I can do that. I only have a day here, and the rules of what I can do are quite limited. I wish I could talk to him. But that, very much, isn't possible."*

William sighed, sadness etched on every part of his face.

A low rumbling noise filled the house, the sound of the garage door opening, and Freya leaped up, racing towards the door.

"Hi Freya," Jax said, scooping her up in his arms and holding her close to his chest, just as William had not long before. Freya was excited for him to see William, now standing in the middle of the living room, but he walked right past him, without paying any attention to his former husband.

Freya turned from Jax to William, looking back and forth before letting out a low meow of confusion.

"What are you looking at, Freya?" Jax asked her.

*"He can't see me, Freya."* William said sadly.

But Freya could. Because she was far more important than a lowly human, clearly. They couldn't even compete with... what had William said? A goddess?

She liked the sound of that.

Freya wiggled out of Jax's arms and leapt to the floor, following Jax around the house as he made himself dinner, and more importantly, fed her. William trailed after the two of them as well, eyes fixed on Jax all the while.

There was a deep love in those eyes, one that Freya knew as the love of a mother cat to her kittens. Here, it was different, and yet the same. William loved Jax. They were separated by different realms, and yet they still loved each other.

And for both of them, that separation had turned the love into grief.

After dinner Jax settled on the couch, turning on the TV to some sort of game that involved kicking a ball around with no birds in sight. Boring.

Freya tried her best to get a hold of the remote so she could change it to the nature channel, but Jax was always too quick for her. In the end, she had to settle for snuggling up on Jax's lap and letting him stroke her fur.

William sat on the left side of Jax, not focused on the TV at all but instead focused on Jax's face, staring so intently it seemed as though he was memorizing every wrinkle in his face.

*"I wish I could talk to him,"* William said. *"I'd tell him that I love him, but that he needs to move on. He needs to get out more and see his friends... and go on some dates, maybe. I wish I could tell him that I would rather see him happy than see him hold onto his grief. But instead, I'm talking to his cat."*

Freya was forced to correct him on that. Jax was her human, not the other way around.

Jax looked down as she meowed, stopping his petting. "You alright, Freya?"

He turned the way that Freya was looking, to William, but his eyes stared unseeing past his former husband, even as William reached out as though to cup his face.

*"Oh, my sweet Jax. You look so much older and yet the same as the last day I saw you. I don't know if I can leave you alone once more, but I'll have too, won't I? It's not like I have a choice in that matter. I wish... I wish I knew you'd be okay. I wish I knew you could be happy."*

Freya could sense what William was talking about. Jax's deep sadness, that he carried around with him always. She hadn't ever thought to question it because it simply always had been that way. But now, she saw. And if Jax was sent here to take care of her every need that she could possibly have—he'd do a lot better job if he was happy while he did it.

He needed to face his fears, as William had said.

Freya jumped down from the couch before leaping on top of the counter and then to the mantle. She nearly knocked over an ugly vase as she landed, but avoided it by a whisker's inch.

"Freya! Get down from there!" Jax called.

Freya ignored him, climbing over a few other knick-knacks on the mantle before she reached the picture frame that held the picture with William and Jax in it, grabbing it firmly in her mouth.

She jumped down from the mantle, bringing the pictures with her as she carried it over to Jax's lap.

"Freya, what have you done this time—" Jax said, as she dropped the frame in his lap. He stood, seemingly to put it back on the mantle, before he paused and sat back down, staring at the picture.

"I didn't really think about it until my mom called this morning, but it would be a year ago today, wouldn't it?" Jax whispered, as Freya snuggled back in his lap. "It would be a year ago today. We knew it was happening. We knew it was going to come. But I didn't really understand what it meant until it was there. Until I held William's hand in my own and heard him take his last breath."

Jax was crying now, the tears falling down his face, a few of them landing on the photo he was holding in front of him.

William was crying too, and Freya saw him reach out and put a hand on his husband's shoulder, a hand that Jax couldn't feel, but Freya could see.

"And then... everything I had ever loved felt like it had been snatched away from me as soon as I had understood how important it was. And I couldn't deal with that."

Jax looked down at Freya, who gave a soft meow at his

words. Encouragement. Telling him to keep going.

"I got you just a few days later, you know that?" Jax said, "Maybe it wasn't a good choice, but I needed something to fill the void. And I knew that the local shelter had a mother cat give birth... and I promised myself I would just go and look. But you were just sitting there so prim and proper, and before I knew it the papers were signed, and I was bringing you home. And you meant everything to me, Freya. You helped fill the void I felt in my chest, ever so slightly. And I felt guilty for that. I still do, for replacing my husband with a cat."

Jax gave a laugh even as he was continuing to cry.

*"No, it's good that you did what you did. I'm glad that you found something to be grateful for, Jax. Please, I am."*

Jax, of course, didn't hear William's pleas, but Freya did, and she snuggled into Jax's chest even tighter.

"I can't believe it's been a year. It feels like only yesterday, but at the same time an age."

Jax took a deep breath. "Thank you for listening, Freya."

Freya meowed in response, trying to get across the words that she knew Jax wouldn't be able to hear, but she said nonetheless.

"And... I think it might be time to stop hiding. A year seems like far too long to hide. Maybe I need to actually... try to return to some semblance of normality. Even if that feels like betraying William's memory."

*"Oh no, darling, that is exactly what I want."*

"But it's time to stop hiding. It's time to open back up." Jax looked down at Freya once more. "Thank you, Freya."

William reached over and stroked gently against Freya's fur. *"I Thank you as well, Freya. I can see that I'm leaving Jax in more capable paws then I thought I would. Look after him, will you?"*

She meowed in agreement.

"I know you will. Thank you, Freya."

William disappeared, leaving Freya and Jax alone as Jax opened up his cell phone and called a number with trembling hands.

It rang for a moment before the other person picked up.

"Hi Mom."


*18-YEAR-OLD SIENA BUCHANAN is a student of biology in the pacific northwest. In her limited free time between school and writing, she enjoys long walks, swimming, watercolors and reading epic fantasy novels that are large enough to seriously injure someone with. This is her debut publication.*

# THE PLACE THAT YOU'VE MADE

## BY JEFF OLIVER

*Life is nothing but a maze.*
*The twists and turns will drive you insane.*
*You're pushing every button as you try to escape the*
  *craze.*
*You try repeatedly to escape the haze.*
*You're locked away without keys to your cage.*
*It's just the place that you've made.*
*A battleground of emotions conflicting in a never-*
  *ending rage.*
*The illusion has always been the escape.*

*Thoughts are very deadly.*
*Bullets and blades mean nothing within.*
*You can't keep your hands steady.*
*You can't stop shaking for shit.*
*Everything that you do feels like you're failing.*
*The depression of these thoughts is constantly*
  *impaling.*
*They tear through your brain matter like parasites*
  *in heat.*

*Looking to lay its vile eggs that are planted by a
    beast.*
*A beast that you'll never see.*
*You will always feel it inside.*
*There is nowhere to hide from the monsters that
    consume your mind.*
*From birth, they begin to eat you alive.*
*We carry these monsters for our entire lives.*
*No matter how religious you are, you have them.*
*No matter how high and mighty you think you are...*
*You're still a vessel to them.*
*A vessel feeding these pus-leaking freaks.*
*A vessel made of nothing more than meat.*
*Open your eyes before you decide to fucking preach.*

*Life is nothing but a maze.*
*The twists and turns will drive you insane.*
*You're pushing every button as you try to escape the
    craze.*
*You try repeatedly to escape the haze.*
*You're locked away without keys to your cage.*
*It's just the place that you've made.*
*A battleground of emotions conflicting in a never-
    ending rage.*
*The illusion has always been the escape.*

*The illusion has always been the escape!*
*This is the place that you've made.*

*Jeff Oliver was born in Baltimore, Maryland on April 6th, 1982. A
poet by passion and father of eight beautiful children, his dedica-
tion to his family and his craft is second to none. Currently
residing in Western New York State, he is a writer of intense
emotions, having started composing his dark poetry at just 11 years*

old. His gift for transforming darkness to words shone brightly from a young age. Jeff Oliver's poetry has an ethereal quality. When others may have been destroyed from such a devastating darkness, he manages to weave lyrical justice into an otherwise unfair world.

His published works include Venomous Words, Strange Sounds, Poetic Fiction: Journals of Silent Screams, Scattered Thoughts: Volumes I, II, and III, New World Monsters, INKBLOTS: A Poet's Perception, and Infinite Black: Tales from the Abyss.

# ACKNOWLEDGMENTS

*Noncorporeal* emerged from our desire to step into the shrouded world of ghostly tales. We have many fans of our other anthologies who have expressed their interest in these kinds of stories. We were pleased with the results.

Inkd Publishing would like to thank Heather Lewis, April Davis, Tony Cioffi, Heather Norris, and Kevin Davis for their relentless hours helping A. Balsamo read through all those stories. They brought the best to you.

*Noncorporeal* is a reality due to the support of amazing fans, first is our **Kickstarter Patrons**:

Stew Buchanan, Joy Kristen Allen, Jared Nelson, Alicia Cay, Michael J Wyant Jr, Zack Fissel, Morgen Rochelle Campbell, April Davis, Mary Jo Rabe, Paige Vest, Jessica Phillips, Mark Lindberg, Melissa Tabon, Aubrey Caulfield, Jessica, Boris Veytsman, LA Selby, Joanna Schmidt, Jessica Springer Guernsey, Ryan, Billy Seale, Luke Stemple, Jill S, JT, Melanie Briggs, Michael Axe, Mitchell Hardy, Rasarr, Tracy Hughes, Kyle Crawford, Campbell Royales, Starkaster, Suzanne M, Tim Lewis, Kimberly Gier, Erin Scrogum, Jose Ayala, Chesh, The Creative Fund by BackerKit, Ashleigh

Floyd, Heather Norris, Colleen Feeney, Edward Abbott, Richard O'Shea, Rain Carling, Paul Trinies, Keenan Locher, Joey, Amanda Meyer, Ronald Miller, Lisa Kruse, Mike James, Windi LaBounta, Katharina Pierce, Tiffany, Jonathan, Giusy Rippa, Eron Wyngarde, Wendy Danger Vigo, Kayla O'Hare, Courtney Sangis, Claincy

A special thanks to Erin Scrogum and Heather Norris for their **Kickststarter Tuckerization** in two stories. Brenda Carre added Heather Norris into her story, *The Mount of Haunted Krisko*. Thank You. Erin Scrogum joins the tale of *Bosque Bello* by Kevin A Davis.

Please sign up for our mailing list at InkdPub.com

ALSO BY INKD PUBLISHING


*Hidden Villains*

*Hidden Villains: Arise*

Please visit us at InkdPub.com or Facebook.

Coming soon: *Behind the Shadows* - a horror anthology, and *Hidden Villains: Betrayed*.